They are casting their problems at society.
And, as you know, there's no such thing as society.

– Margaret Thatcher,
from an interview in *Women's Own* magazine (1987)

...Go together
You precious Winners all

– William Shakespeare, *The Winter's Tale*

Sunshine flooded the spot where I stood.
Then I defiled the day by entering.

– Walter Benjamin

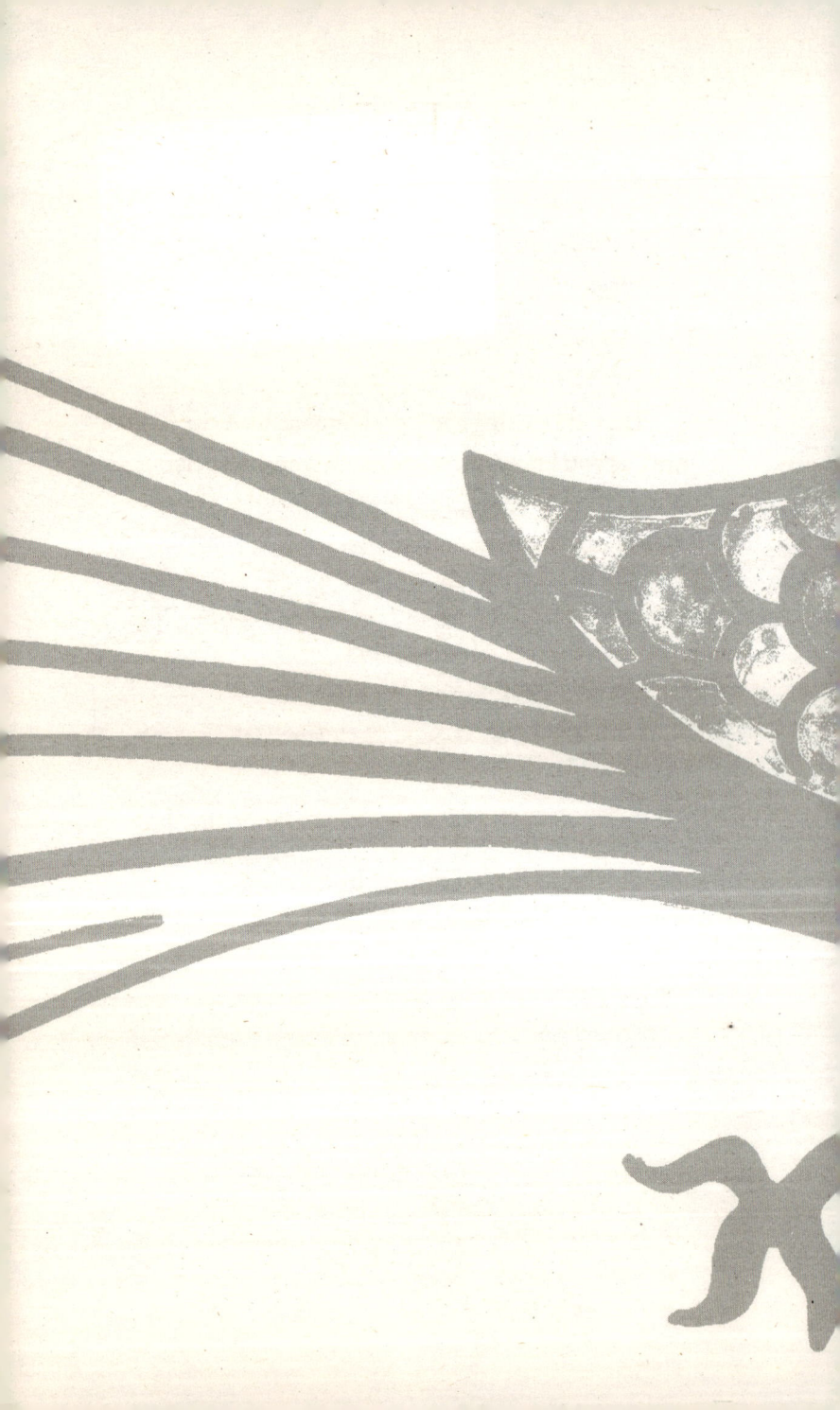

STEF MACBETH

FOLK

Stef Macbeth is a freelance writer and commercial creative based in Berlin. He grew up in the southwest of England, studied at the University of Glasgow, and received the Edward Caird Medal for Philosophy in 2005.

In the early 2000s, Stef was part of the creative team at Sub Club, Glasgow, where he worked with artists such as Optimo and Harri & Domenic, and helped steer the narrative of one of the UK's longest running independent electronic music venues.

Since moving to Berlin in 2013, he has been involved in a series of collaborations with artists, companies, social enterprises and cultural institutions, both in Germany and the UK. His work has appeared at international shows including Borealis Festival and Cannes Lions.

In 2023, a version of FOLK was longlisted for the McKitterick Prize, awarded by the British Society of Authors each year to a first novel by a writer aged 40 or over.

First published by Velocity Press 2025

velocitypress.uk

Printed and bound in Great Britain by Clays Ltd, Elcograf S.p.A.

Cover design Hayden Russell

Typesetting Paul Palmer-Edwards

Editor Paris Ferguson

PRINT ISBN: 9781913231934

EBOOK ISBN: 9781913231941

GPSR

Publisher: Velocity Press, London, United Kingdom

EU Authorised Representative: Easy Access System Europe:
Mustamäe tee 50, 10621 Tallinn, Estonia, gpsr.requests@easproject.com

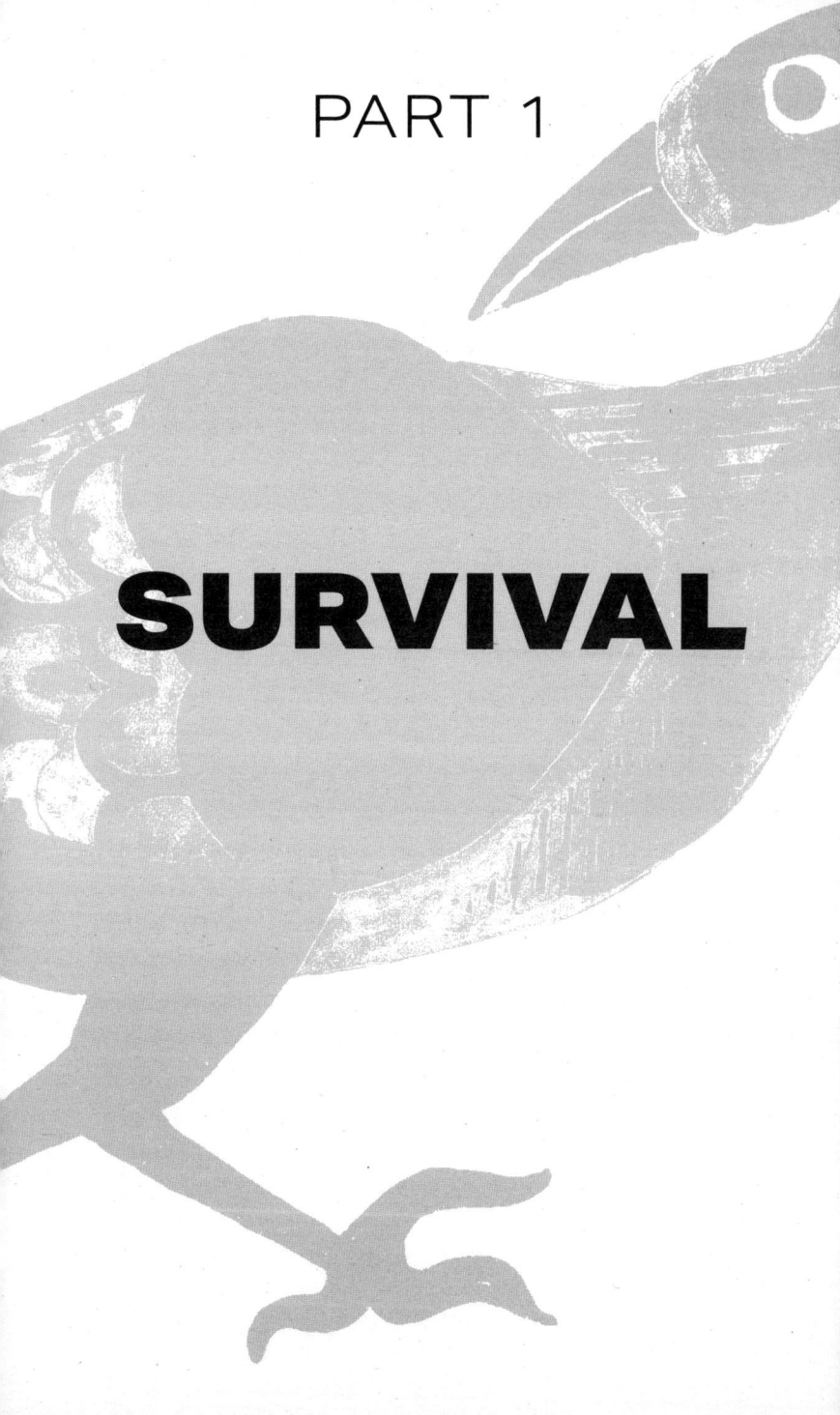

PART 1

SURVIVAL

Chapter One

His name, we're told, is Jason Templar. My head only goes up to his jaw, which appears to already justify the daily attention of a razor. He turns up one night at Folk. Gerry says he's seventeen.

It is 1994.

As well as running Folk, Gerry is active in peace circles and publishes a periodical by the name Juggernaut Press. When my parents still went on CND marches Gerry would be there, up on stage, waving a megaphone and working the crowd. 'Can you hear that, Mr Major?' he'd say in a mocking voice, and a chorus of MAGGIE, MAGGIE, MAGGIE! (OUT! OUT! OUT!) would erupt, for while Mrs Thatcher was no longer Prime Minister, the wounds were still raw, if only in the imagination. 'That's right,' Gerry would yell, as if he'd just served the government a damning indictment. 'The people have had enough!' And he would list all the things about which the people had had enough. Corporate Greed. Police Brutality. Ecological Destruction. Western Imperialism. Racism. Apartheid. Poll Tax. The list was long. There was much to be angry about. Unlike most of our friends' green-leaning parents – the dads especially – Gerry has charisma.

Folk convenes once a week at the community centre canteen, an outhouse attached to a sprawling labyrinth of a building that has been constructed, reconstructed, extended and renovated at various points in a legacy going back to Queen Victoria. The canteen is a more recent, rather unspectacular, addition. With its pea-green walls, frosted glass and strip lighting, it has the air of an institution from a bygone era. Usually we can guess from the smell what the kids had for lunch; cauliflower, liver and boiled potatoes being a particular favourite of whoever plans the menus.

While the canteen has changed little in the time we have known it, Folk has undergone major transformations in recent years, most conspicuously in its numbers. From a peak of thirty-three young people and three leaders in the late 1980s, we are now down to a hard core of eight. Nine if you include Jason.

Jason comes with the spring. The cherry blossoms are everywhere, all through the lane that runs around the back of the community centre, clinging to boots in the rain, coating them in a fine pink powdery dust.

And it had been raining on this particular day, the day Jason Templar entered our lives. I see him the moment I turn the corner. Dressed all in white, he appears like an apparition, glistening in the evening sun.

'Mark!' Gerry waves me over. 'Come and meet someone!'

His eyes – his whole face – is hidden by a baseball cap. His jacket is shiny and zipped all the way to the chin. His trainers are gleaming and pristine.

'This is Jason,' says Gerry. 'He'll be joining us.'

I smile at *Jason* and try to look non-judgmental. He lifts his head, and finally I get to see his face. He looks rough. Like you're not sure whether to offer him your hand or your wallet, I will later recount. A long silver stud sticks out of his left eyebrow.

'Mark's been coming here for years,' Gerry continues, and laughs as if he's cracked a joke. 'I go way back with his folks.' He laughs again, and says: 'June still singing at the Dog?'

June is my Mum. The Dog is the Dog's Whistle, a pub out of town, taken over a few years earlier by a couple of ageing hippies belonging to a time that Gerry calls Way Back When. They held live sessions in the back room, where Mum was a regular and much admired performer.

Gerry leans in. 'Mark's mum,' he says, dropping his voice as if sharing confidential information, 'is a supremely gifted jazz singer.'

I attempt an ironic wince for Jason's benefit. It is not clear, even to me, what I expect this poorly executed gesture to achieve. Solidarity? Recognition? Rapport? I am trying, I suppose, to make a connection.

'Safe,' says Jason, not looking at me.

Jason's voice. I have heard voices like it before, but only on the telly. It is the voice of someone from a world that is both exotic and familiar. Is it real? I do not recall my parents ever watching soap operas when I was young, but Nomi – Zee's middle sister – loved them, and I recall us all sitting together, me and the three sisters, devouring the melodrama, one soap frothing into the next; Nomi bringing us up to speed, with the names of the women screaming at each other, and details of who is having affairs with whom and which one has a gambling addiction. 'Oh yeah,' she says one time. 'Mark's got AIDS.' 'HIV Positive,' Zee corrects her. 'Mark's HIV positive.' 'Same difference.' 'Not to Mark.' And then Megan, who must be about six at the time, pipes up: 'Are you Haitch-I-Vee Pos'tiv, Mark?' and we all have a good laugh because Megan is cute, but I still wonder whether it really is only the fictional Mark they are talking about or whether they know something I don't. Don't Die of Ignorance, warned the adverts from our childhood, with looming tombstones and icebergs inscribed with the word AIDS to hammer home the point. Of course, I am low risk, being a virgin and not a drug user, but that doesn't stop me from worrying.

Anyway, that's Jason's voice. Gerry is still smiling. I try to think of something welcoming to say, but all I can manage is:

'Do you like music?'

The moment this question pops out, I know how weak it is, and I rue my inability to keep my mouth shut. Gerry's comment had not required a response. It could have just been left there.

Jason does not answer, at least not with words. Only a tiny curl of the top lip betrays what he thinks of my question.

Gerry comes to my aid, requesting assistance. He wants help fetching some things from the car.

Once we're out of earshot, he begins to talk. 'Mark,' he says. He always uses my name. 'I need you to do me a favour.' He hesitates for a moment and lowers his voice. 'It's Jason.'

We look back at where we've left him. He's still there, obviously. He has removed a pack of cigarettes from his pocket. I watch him insert one into his mouth.

'He seems nice,' I say.

At the car Gerry opens the boot and begins exploring the chaos. The boot of Gerry's car is like a permanent car boot sale, full of weird, unwieldy items that offer no obvious connection to each other or to anything else. So a box of macrame will be squeezed in next to a garden hose, a vacuum cleaner, some yarn, some dog food (Gerry doesn't have a dog), an axe, several jars of pickles and a parachute. We sometimes say that all of life is contained within Gerry's boot. For example: say you need a particular tool or a valve or a plug or a stopper – mention it to Gerry and he'll say, 'Ah, you might be in luck there,' and he will nip out to the car and, nine times out of ten, he will return with exactly what you're looking for. Who needs Mary Poppins' handbag, we joke, when you have Gerry's boot?

'Jason's new here,' he calls back, his voice slightly muffled. 'Doesn't really know anyone.'

He pulls out a plastic ringbinder, clutching it with an air of triumph. 'Ah-ha!' he exclaims, and I laugh.

Gerry's approach to paperwork is notoriously haphazard. 'We'll save the rainforests,' he would say, depositing official forms and guides into the recycling bin, barely giving them a glance.

He hands me the folder and bangs the boot shut in that nonchalant, confident way that he has. We start walking back towards the canteen.

'He's not had it easy, y'know?'

'Right.'

'He's a good kid.'

'Right.'

'I'm telling you, Mark, because I think you're more mature than some of the others.'

'Right.'

'You don't have to do anything special. Just make him feel included.' He stops and turns, squinting slightly, head cocked to one side. 'Can you do that for me, Mark?'

I nod. 'I can try.'

There are voices up ahead. Gerry grins and puts his fingers to his lips, letting rip one of his ear-splitting wolf whistles. The sound ricochets off the brickwork, startling the pigeons and threatening to shatter the community centre windows. Every head turns. 'Evening, campers!'

One head in particular is looking more vibrant than usual this evening. Anna has been at the peroxide again. When she moves, she displays a kaleidoscope of tones, from amber roots to radioactive ginger and burning white tips. Anna's hair is a constant source of concern, and fascination, for us all.

'It will fall out,' Zee will have cautioned.

Completing our little gang of four is Seb, crouched down and rolling himself a rolly, his long fingers dextrous from years of dedicated guitar playing. With his dirty straw-coloured hair and scraggly beardy bits, his famous lookalikes are either Kurt Cobain or Shaggy from the Scooby Doo cartoons. This depends on one's points of reference and whether we're trying to wind him up. Normally I'd join them but I've just agreed to look after Jason.

'What should I do with this?' I ask, holding up the ringbinder.

'Oh,' says Gerry, absently. 'On the counter, buddy.'

* * *

Jason has already gone inside. I find him staring at a child's drawing of a burning house. The rescue workers are trying to free someone on the top floor, who has a speech bubble coming out of their face with the word HELP!

The scene is rather harrowing for a child, and I wonder how it can be that I must have walked past this picture so many times and never paid any attention.

'The school next door,' I explain. 'This is their canteen.'

Jason flinches, as if I had struck him, and turns to me. The stud, I note, is a bit longer than ones I'm used to seeing, more like the piece of metal Anna once stuck through her belly button. (A party at Seb's, a bottle of surgical spirit and a needle from Seb's mum's sewing kit. The piercing went septic after three days and Anna wound up with a nasty scar, which didn't stop her from wearing crop-tops.)

'Did it hurt?' I enquire, touching my own eyebrow.

'Naw, I had a couple of biffters first.'

'Right.'

I'm trying to look at something that's not his eyebrow. I follow his eyes as they move around the room. They stop on Zee, who's chatting with Seb, in the corner by the stacked chairs.

'Who's the girl?'

My cheeks burn. The stubble above his top lip twitches.

'You fuck her yet?'

Zee whispers something to Seb, which provokes an explosion of laughter, and then she's coming towards us, her hair pushed up high by a yellow silk scarf. Her cherry-red Docs squeak on the lino.

'Hey, babe,' she says, giving me a chaste hug.

If I wear my boots we're the same height.

She turns to Jason. 'Hello, stranger,' she says, offering him her hand.

They shake hands. His hands, the skin so pale against her skin, are much bigger than hers. Man hands. There is scarring around the knuckles.

'Jason, meet Zee,' I pronounce with a flourish. 'Zee, meet Jason.'

She looks him up and down, openly checking him out, like she would a painting or a curiosity in a museum.

'You know, my mother once said,' she begins, and I know what's coming. She's going to use the pantomime voice that she sometimes adopts to impersonate her mother who, it should be noted, doesn't even have a West-Indian accent, or whatever accent Zee is doing: 'Don't never trust a man who wears more jewellery than you, girl!'

I'm watching him closely to see what he will do.

What Jason doesn't know – what he can't know – is that Zee's mother sounds nothing like this person. Yolanda grew up in the north of England after coming to this country as a baby. She got accepted into a grammar school, then Oxford, followed by a series of research positions and fellowships and eventually professorships at the UK's top universities. She has written books. She's been on telly. She's met the Queen.

But Zee does this with new people. Especially if she suspects they might be a bit – or a lot – racist.

We wait for his response. His lip does its twitchy thing again.

'Well,' he says. 'Mum knows best.'

Zee grins at him. She likes this answer. Their eyes meet.

'Not mine, Jason. She's a complete fucking disaster.'

'Erm,' I cut in, 'I think it's Circle Time.'

Chapter Two

Gerry needn't have worried. Jason proves to be an instant hit at Folk.

One evening, a few weeks after his arrival, we do skits. Jason is in a group with me, Anna and Merlin. We do a routine, which we've done before, where Anna is blindfolded and has to feed jelly to Merlin, who is also blindfolded.

Jason and I are 'the eyes'. Our job is to guide her spoon to Merlin's mouth by shouting out 'left!', or 'up a bit'. Each time I try to correctly instruct Anna, Jason tells her to go the other way. The result is that she keeps spilling jelly down Merlin's front, to howls of laughter from everyone.

Jason, it is agreed, is a pretty cool guy.

Zee says afterwards that it's as if Anna had the devil on one side and her conscience on the other.

'Bit harsh on Merlin,' I reply, smiling, because I don't want to sound poe-faced and humourless.

The image of Merlin shivering in the cold strip lighting of the community centre canteen, drenched in raspberry jelly, indignant and upset, is hard to shake, no matter how funny it might have been at the time.

People often think that Folk is very *crafty*. What's true is that Gerry is good at making things. One year, for example, he carved an African chess set. There was some connection to the Free Nelson Mandela campaign, and we all followed its progress, admired the precision of the knight's mane and the cold, faceless bishops. We discussed the cultural meanings of the Bapedi design Gerry had chosen. Our own craft skills never get much further than gaudy friendship bracelets, tie-dyed T-shirts and whittling.

Whittling is Merlin's great passion. He carries a piece of wood around with him everywhere he goes, and scrapes away at it with his penknife in the same way that other people bite their nails or smoke cigarettes. He never seems to make anything. The whittling is the thing.

Merlin is home-educated and weird even by Folk standards. His family, the grandly named Cooper-Clarkes, are self-sufficient and described variously as artists, conservationists, radicals and tree-huggers. They practice permaculture, generate their own energy and are distrustful of conventional medicine.

They live in a converted barn on a smallholding somewhere north of Nowhere. I went there one time after a trip, because my parents were too wrapped up in their own affairs to fetch me. So Merlin's parents had stepped in and taken me and Merlin back to the Cooperage.

Merlin has no siblings and he doesn't call his parents Mum and Dad. Instead they are Mary and Spencer. M&S, or S&M, we joke.

We were given orange squash that day, which surprised me because I would have thought of them to be *freshly squeezed* people. We sat on a bench in front of the house. The bench had been constructed by the S half of M&S out of wood from their own woodland. We sat there and Merlin scraped away at his stick, the strips of bark peeling off in long shreds, curling like the skin of an apple. I watched him – it was quite mesmerising. But what really sticks in my mind is the sound of Merlin's breathing, which was wheezy at the best of times, and on this occasion was exacerbated by a heavy cold. At one point there was this glob of snot at the end of his nose, just hanging there, and I wanted to knock it off or at least give him a hankie. I didn't, obviously; I just politely pretended not to notice.

'You're sounding quite judgmental, Mark,' Mum remarks on the way home. 'Folk is a good outlet. For Merlin, and for you.'

The comment riles. Folk is not an *outlet*, and certainly not a 'good' one. She makes it sound pathetic.

Folk is lots of things:

It is jumping in icy lakes and warming up again beside the fire.

It is sleeping under the stars and talking about things that demand capital letters: Truth, Art, Love, Life.

It is drinking too much cider and getting off with your mate.

It is Zee Adams.

It is not having to justify yourself constantly to small-minded provincial people with their mini-lives, people like my parents and their friends.

It is Gerry.

And, fundamentally, it's mine.

She has no right to express an opinion.

Her opinion is void.

'Did I tell you,' she says, 'I saw Gerry at the Dog's Dinner?'

I refuse to smile. The joke is so tired it has ceased to be a joke at all.

'He's very fond of you, Mark. You know that, don't you?'

* * *

Jason frequently talks about a brother, who is some kind of DJ, in London.

'He's a *junglist*,' he announces one evening. We're outside the community centre canteen waiting for Gerry to arrive. 'You know Chime.'

This isn't so much a question as an instruction. I just stare at him but Anna, whose own brother is involved with such things, says she thinks it might ring a bell.

'Hyperbolic?' Jason continues, and reels off more names in a kind of dreamy roll-call of gods and idols. 'Randall, Nookie, Mickey Finn, Knuckleheads...' The words mean nothing to me, he might as well be speaking another language, and I wonder: is this a test? Is he trying to see how far he can push us?

'I'll be getting my decks soon,' he says. 'Then we'll have a rave.'

'Cool,' I reply. 'Maybe your brother can play?'

'Yeah,' says Jason. 'Maybe.'

* * *

It is a glorious evening in the middle of May and Gerry has laid out trays of seedlings, trowels and bags of soil in front of the community centre canteen, like a stall at a jumble sale.

'I thought we could do some gardening,' he says with a grin. 'Sow the seeds of change, and all that.'

There is a small communal garden behind the community centre, which some people use for smoking, the pergola providing shelter when it is raining. The community centre manager often complains about the cigarette butts that get left behind, and in the past he has pointed the finger at us, which isn't fair because the butts are usually for B&H or Lambert & Butler or Royals, brands that kids at my old school smoked but which no one at Folk would lower themselves to poison their lungs with, or at least only in an emergency if there really was nothing better to blag.

The response to Gerry's suggestion is pretty muted. Most of us have gardens at home. We don't go to Folk for stuff we can get at home. Gardening is pretty boring.

But Gerry's still grinning. He has that glint in his eye that tells you, once you know him well enough to spot it, that he has a surprise up his sleeve. And, sure enough, it soon becomes clear that when he says 'gardening' it is not your standard geriatric Sunday afternoon leisure pursuit he has in mind.

'You'll have heard of the Green Guerrillas, I imagine,' he says.

Anna sniggers. 'You been smoking that Whacky Backy again, Gerry?'

Gerry ignores her. 'Liz Christy? New York? The Lower East Side?'

Our blank faces reveal that none of us has a clue what he's talking about.

'Honestly,' he says, pleased with himself, 'I don't know what they teach you these days.'

And he explains that the Green Guerrillas are an influential group of New York artists who took it on themselves to reclaim neglected urban spaces, beautifying them by planting gardens in the city's cracks and crevices.

'Of course,' he continues, 'Liz Christy and her crew weren't the first to practice this type of activism. As with a lot of these things, Britain has a rich history in this regard that no one knows about. It goes back to the seventeenth century and a group of dissidents known as the Diggers. You should look them up, they were real pioneers.'

He starts handing around the tools and bags of seeds. We are to divide into pairs. Zee and Seb, Anna and Jason. I'm left with Merlin, but I don't mind. Merlin's quite good on horticulture and growing things and I'm clueless about this stuff, having never even tried to grow marijuana.

'Is this legal?' someone asks.

'It's a grey area, as far as the law goes,' says Gerry. 'But there are rules. Avoid going onto private property and don't do something that will cause damage. The best tactic is to go for the places that no one cares about. Find the most unloved, unlovable patches of dirt. If there are weeds already growing there, that's a great sign that something more uplifting could thrive in their place.' He nods, and adds: 'And remember, if you are stopped by the police or some irate resident or council apparatchik, you don't have to say a word. It's up to *them* to prove that you're doing something wrong.'

The suggestion that we could get ourselves arrested has the instant effect of turning us all into enthusiastic Guerrilla Gardeners, part of a long line of dissidents and artists and daredevils, fighting for the right to cultivate the land.

We set off, armed with our trowels and bags of earth, ready for anything. Our long shadows fill the lane, making us feel ten feet taller, with virtue on our side.

At the end of the lane we part. Zee and Seb head up to the leafy streets where I live. Anna and Jason go down towards the river. This leaves the new-build estates at the sketchy end of the street for me and Merlin.

As soon as we pass the first corner and the lane is out of sight, Merlin seems anxious, looking around him as if he might have landed on another planet rather than a few streets beyond the community centre canteen.

'Do you know where to go, Mark?'

'Sure!' I say, though in truth I don't yet have a plan. To prove that I'm a native to the area and not just making it up as I go along, I turn off into an alleyway that runs to the back of some of the shabby new-builds. 'Come on,' I instruct. 'I'll show you.'

The estate was built sometime in the 1970s and the flats still feel out of place, while at the same time showing obvious signs of decay, as if they are much older than they really are. My father, who knows about these things, says the development has never succeeded in 'bedding in'. He says it was poorly planned and built on the cheap, so it's not surprising. Gerry calls them 'dinky homes'. Everyone agrees that they are *ugly as sin*.

But for our purposes, as illicit gardeners, this unloved dumping place for poor people is perfect.

We soon find our first patch and Merlin gets to work, crouching down on his hands and knees. He picks up some soil in his hand and inspects it.

'It's quite fine tilth already,' he says, showing it to me. 'Look at the way it crumbles, Mark.'

I look, and nod. I have no idea.

He removes a bag of seeds from our Seeds of Change pack. There is a hand-drawn sunflower on the front.

Merlin glances up at the fading light, checking the position of the sun. He nods, evidently satisfied, and tips the seeds into the palm of his hand. 'These Teddy Bears should do well here. South-facing.'

I grin. 'Teddy Bears?'

'That's what they call them, these ones. They grow up to ninety centimetres!'

'Who has a ninety-centimetre soft toy?'

'Well, I did,' he says, smiling.

'Actually,' I admit, recalling a prize I once won at a summer fete, 'I did as well.'

Merlin laughs and we get down to the serious business of planting the future and sowing the seeds of change. I help by pulling out weeds and discarding larger stones, cigarette butts and assorted litter.

When we're done we stand back and admire our work. 'There!' we exclaim simultaneously, and we chuckle at our synchronicity, and because it's the sort of thing neither of us would usually say, not in that tone, at least not in the company of our peers. But with Merlin it's okay to sound like my parents (or maybe more like an imagined version of them if I'm honest), and I am happy for him to instruct me in the ways of sunlight, soil and giant sunflowers.

We press on. We are hunters, scouring the paths and dead ends for scraps of earth and signs of life. Viewed in this way, it is like I am seeing this unpromising corner of the town for the first time.

We plant more seeds and saplings. Merlin shows me how much space to leave between them, and how deep to go. The latter he tells me is called 'drilling', and we have a good laugh about that as well. No one ever told me gardening offered up so much ludicrous language and silly names for things.

At one point an elderly couple come over wanting to know what we're doing. We explain that we're urban gardeners, beautifying the neglected patches of the neighbourhood. They smile and call us 'good boys,' and the man, who has a hacking cough, adds gruffly, 'not like them 'round here.' When he says this we all look around, but there is no one else in sight, so he must be speaking in the abstract.

It is only when the sun is almost completely below the rooftops that I check my watch.

'We should get back,' I say. 'Mission accomplished?'

Merlin nods, indicating the near-empty Seeds of Change pack. 'We did all right, didn't we?'

I smile. 'We did.'

The only issue is that I've not been paying attention, which means I'm not quite sure where we are, at least not in relation to where we need to be. We start walking and immediately come up against a dead end and have to retrace our steps. The light is fading fast.

Merlin frowns. 'Everything okay, Mark?'

I am conscious that I must act quickly in order to reassure him, and myself, that I know what I'm doing. I spy a passage. With a bit of luck, it will take us out of this maze. But instead of leading us to the street, as I had hoped, we enter a square.

'Square' is perhaps not the right word, though when it was designed, it was probably imagined as a vibrant piazza where residents would gather, drink Italian coffee and play *boules* or something. This evening, though, those gathered are drinking super strength cider and bear an uncanny resemblance to the shady characters who used to hang around outside my old school, selling the kids Lambert & Buttler for fifty pence a smoke, and probably plenty else besides if you asked.

I can feel Merlin's unease and I'm about to suggest we walk the other way to avoid the group, when I spot the perfect piece of ground – an elevated section of earth, sheltered from the wind yet exposed to all-day sun. The patch is simply crying out for sunflowers. It is as if the developers understood this, but never got around to doing anything about it, putting in a raised bed and then leaving it empty.

And, as luck would have it, we have in our Seeds of Change pack one final bag of Teddy Bears.

I glance at Merlin. He is looking at the patch of higher ground too. I can see him weighing it up in his mind. The triumph of completing our mission versus the potential threat posed by the local youths.

'I'm up for it if you are,' I say, holding up my trowel.

As we cross the square I can feel our every move being observed, though no one says anything at this point. I remind myself that they may look rough, the youths, but they're just people – just like us. They deserve some beauty in their lives, too. This is what Folk is all about, I tell myself.

Feeling the fear and doing it anyway, we clamber up the wall and set to work preparing the ground.

Up close it's a real mess, more stony than it looked from below. Had I known, I would not have suggested we attempt to rescue the site, but it's too late to back out now.

At last we manage to plant the seeds.

Wiping the sweat from my forehead, I turn around to leave. The group of youths has moved across the square. They are staring at us. It is like every zombie film I've ever seen. We are surrounded.

I glance at Merlin. His lower lip trembles.

'When I say so,' I whisper, 'we run, okay?'

'What's that, then?' one of the youths demands.

'All right, lads?' I call back.

Then, to Merlin, I hiss, 'Now!'

We jump down from the wall and race across the square. There are several shouts and what sounds like a stampede of horses behind us.

We make it to the other side and dart into a dark alley. We turn a sharp left, then right, then down some steps, two at a time, not daring to look back. Every passage looks the same in this 1970s hellhole estate. At every corner I pray for an exit, which never materialises. It's just more of the same. More passages, more closed doors and net curtains. Where is everyone? After a while, I begin to suspect that we have gone in a circle.

At last we reach a spot where the wall on one side is lower. We pause to catch our breath and I reach up and touch the top of the wall.

'I reckon we could get over this,' I say.

Loud footsteps echo behind us. A shout goes up. It's like the fox hunting videos that Gerry's friends from the League Against Cruel Sports showed us. We are the foxes and there are no saboteurs to put up a fight or document the atrocity on film. Suddenly, they are everywhere, coming at us from both ends of the passage. We are cornered and it is as if they have multiplied: there must be forty of them, perhaps more.

'Quick!' I shout, dropping my trowel and the bag of litter we had collected. I heave myself up onto the wall. Merlin does the same. And there, stretching out before us like promised land, is the road.

Parked cars mark the boundary where the estate ends and civilisation begins, and I know that if we can just get to the road we'll be safe.

The drop on the other side of the wall, however, is bigger than I'd anticipated. 'Shit,' I say, staring at the concrete below. It's a good six feet at least.

But Merlin shows less caution. He doesn't hesitate in leaping to the ground.

I hear him land. I hear the cry of pain. Maybe he didn't see the drop. Maybe he was too scared to think.

'Merlin!' I shout. 'Shit, Merlin.'

I carefully lower myself down, gripping the top of the wall with my fingertips to reduce the fall, so that when my feet connect with the concrete it is only a minor jolt that I feel.

Merlin, though, is still down.

'I'm all right,' he winces, clutching his ankle.

I crouch down next to him. 'Shit, man, you're really hurt.'

He tries to smile. 'That was a close one, eh, Mark?'

I shake my head. 'What were you thinking?'

Because… what I'm thinking is that we might have overreacted; that what we took to be menace from the locals may have been genuine curiosity. That they might not have meant us any harm.

'What do you think they'd have done?' Merlin persists, unable to let it drop.

'If they'd caught us?' I shrug and look away. 'Maybe nothing. Maybe roughed us up a bit. I dunno.'

His face drops, like I've just emptied his milkshake over the ground. I don't know why I'm being so unkind to him.

'Come on,' I say, more gently. I try to help him to his feet, which is difficult because even though Merlin's not much bigger than me, I'm not exactly strong.

'Is he all right?' comes a voice, and I turn to see two lads approaching, walking slowly towards us from one of several passages leading into the warren of flats. I think I recognise the bigger of the two from the group on the square. He steps forward now and hands me the trowel I had abandoned in the alleyway.

'Why'd ya run?' he says, shaking his head. 'We was only messing with you.'

I do not answer. There is nothing to say.

They help Merlin hobble to the edge of the estate. They offer to take us further. Fortunately, at this moment I spot Anna at the far end of the street, her radioactive hair acting like a beacon in a storm, and I've never been more pleased to see her.

'Anna!' I yell, finally finding my voice.

She turns and I notice that Jason is with her, and that too is a relief, although not because I think we're in danger any more.

'We'll be okay from here,' I say, turning to our Good Samaritans. 'Erm... thanks.'

The one I recognise shakes his head again and exhales a long breath. 'You're Mark Fisher, in't you?'

I frown at the sound of my name on his lips.

'Do we know each other?'

'My brother went to school with you.'

'Oh, right,' I say, burning with shame. 'I... er... didn't realise.'

Another shake of the head, but there is now a half-smile on his lips. He is watching me squirm. I cannot say if he is taking pleasure in my predicament, but he has noticed.

'Sorry,' I mumble.

'Yeah,' he says, walking away, still shaking his head.

When Anna and Jason arrive, we don't mention the youths, or the chase. Merlin's injury (it turns out to be a sprained ankle) is explained away as an accident. After that, there is no more guerrilla gardening. It is understood that Gerry receives a serious reprimand from Merlin's parents.

Part of me is desperate to confess. It is not, after all, Gerry's fault that Merlin and I are such snobs, and such cowards, that we chose to run away from the residents instead of talking to them like human beings. Of course, I remind myself, it is possible that had we stuck around we would have been beaten up anyway. And so I say nothing and hope that the whole thing will be forgotten, buried in the annals of mishaps that for one reason or another always seemed to happen to Merlin.

Chapter Three

There's a meadow we use. It is more wasteland than lush rolling hills but it has earned the title of 'meadow' on account of the long grass and the deserted nature of the spot. We call it Top of the World. From this spot you can see across the valley to the real countryside. Top of the World is Anna's discovery. She had overheard her brother describe it as a good place to do acid. We'd kept it secret, a Folk thing. I'm not sure about showing Jason but the others insist.

It'll be fine, they say.

The meeting point is at the end of my street. I borrow a picnic hamper and raid the kitchen for provisions. Zee has her ghetto blaster and Jason has a two-litre bottle of 8.6 per cent abv. White Pearl.

'Seb's got to work,' Anna says on arrival. Seb is the only one of us with a job. Sometimes we all go into the bakery where he works as a counter assistant, to annoy him, and to try to blag pies and free cakes.

Zee leads the way, marching ahead with her ghetto blaster tucked under her arm. She has put glitter around her eyes and wears a beret, like in the Prince song, although hers is navy rather than raspberry. Her jeans have specks of paint on them. The colour is called *Sapphire Salute*. We chose it together the previous summer when I painted my room and Zee helped. My parents thought blue might be a bit cold for a bedroom, but I insisted and Mum said, 'If that's what he wants,' and so we'd gone ahead with it. Painting the room had felt like a bit of a rite of passage, although we both went right off the colour before the paint had even dried, but it was too late by then to change it, so I kept my doubts to myself and pretended it was exactly what I'd wanted, which in a way is true.

We continue on towards what looks like a dead end and push back the foliage to reveal a dark track leading to a rusty gate that doesn't open. Zee hands me the ghetto blaster and climbs over, revealing more Sapphire Salute and earning me a poke in the ribs from Jason, who can't resist an opportunity to tease about Zee.

The path opens onto the meadow. The sudden brightness as we emerge into the daylight is dazzling, like that bit in Raiders of the Lost Ark, and Zee breaks into a run, swinging her arms around and singing at the top of her lungs 'The hills are a-LIVE with the sound of muuuuuusic...' Everyone joins in, except no one can remember the next line, so we just do the *dahs* and repeat the lines we know over and over again.

Anna finds an abandoned shopping trolley and we take it in turns to push each other down the hill.

Someone suggests getting out Anna's brother's home-grown she's brought along for the occasion. For a moment I long to be able to do things like this – being out in nature, spending time together – without the excuse of getting off our faces to justify it.

Zee lies down in the long grass, exhausted by her exertions. She is dappled in sunlight. I stretch out next to her and together we stare at the endless expanse of nothingness above our heads. A pigeon coos. The grass tickles.

'Is it all just bollocks, Mark?'

'What?'

'This.'

I can smell her shampoo. Honey. Citrus. I long to reach across and stroke her face. Is she right? Is it all make-believe? This? Us? Folk? In my mind Zee and I will be forever in each other's lives, if not as lovers then as stand-ins, and one day we will have our own kids, probably with other partners, but still – our children will also have Folk, or a version of it, updated perhaps for the times but fundamentally the same.

'Dunno,' I say, and she smiles and touches my hand. It is the briefest of touches, a brush against the skin, nothing more, yet it shoots through my body and every nerve is awakened.

We kissed, just the once, drunk at a party. The next day she said that she didn't want anything to get in the way of our friendship, and then she got together with a guy from my school, and while the boyfriend didn't last long ('he was a bit of a prick, Mark'), we never resumed where we'd left off.

Regarding her in this moment – the dew, the sun, the glitter – it feels all in concert to make Zee more lovely than ever, as she stares up at the sky, the clouds billowing and floating away, her lips slightly parted. She closes her eyes, opens them again.

'Do you like Jason?'

The question catches me off guard and it takes me a moment to recover enough to ask: 'Where did that come from?'

'I think he's jealous of you.'

'Of me?'

I glance over at him. He is sitting cross-legged in the grass, deep in concentration, building what Zee and Anna have begun calling *one of his magnificent specimens*.

'I'm serious,' she says. 'Do you?'

'Do I what?'

'Like him?'

'Er. Of course. Why wouldn't I?'

Zee puffs her cheeks out. 'Sometimes, Mark, I think you despise him. But then, sometimes, I think you despise us all.'

'How can you say that?'

She shrugs.

'Look,' I say, magnanimously, 'I just think maybe he goes on a bit too much about his brother.'

'He's proud of him, Mark!'

She turns her gaze on Jason, cocking her head. It is as if she is considering him as a philosophical problem. 'I think it's quite sweet, actually.'

He gets up slowly to his feet, ambles over to Anna.

'Oi!' Anna yells in our direction. 'You having some of this bad boy or what?'

* * *

Cider is served and the joint passed around. Jason's thigh has become Zee's pillow. She shuts her eyes and smiles contentedly to herself.

'Tell your brother,' she says in a BBC costume drama voice, 'that I find his green fingers very much to my liking.'

'May I venture,' Anna returns in her breathiest, mock-posh accent, 'that the source of your satisfaction has rather more to do with your current situation than my brother's horticultural exploits.'

Jason looks confused. He's not yet familiar with Zee and Anna's impromptu little skits, the way they slip in and out of character without warning.

'Nonsense, my dear,' says Zee, still in character.

'Ah, but you betray yourself, Miss Adams.'

Zee and Anna are tight, like sisters, people say. They can be mean to each other and fight and tease without inflicting lasting damage. That couldn't happen in my family, but then I've never had a sister or a brother.

I have always longed for a sibling, always loathed being an only child, a *lonely* child – for years that's what I thought it was. It sounded so sad, and I couldn't understand why any parent would choose to inflict loneliness on their offspring.

It is time to change the topic, I decide. When they are stoned Zee and Anna can go on like this for hours.

So I say: 'Do you think Gerry's Survival Night will go ahead?'

This breaks the spell.

Anna looks up. 'Here,' she says, her normal voice returning. 'We should do it during mushroom season.'

'You're such a stoner, Anna,' says Zee.

'All *au naturale*, Zeenah D. No chemicals.'

Every summer we go camping with affiliated groups from across the United Kingdom and sometimes also Europe and around the world. And every year Gerry runs his Famous Survival Overnighter. Numbers are strict, and he is picky about who he takes, so it is something of an honour to be invited.

To my knowledge, no one has ever expressed any serious concern about the event in the past, so the veto that has now been issued by District Council following a risk assessment that was carried out without Gerry's consent, feels like an affront.

Gerry has never held Council in high esteem. Their meetings, he says, are rather like Andrew Lloyd Webber musicals: tedious, self-satisfied and without substance.

Since the ruling, diplomatic relations have deteriorated and any remnant of good faith is gone. Gerry says it's a witch hunt, an attempt by certain members of the committee to discredit him and turn the movement into a banal and fundamentally empty babysitting service. It is a betrayal of the movement's values, he says. They talk about *safeguarding*, he says, but what are they guarding? Certainly not the principles that brought him to the movement.

We agree. We think it's stupid. We think they're out of touch. We think How Dare They. We think we should not be treated like children.

We respond (Gerry responds). We escalate the matter to the national Powers That Be. But those powers uphold the decision by District. The committee applauds the energy and commitment that Gerry has shown over the years, but concurs that the Survival Overnighter in its current form falls short of their standards for care and protection. They suggest certain steps that could be taken to bring the event into line. None of these proposed measures are acceptable to any of us, removing as they do the *Survival* part of the Survival Overnighter.

'What I don't get is this,' says Gerry, breaking the news to a roomful of disappointed Folk, 'I've been taking groups on these things for fifteen years. In all that time we've never had a complaint. What's changed?'

There must be something we can do, we say. The decision, we all think, represents more than just the Survival Overnighter. It is, in effect, an attack on our values.

There is, it transpires. We can go it alone; break with the national network of youth organisations which, for all its talk, had become stuffy and parochial, driven by egos and personal agendas.

Independence will not be easy, Gerry had warned. We would almost certainly lose our charitable status, which would affect our funding. And linking up with other groups, at least officially, will be difficult. No one had ever declared independence before. In doing so, we would be entering uncharted waters.

It is put to a ballot. The result is convincing, if not unanimous. The formal split is completed just weeks before the arrival of Jason.

'It'll go ahead,' says Zee, quietly. 'Gerry's fought too long, and too hard, for it not to.'

Chapter Four

Gerry has a house. It's on Mount Pleasant Road, which is neither a mountain nor very pleasant, but it is a road, a busy one, and when the windows are open the roar of the traffic can make conversation nigh on impossible.

Most of the houses in this area have been crudely chopped up and divided into single-occupant bedsits with shared bathrooms and kitchens, and absent landlords who provide the minimum level of upkeep that the law requires. In reality it is often considerably less, knowing as they do that their tenants have neither jobs nor lawyers and are mostly just grateful to find a landlord that still accepts DSS payments. In other words, it's not the sort of place you're going to find many Folk people, unless they're visiting Gerry.

Gerry's house is large and chaotic, and filled with things in various states of disrepair. He always has a couple of lodgers, a shifting cast of figures – Gerry's Waifs and Strays, my parents call them. Gerry jokingly refers to them as his children. Some stick around for a while, others you see once and never hear of again. If money passes hands, it doesn't do so officially.

One of these characters, known only as Badger, plays drums for a band that some people have heard of. When he's not on tour, he sometimes sells a bit of blow on the side, which is how Anna knows him. He lives in one of the rooms at the back.

Then there's Kay, who knows about crystals and uses words like 'aura' in normal conversation. She has a grown-up daughter, somewhere, who she doesn't see very often.

Gerry says there's always more to people than they present.

They all call me *Gerry's boy*.

Generally, I only go there to pick up some copies of the latest issue of Juggernaut to give to Mum to take out to the Dog (the pub, that is).

I enjoy this role, for it makes me feel of use, and contributing to a cause that is bigger than myself, bigger even than Folk. This, I'm told, is how the movement grows: changing the world, one pamphlet at a time.

The relaxed disorder of Gerry's open house is a welcome break from the silences and meanness of our house, a house that Mum (according to a recent argument) had never liked. (She may not like the house, but it proved to be a canny investment, thanks to buying *at the right time* and a buoyant property market that has seen house prices in the area rise and rise beyond belief – as Dad, in the same argument, pointed out.) Of course, I already know (from a previous row) that Mum wanted to stay in London, and had it not been for Dad's insistence that the provinces would be a better place to start a family, they would have remained in the cosmopolitan world of theatre and late-night jazz clubs and friends with interesting backstories – the world that had brought them together. Had they stayed, she might have succeeded in her acting career, and maybe the marriage would have been a happier one, or perhaps they'd have split up sooner. Mum would have got bored, probably. Dad would have been pulled by his provincial roots. And I would never have been conceived – an outcome which, from their perspective, on one level at least, may have been a good thing. Do I believe that? Yes, I do. Maybe. Perhaps.

It is a month or so since Jason turned up at Folk. It's been a while since I last visited the house and I'm momentarily shocked, though I should be used to it by now, by the excessive noise and dirt of Mount Pleasant Road.

The door is open, so I go straight in, calling, 'Gerry! You there?'

'In the kitchen!'

The kitchen looks out onto a back garden, also filled with junk. There's an ancient bathtub, a bent bicycle wheel, some bags of cement – Gerry always says he's going to do something about it, but he never does.

I fight my way past the various boxes and jackets and tools and unclaimed mail in the hallway and eventually come out into the light of the kitchen.

Gerry is sitting at the table with a pile of Juggernauts. At the window, wearing only a pair of boxer shorts and a T-shirt, is Jason.

'Hello, Sparky,' he says.

'Ah, yes,' says Gerry, not looking up from the envelopes he is preparing to send out the magazines in. 'Jason's staying for a bit.'

'Right. I see.'

'Just for a while,' Gerry adds, licking the gum on the envelope. 'Just until we can sort out something more permanent.'

He pulls out a chair for me to join him at the table. Jason stays where he is. His T-shirt has the words 'Spiral Tribe' written across the front, with a graphic of a deformed smiley face, all teeth and wide eyes, like a skeleton or a poltergeist.

The other lodgers aren't around. Badger is on tour, somewhere in eastern Europe, Gerry thinks. It is the band's first trip behind what used to be called the Iron Curtain and is now all these countries I never knew existed.

Belarus, Estonia, Lithuania. They sound made up.

We watched the Berlin Wall on telly. They showed it live, all these folk climbing over a particular section that was somehow significant, which didn't look *that* high. I knew I wasn't supposed to think that, given all the fuss, and because people died, but it didn't look that forbidding.

Truthfully, it seemed more a party than an epoch-making moment in the history of mankind. The music and the dancing were terrific. We liked watching the people holding hands and waving sparklers, and I would definitely have been one of the ones hammering away at the bits of wall for some good memorabilia.

Gerry says he can remember The Wall going up. 'No one predicted it that time, either. But that's how change works. You might wait years, decades, centuries, and when it does *finally* happen, it's all over within a few hours and then no one can believe that it was ever otherwise.'

'Of course,' he adds, 'I was just a kid. But I knew something big was happening.'

Kids, we agree, are aware of more than most adults give them credit, and obviously I think of my parents still pretending they're happily married.

'So, er, Jason. Have you got Badger's room?'

Gerry laughs. 'No, no – I wouldn't do that to the kid. No, Jason's in the wee room at the top.'

'Right.'

I know the room he means. It is a room he doesn't normally let out to lodgers, and I feel inexplicably and unjustifiably hurt that Jason has been offered something that was never offered to me.

'Full house,' I say, rather spitefully I may add.

Jason picks up the packet of Marlboro reds on the table. The ashtray is overflowing. Gerry and the rest of the house only smoke roll-ups and joints, so Jason's stubs stand out for their brightness and chemical quality.

I wouldn't really want to live at Gerry's, I tell myself. I wouldn't be able to live with the squalor and the disorder. It would get to me. There is, however, an appeal to all that looseness, all that absence of manners.

'Is this the latest, Gerry?' I ask, picking up a Juggernaut.

The cover is given over to the Criminal Justice Bill, which I'm now following quite closely. Everyone is angry with the shadow home secretary, a young man called Tony Blair who, despite the protests and the solidarity, is still refusing to fight the legislation. Indeed, people seem even more angry with this Blair guy than they are with the real bogeyman, the actual home secretary, Michael Howard, who Gerry calls 'a weasel of a man'. It is, however, not all plain sailing for the government, because leading members of the judiciary have come forward to publicly condemn the proposed legislation, which they say overturns centuries of legal traditions, especially in regard to laws around trespass and public nuisance, but also in relation to police powers to conduct what is known as Stop & Search operations, which they warn may be used disproportionately to target certain parts of the population.

'It's a bonfire of rights,' says Gerry. 'And Her Majesty's opposition are running scared in case the *News of the Screws* or the *Daily Mail* accuses them of being soft on crime. Which is why we must fight this thing, fight it tooth and nail. We can't leave it to Westminster elites to do our bidding. We have to force them to listen, make it so that they can't *not* listen.'

I'm smiling, because this is quintessential, peak Gerry.

'Power to the People,' I say, glancing at Jason, who has that familiar look of amusement on his face.

'Fuck 'em and their law,' he adds.

It's an odd coalition that the Criminal Justice Bill has rallied: High Court judges, ravers, travellers, ramblers, environmentalists, road protesters and occasional protesters like my parents. Commentators question how long the unified front can last. Everyone agrees that this is a moment of seismic change. Someone has called it the end of history. The Second Summer of Love, thirty years after the first one, has been and gone, and apparently that's all over. Kurt Cobain is dead. Freddie Mercury is dead. Guitars are dead. Something else is coming. Something has to fill the void.

Spiral Tribe.

Gerry sends Jason out to fetch a box for the newsletters. Once he's gone, Gerry turns to me and says, 'Probably wise, Mark, to keep this one under your hat. About Jason, I mean, living here. It's not a secret or anything. Nothing like that. It just might get a bit... complicated. You understand?'

I nod. Yes, Gerry. Understood. Mums the word.

Jason returns with a box and helps load the newsletters for Mum.

I'm wondering if Zee and Anna already know about Jason living there. It had not occurred to me to ask Jason where he was living. Of course, I did think it a bit strange that he never complained about his parents, so maybe I did know – not that he was living at Gerry's, but that he wasn't living in a normal family home?

Mum and Dad, at one time, had toyed with the idea of becoming foster parents, of taking in vulnerable kids like Jason Templar and giving them opportunities and stability, the sorts of things that have so far been denied to them in their miserable lives.

I know, because I've heard them talking, and because I know them, that not having a second child is a great disappointment for them and one of the reasons their marriage is so crap.

All my life I've felt the absence of this missing brother or sister that never was. The house has always felt a little echoey, though it is not a particularly big house, not in comparison with other people we know, nor do my parents show much restraint in the accumulation of stuff.

I can, of course, see why fostering might have appealed to them, filling the gaping void in their lives on the one hand while always giving them something to feel good about. Their dreams, however, are dashed when the social worker comes around to assess the application, and the questions – indeed the whole *focus* – is all wrong and not at all what Mum and Dad had expected. And so the plan is modified, meaning instead of taking in a damaged child they get a rescue dog – an incontinent Jack Russell, who is always molesting Dad's leg, and who no one likes. After a few hellish months, the dog is returned and the only rescuing that anyone is talking about is the rescue effort required on the upholstery, which now stinks of pee and Febreeze.

Chapter Five

One drab morning, early enough in the summer that it still feels as though there's plenty of summer ahead, I go out straight after breakfast. Mum and Dad have been arguing on and off for about a week, in that way they do, not actually saying anything. Just quietly despising one another for nothing in particular, just for being. And so I leave the house without a plan, without even an idea of where I might go or who (if anyone) I'll see.

I take my bike. Maybe I'll swing by my favourite outdoors specialist. I've had my eye on a 3.5 Seasons sleeping bag with convertible inner, and a few other items of kit. None of it is cheap. I'm conscious how lucky I am to receive the generous allowance that my parents pay into the bank account they helped me to set up. I'm aware that other people have to get jobs, that other people must resort to cheaper (substandard) kit that breaks and leaks and is really heavy and cumbersome and just a bit rubbish. My own gear, it must be said, is not the very best, but it's pretty good nonetheless. The guys in the shop know me. They know I'm properly into it, not just a fair weather walker or someone who buys the equipment and then never uses it, just sticks it in the loft or the garage. They're the worst. But I do know

I'm lucky. Privileged. That's the word. Sometimes I wish I didn't have to be one of the privileged ones and that I had something legitimate to complain about, but I know you're not allowed to say that out loud, or even think it, because there's nothing more privileged and entitled than someone privileged and entitled whinging about their privilege and entitlement.

Town is the usual. I spot a couple of girls I knew at school, but not to speak to. School feels a world away now I'm at college and it's weird to think that I may never have to associate in any meaningful way with people like these girls again. Nothing against these girls in particular, just generally, the sort of folk who went to my school.

Me and Zee, Zee and I, we went to the same primary school, then she moved out to a village and when they returned, a few years later, Zee had enrolled at the more *academic* secondary school on the other side of town. For a long time I resented my parents for sending me to the crap school and not the good school with Zee. I have become more philosophical about it. It is not a given that the friendship would have held had we attended the same school. People behaved differently in school and we would probably have fallen into quite separate friendship groups: Zee would have been with the cool kids.

I am aware that in thinking this I'm being unjust, both to my ex-school friends, who weren't such a bad bunch really, and also to Zee, who has always been quite capable of deciding for herself who she wants in her life. She is not, and has never been, pulled by notions of popularity or the need to be accepted by a dominant *in-crowd*. She is, after all, a *Folk* person, not a *School* person. And yes, I'm aware of the shortcomings of my reasoning, but I am forever dividing the world into *Folk* people and *Non-Folk* people.

So, yeah. I mooch around town for a bit, but there's nothing going on and I'm getting a little tired of my own company. My thoughts are starting to bore me. I want to stop thinking and start, you know, *living*.

I find myself cycling in the general direction of Zee's house.

Something else I deplore in myself: my lack of spontaneity. I hardly ever just knock on someone's door or do anything, really, without checking diaries and making a prior arrangement. It's pathetic. Really.

Yes, I need to stop thinking.

* * *

The Adams family live up by the university in a red brick Victorian mansion. One side of the house is completely covered in wisteria. There is an epic treehouse out the back.

The front door is open so I go into the entrance hall, through the beautiful stained-glass inner door.

'Hello?'

I can hear a TV on in the front room, the volume turned up very loud. I poke my head around the doorway.

A skinny thirteen-year-old is sitting cross-legged on the sofa eating Super Noodles out of the saucepan. A re-run of an American cop show is playing, although her attention seems to be on a magazine that's open in front of her.

I recognise the title because it's the same one the girls at my old school used to bring on school trips, and which everyone – boys and girls – would pore over for the sex stuff, reading aloud the agony aunt letters from readers fearing they might be pregnant from kissing, etc.

'Hey, Nomi.'

'Oh, it's you.' Nomi is not one for niceties. 'They're upstairs. You might want to knock.'

I thank her and go out to the hallway. I remove my boots and stow them in the rack next to Zee's Cherry Reds. They look good together.

The door to the music room is open. I can see Beethoven above the fireplace. The girls were all encouraged to learn instruments, but Zee's youngest sister Megan is the only one who displays any talent for it. She plays second violin in a local Youth Orchestra.

Zee's still got her cello but she never practices. I regret not learning an instrument. I had piano lessons for a while but I never got very far with it. Part of the problem, I think, was the location my parents chose for the piano. It sat in the front room, so that every time I practiced I was 'serenading' at least one of my parents and usually half their friends. They would say encouraging things like, 'Oooh, I didn't expect a concert!' or 'He's getting very good, isn't he?'

After Zee's parents split up, Zee's Mum got together with Polly, which caused a mild stir, even among the less bigoted parts of the community.

They both have what people call, with a mixture of envy and disdain, *Big Jobs* up at the university. As well as standing out as the only black professor in the faculty, Yolanda has written books on cultural theory and semiotics that people have actually read, so folk who don't know her personally *feel* they know her, at least to the extent that they feel permitted to comment on her personal life and motivations.

Everyone seems to like that they know Yolanda and Polly. People admire them, but it is sometimes said they're a little aloof, a bit high and mighty.

Yolanda and the girls are, of course, the only black people anyone we know knows. There's the nice family that run the corner shop, but having never had an actual conversation with any of them they don't really count as friends.

On the stairs I pause to look at the family photos: trips to the seaside, adventures in forests, glens, rivers, mountains. The girls in New York City. The photos go all the way back to baby Zee, chewing on a dandelion. Before even, to Yolanda's parents (how formal they're dressed!) and Polly's conspicuously white parents and younger brother (who died). There is so much life spilling out of this wall, so many stories, so many characters, places, voices, sensations. The contrast to the photos we have on our walls couldn't be starker. For a start, there aren't very many, and of the few there are, every one of them feels contrived, taken at some choreographed life event – wedding, fortieth birthday, school play, etc.

I steal a peek into the study. They have an amazing study; floor-to-ceiling books and big windows looking out onto the mature trees behind the house. There is an enormous desk piled up with papers, academic journals and notepads.

If Yolanda or Polly were there, I would now be summoned in for a conversation, and not just about nothing but about something: a question relating to what they're working on, something in the news or a philosophical problem that they want my opinion on.

From a young age the girls were included in discussions and encouraged to speak with confidence and openness about anything and everything. This is utterly foreign to me, growing up in a house where conversations are more practical and thorny topics are avoided.

The stairs get steeper and the ceilings lower towards the top of the house, which gives it a fairytale castle-like quality.

Rapunzel, Rapunzel! Let down your hair!

Zee would probably hit me if I called her a princess.

Her room is all the way up. It has sloping ceilings and a large skylight. It is probably – definitely – my favourite room, in any house, anywhere I've ever been.

The thud-thud-thud of machine-music drifts out. There was a time, not that long ago, when we'd listen to, I dunno, the Waterboys and Joni Mitchell. Like, *actual* songs.

The smell of joss sticks suggests they're already on the weed, and I'm all set to chastise Zee and Anna (I assume it's Anna) for being such wasters, sitting around all day getting stoned when the world is filled with injustice and there's a hole in the ozone layer, and people in Africa (and other continents) are starving and being persecuted, or getting blown up by western forces, or having their livelihoods destroyed by corporate capitalist greed.

I knock on the door. There is a hurried movement on the other side.

I wait a few beats, and go in.

'Sparky! All right, mate?'

They are sitting up in bed. Zee and Jason. Zee smiles. She is relaxed, not the least bit concerned that I have walked in on them.

She is wearing his Spiral Tribe T-shirt. I can't tell if she's wearing anything on the lower half of her body.

'Did you see Mum?'

'No, only Nomi.'

'Only Nomi,' repeats Jason.

I consider whether to try to squeeze onto the bed with them. I decide that's a bit much. There's a beanbag in the corner. Probably a better idea. To buy a little time before having to commit, I kneel down beside the stereo and flick through some cassettes and CDs.

'Jay got a new Cloud 9 mix yesterday,' Zee calls, as if this might mean something to me.

'Right.'

It dawns on me that Zee's music collection has become an assorted mass of names and graphics that exist in a space that is entirely divorced from any sound, emotion or specific memory or place.

The clatters and clicks and claps and beeps and booms and bursts of melody coming from the speakers seem artificial and empty, each element processed and replaced by approximations of the original thing: the musical equivalent of a Big Mac. There are no songs, only sounds, and the sounds are all synthetic or stolen. Call me old fashioned but I miss having a beginning, a middle and an end. I don't like this drifting, this not knowing where I'm at. Zee says that's because I'm a control freak.

'This place must seem like such a backwater to you,' I call over the music. 'You know, compared to London?'

Jason shrugs. 'Nah, safe here.'

He winks at Zee as he says this, and she sticks her tongue out.

Jason breathes a thick cloud of smoke from his substantial mouth and nose, like a dragon.

Then he offers me the joint. It doesn't matter how many times I refuse, he continues to offer. I suppose he's just being polite and inclusive, but I also wonder if he might not also be trying to corrupt me.

I get up and go over to the skylight, which is propped open to air the room. Zee's not really supposed to smoke in her room – Yolanda and Polly are critical of drugs, and they include tobacco and alcohol in this, not just for their effects on society but because people use them to hide behind and *negate* themselves. Zee finds this talk hilarious and sometimes jokes about being in the mood for a bit of *negation*, before grabbing a bottle of White Pearl or skinning up. Yolanda sometimes tells Zee she can be too arrogant for her own good.

The breeze brushes against my cheek. The sun is trying to break through.

Zee suddenly sits up straight. 'Let's do something!'

'Right.' I'm doubtful. 'Like what?'

She inhales deeply. You can hear her brain ticking, considering the possibilities. 'Let's go somewhere.'

'Go somewhere?'

'Yes!' she cries, leaping from the bed and pulling on a pair of jeans that are lying on the floor.

'Come on! It'll be fun!'

I glance at Jason. He's amused. He's really into her. Of course he's really into her.

'You mean... all of us?'

'Absolutely. Why not?'

Okay, her enthusiasm is infectious. She is so beguiling.

'I dunno...'

'Come on,' she cries, and now she really sounds like Julie Andrews. 'It'll be good for us to get out. Fresh air. Exercise. We'll take a picnic!'

'Are we talking Top of the World here, or will we be needing the National Trust card?'

Jason laughs as if I'm the wittiest person in the world.

The only snag, we realise, is transport. Me and Zee, Zee and I, have started driving lessons but neither of us have passed the test, and in any case we don't have a car. Jason offers to hot-wire one and it's not one hundred per cent clear he's joking.

'How about Stoke Woods?' I suggest.

Zee approves wholeheartedly.

'We'll *bike there*,' she says, gaily. 'It'll be like *Jules et Jim*.'

Jason thinks that's a kid's TV show, so we give him a short précis on Truffaut, Goddard and French New Wave cinema.

'It's all about sex and freedom,' says Zee.

'And friendship,' I add.

* * *

Zee finds an old bike for Jason at the back of the garage. She pumps the tyres and oils the chain.

'There you go, darling,' she says. 'Want to give it a test drive around the garden?'

He gets on, unsteadily, and almost wipes out into the Begonia. He tries again, his hands gripping the handlebars as if the front wheel might at any moment fly off. He wobbles along the path, narrowly avoiding Polly's prize marigolds, and comes to a standstill in front of the old treehouse. He seems relieved.

'Been a while,' he says, blushing.

We've not seen him embarrassed or shy before. What kind of childhood did he have if he never properly learned to ride a bike?

Zee grins and gives him a peck on the cheek.

'Bit like riding a bike, eh, Jase?'

We're about to get going when Zee suddenly rushes back into the house. She returns a few moments later waving around her Super8 camera.

We set off, Zee going in front, cycling with one hand, filming with the other. A car whizzes by, its horn blaring.

She doesn't care.

The first section is all downhill, so we freewheel the whole way, yelling and whooping into the wind.

We pause at a petrol station for pasties, bottles of water and juice, and a can of Lucozade for Jason. Zee insists on paying for it all.

'My treat,' she says, with a wink. For the summer, Zee is doing a few days a week at a shoe shop in the only alternative shopping street in the town.

The day is mild, a little overcast, no sign of rain. I'm conscious that we have nothing sensible with us. No waterproofs, no map, no first aid kit, and it crosses my mind to care, but I don't want to be boring, and it is only Stoke Woods.

It's not exactly Gerry's Famous Survival Overnighter.

At the woods we lock the bikes together. There's no dilly-dallying about which way to go, we just go. It doesn't matter. None of it matters. Nothing matters. We are free. We are young. We run green. We are alive. We are the next generation. We are the future.

Avoiding the paths, we soon lose the other visitors to the woods that day, and from there on in the place feels like our own film set as we take it in turns to film each other and whatever else piques our interest: phallic shrubs and gnarled trees, butterflies and bees and rabbits and brambles, and copulating beetles.

Jason runs on ahead and hides, springing out from trees with a roar. One time he lands awkwardly, almost crippling himself and losing his shoe in the kerfuffle. The next half hour is taken up with hunting for his missing

Air Max. He hobbles a bit after that, but insists it's fine.

On the trunk of a fallen oak, we sit and eat our picnic, the crows squawking and circling, hoping to pinch some pasty. We watch them in silence, chewing on unspecified material wrapped in shortcrust pastry.

'You know the four and twenty blackbirds,' says Zee, presently. 'The ones baked in a pie and set before the king?'

'What about it?'

'I've always wondered, why is it the domestic servant, hanging out the clothes, who gets mutilated?'

'Mutilated?'

'Yes. What would you call getting your nose pecked off?'

'Well, yes, if you put it like that.'

Zee is right. Framed in this way, the maid getting her nose pecked off is no laughing matter. I have to think about it for a moment.

'Isn't it about revenge?' I say at last. 'The blackbird is avenging the deaths of its brothers and sisters and children, the ones that went into the pie.'

'So, like a punishment attack?'

'Yeah, if you like.'

'But why the maid?'

'Why not the maid?'

'Why not punish the king in his counting house or the queen in her parlour? It's their pie. They ordered the killing. They are ultimately responsible for the death of the four and twenty blackbirds.'

'Maybe the blackbird would have done the cook, or whoever it was who butchered them, but they weren't available?'

'I think there's some truth to that,' she says. 'We punish those who are available. If we can't get to the king or queen we go after the easier targets. It's like people who commit tax fraud. Fiddle an expense claim and you get in big trouble. Steal a million and you get to keep your money because you're too big to catch.'

'Didn't we watch a film about that once?'

'So,' —Zee is on a roll, she does this—'Let's say the maid was the only one available. You know, wrong place at the wrong time kind of thing. But I think there's more going on. I think it's about status and where the domestic servant stands in relation to the bird.' She smiles. I'm conscious that Jason is looking at us as if we've lost our minds, but he's also quite amused. 'Stay with me,' she instructs. 'I'm getting to it. So, imagine, you're the blackbird. Yeah? You've just witnessed the slaughter of your people.'

'People?'

She smiles again. 'Birds. You know what I mean.'

'Are we still talking about the nursery rhyme?'

'Now even if the facts of the case are that the maid had nothing to do with the killing of the birds, she's still a more attractive target for a revenge attack. Not because of her role in the killing (she didn't have one), but because of who she is and where she stands in the, er, pecking order. Because – from the bird's perspective – she *ought* to know better. She's oppressed by the monarch. So are the birds. So her betrayal feels greater even though she's technically innocent.'

'That's one sophisticated blackbird.'

She shrugs. Her eyes are twinkling but she manages to remain completely deadpan. 'Birds are clever.'

We all laugh.

'This one is,' says Jason, and without warning, he swoops down and pretends to grab my nose, holding his thumb between index and middle finger like a trophy.

The day rolls on. We do some more filming until the batteries in the camera run out.

We find a rope that's been tied to a tree as a swing. We do that for a while and Jason pretends to be Tarzan, which feels a bit off to me, Tarzan being a bit on the racist side for 1994, but Zee doesn't seem to mind.

Eventually we agree it's time to call it a day. We've run out of food and drink, and people – parents – might be beginning to wonder where we are.

Confident in our knowledge of the woods, we've naturally paid zero attention to where we are or to the signposts and waymarks. Mostly we've managed to avoid proper paths, taking only the tracks made by foxes, badgers, deer and whatever.

To get our bearings we climb to the top of a hill. In a gap between the trees we spot the railway, the river and the road, and from all this it's easy to gain a sense of direction.

It's only when we begin walking in earnest back to the bikes that the strangeness of the signposting becomes apparent. Having just seen, with our own eyes, where certain landmarks are in relation to other known landmarks, it is disconcerting to find a sign that claims a different reality. And we're not talking just a small deviation that could be accounted for as necessary, or even desirable, to avoid an obstacle or offer a more scenic route. These signs, if one was to follow them, would send you in completely the wrong direction. Worse, the signs frequently contradict one another, meaning that a devoted follower could quite easily end up trapped in a labyrinth of misdirection and deceit.

There is one signpost that mocks objective reality with such flagrance that Zee decides she cannot let it go. She gets down on her hands and knees and begins to examine the ground around the signpost.

'Here,' she says, pointing to where the earth has been disturbed. 'Someone's been at this. You can see where it's been twisted.'

'Bloody kids.'

Going to a school like mine, I had obviously heard of these sorts of pranks, carried out by folk who think that sending tourists and weekend walkers the wrong way is the pinnacle of hilarity.

Jason joins her in the dirt. He reckons he can fix it. I'm not so sure it's a good idea, but I'm also desperate for a pee, so I dive off behind the trees to relieve myself and leave them to sort out what, if anything, should be done about the offending signpost.

When I return, voices are raised. A couple of older walkers, dressed in choreographed leisure wear, came across Zee and Jason while they were moving the signpost into the correct position, and an argument has broken out because the walkers have assumed that Zee and Jason are the culprits who tampered with the signs in the first place.

Something is said to which Zee reacts with fury.

'What's THAT got to do with anything?'

I hurry over to make peace.

'What seems to be the problem?' I call, falling easily into what Zee calls my *Weasel Posh Boy* voice.

This is the voice I adopt when I speak with parents and teachers and college admissions staff and anyone in a position of authority. My presence, and my Posh Boy Weasel voice, brings instant calm and the possibility of dialogue.

The couple explain what happened, as they see it, and I listen politely to their concerns. Yes, I agree, tampering with the signposts is indeed an act of wanton vandalism.

'The thing is,' I add, 'my friends were putting the sign right. We live locally, you see, and we were worried that visitors to the woods might be misled.'

I'm wondering if I'm laying it on a bit heavy, but my Posh Boy Weasel voice has never let me down yet.

The couple exchange glances with each other.

'They're your friends?' asks the man, with undisguised bewilderment.

'Well, yes.'

'Well,' says the man, taking his partner's arm and starting to walk away. 'We'll have to give you the benefit of the doubt.'

'What doubt would that be?' shouts Zee, but the couple pretend not to hear her, hurrying away from us all, as if they think we might rob them.

The ride back is a slog, partly because it's all uphill, but also because the conversation has dried up. All I can think about is how I let down my friends – and myself – in trying to please the Concerned Citizens instead of calling them out on their prejudice, and how typical this is of me, always seeking the approval of others even when those individuals prove themselves to be bigots and bullies.

Zee powers on ahead, and even I struggle to keep up, while Jason puffs away behind us in the wrong gear. At the top of the hill, outside Zee's gate, we part without ceremony.

It is an unfortunate end to what had been a magical and dreamlike adventure.

The following day my legs feel like granite. My head as well, and I wonder if it is divine retribution or whether I am just coming down with something.

I stay in my room and wait for my parents to go out before venturing downstairs and making some food.

I tell no one about our day in the woods, or the way it ended, and the next time I see Zee and Jason it is as if it had never happened.

Chapter Six

The location to which we are headed is top secret. The whole event is shrouded in secrecy. Police have been closing in on unlicensed parties, going in heavy and breaking them up with mounted officers, like cavalrymen in old paintings. They are keen to be seen to be clamping down on the illegal rave scene after the spectacle of Castlemorton two years earlier when 20,000 folk descended on the Malvern Hills, turning a picturesque English country idyll into a giant cesspit – and a media circus.

I've heard about Richie's UTR parties but never been even close to going to one. The only reason I'm invited this time is because Seb had to pull out at the last minute and Zee called saying they had a space in the car if I was up for it.

So, here we are, squeezed into the back of a Ford Fiesta. Me, Zee and Jason, hurtling up the A30, windows down, bass pumping.

One of Anna's brother's friends is driving, and there's another random person I've never met before beside her. They are not the slightest bit interested in the kids strapped in the back. The only reason they're giving us a lift is because we've agreed to pay for the petrol.

After turning off the main road and travelling for a mile or so along a pretty country lane, the homemade UTR signs begin to appear along the roadside.

UTR. Under the Radar.

More of these signs have been tied to trees and telegraph poles at regular intervals. It feels a bit like a treasure hunt. Everyone in the car is getting excited, although we're all too cool to let on.

It's almost dark by the time we reach the site. A gate is opened by a white girl with dreadlocks wearing a hi-vis vest. She checks with the driver how many of us we are, then she points up the field to where some vehicles are parked and a rabble of folk are milling around.

Zee settles the financials with the friends of Richie's (whose names I never got) and Jason hands over some of his cigarettes.

They ask if it's our first UTR. Zee says she's been to one before, but that one was at a different location. They're not interested. They remind us that they can't drive us back, that we'll need to find our own way home, which comes as news to me, but I let Zee do the talking because I trust that she knows what she's doing and that as long as I stick with her we'll get home somehow. I feel a little anxious about the practicalities.

'Don't stress,' says Zee. 'It'll work out, it always does.'

This answer increases my anxiety, but I smile because what else am I going to do? I wonder what my parents would say if they knew. They think we've gone to a barn dance.

'Well,' says Zee, holding out an arm for Jason and an arm for me to take. 'Here we are!'

A dirt track leads towards some trees and that's the way everyone's going, so we follow them. A few minutes later we hear a low rumble, and the trees open out onto a quarry, with dormant bulldozers and heavy machinery scattered around like dinosaur figures in some kind of approximation of a prehistoric scene.

A trail of tea-lights in jam jars leads down into the bowl-shaped quarry, where a marquee has been erected, along with a couple of other (smaller) temporary structures.

As we descend the music seems to grow.

Further along there are self-made signs directing to toilets and medical facilities. The level of organisation is impressive. As a Folk veteran of many years, I've seen enough setups to recognise the hand of someone who knows what they're doing.

This is not, it must be stated, what I'd expected. From everything I had heard and read about raves and illegal parties I had been bracing myself for something more, well, hellish; an apocalyptic fairground filled with zombies and litter and folk passed out or wandering around aimlessly, gurning, lost inside their sad, pickled minds.

'Sick,' says Jason.

'See!' says Zee.

'Goodness,' says I.

People mill around chatting and laughing, fixing lights, tying up guy ropes, cables and canopies. The mood is calm; everything shipshape. With its mix of practical activity and hanging around waiting for something to happen, it reminds me so much of Folk and the first day of camp that I start to relax and feel at home. Okay, so the people are a bit older and a bit crustier, but still. There are definitely more Folk-people than non-Folk-people.

We spot Anna. She's sitting on a folding stool under a ten-foot papier-mâché dragon. She has glow sticks in her hair and a pair of fairy wings on her back. They came up earlier in the day with the sound system, she explains.

Anna, Zee and Jason talk excitedly about the night ahead. They keep mentioning a name of someone they seem to all know who has come over from America for the party. They say Richie's been trying to book him for months.

The girls insist that Jason and I allow them to put glitter around our eyes. When they're done decorating us like a Christmas tree they nod and say boys should wear makeup all the time, that it looks hot.

'I thought you hated makeup?'

'Not this kind, Mark,' says Anna, laughing. 'This kind's good.'

A bonfire has been lit. There are crates and boxes to sit on. Folk are even toasting marshmallows.

At some point Jason goes on a walkabout. He says he's going to see a man about a dog, which even I know means he's buying drugs.

More folk arrive and the place starts to fill up. There's a real sense of anticipation. Zee points out a very tall black man chatting with Richie.

'That's him,' she says.

'That's the DJ?'

I'm surprised because whenever I've seen rave acts on Top of the Pops and the other music show, the one on Channel 4, it's always white blokes, usually dressed in boiler suits or gas masks or wearing T-shirts as long as dresses with big leering smiley faces on them. The man talking to Anna's brother doesn't fit any of my preconceptions of how a DJ looks.

At last the DJ comes on, and everyone who can moves into the marquee, where the glowing ends of cigarettes bounce in time to the music, which isn't the boom-boom-boom stuff I had expected, but slower and more freeform in its rhythms and patterns; sort of stretchy, and I feel my limbs relax. Cautiously at first, my confidence growing as I realise no one is paying attention to me, I move my arms and the upper half of my body. I'm not sure what you're supposed to do with your feet, but it's dark enough that it doesn't matter. The music goes this way and that, bobbling and meandering, layers and rhythms coming in and falling away, like a river, plunging through the valley.

Jason dances up, grinning. He's in his element. These are his people. This is his thing.

'Getting into it, Sparky?'

'Yeah, I am, actually.'

He puts his arm around me. 'We're cool, yeah?'

'Yeah. We're cool.'

He lingers a little longer, then he spots Zee near the front. He asks if I would like to go forward. I promise I'll join them in a bit.

'Can I get you anything?' he asks.

'What, like a drink?'

He clicks his cheek.

'Sparky. You just say the word, mate. We got plenty.'

The music picks up. Everyone is dancing now, me included. It feels as if my limbs have been liberated from my brain and are just doing their thing.

The only issue is Zee. There they are, at the front, dancing together, her and Jason, their bodies in devastating harmony. I want to be cool about it. I want to be able to say, 'No problem!' I want to be happy.

They're being careful to keep it under the radar, as it were, but it's obvious they're all over each other; that at some point, maybe later, maybe not until they get home, but at some point they'll be going at it together in ways I can only dream of.

I fight these thoughts back, determined not to fall into that particular hole.

I am Sparky. Jason is my mate. Zee is my mate. It's all good.

The music is actually quite good. It has melodies and slower bits, when everything drops off apart from the drums or a piano or whatever, so that when the bass and everything comes back in, it seems much louder and bigger than before. And for a little while there I manage to forget about Zee and Jason, forget to feel awkward, forget that we don't know how we're getting home, forget everything, and I'm just there, in among the people, responding to the sounds coming out of the speaker stacks. A snippet of a song (a song!) comes in, just a few seconds of it, and it's a song that everyone seems to know, and there are a few cheers, and the DJ looks up, a wry smile on his face, and then he flicks a switch and it's the song, the one everyone seems to know, and there are cheers and whoops and applause, and he climbs up onto a speaker and punches the air.

When the song finishes, he puts his hands above his head and claps the crowd. Richie goes up to him and they exchange a hug, and Richie looks so chuffed, like this is the best thing that has ever happened to him, and it's not hard to see why he wanted to get this guy to play at his party, because even an ignorant newbie like me can tell that this is rather special, all this joy on display, all this togetherness.

* * *

Another DJ comes on, and for a while it stays good, and then it gets more like what I expected and I'm feeling tired. I check my watch. There's a lot of night ahead, and I don't even know how I'm getting home.

I decide to take a break and go over to the fire.

A few people are sitting around, smoking and chatting. They all seem to know each other. I pretend to look for friends.

'Want to join us, dude?' a voice calls over, and he nudges his neighbour, 'Mate, budge up, will you? Make some fucking space, man.'

I squeeze onto their makeshift bench, and someone asks me if I'm having a good evening.

'Yeah,' I reply, suddenly feeling crushingly shy, conscious of not knowing anyone and not belonging, knowing that I will never belong.

The conversation moves on. I should have asked a question in return, but I missed the moment. I could have said something about the DJ. I could have even name-dropped Anna or Richie. I could have said all manner of things but now they are talking of people and things about which I have nothing to contribute, and now the moment has slipped away I feel that if I was to say something, now, it would just make everyone feel awkward, like I'm trying to impose myself onto them, and so I stay quiet.

I am a tourist, an imposter.

I stay a little longer, staring into the flames, tracking the trajectory of the fire, which has been well constructed by someone who knew what they were doing.

No one seems offended or surprised when I get up. I mumble something and move away, as if to go back into the marquee, and the guy who invited me into their circles calls out: 'Catch you later, dude.'

I just want to get away, and I'm wondering how I'm ever going to fill the hours before it gets light.

Standing there, alone in the shadows, feeling neither fully present nor absent, a familiar darkness descends on me. I can't blame the music. I can't blame the strangers sitting around the fire, who were perfectly friendly and would have been quite happy to speak with me had I managed to actually open my mouth and say something. No, the music is decent, the people are nice. It's an excellent party.

I can't even put it down to jealousy. The Zee and Jason thing doesn't make it any easier, but even if that wasn't going on, I know in the part of my heart that's honest I would still be feeling this way.

And it is this thought, more than anything else, that alarms me, because it means the darkness is all mine and it is me that prevents me from being able to enjoy things that for others appear to be straightforward and easy and joyful.

One option would be to leave, to go out into the woods, build myself a bivvy and hide there for the rest of the night. And it is, for sure, tempting.

Keeping to the shadows, I walk around to the other side of the marquee, feeling the cleanness of the night sky, free of the distorting orange haze of so-called civilisation.

It is a clear, cloudless night. The Big Dipper, the Great Bear, the Little Bear and the Hunter are all visible, along with a perfect crescent moon, and I am not ready to give up.

There is a refreshment stand set up with rows of fizzy pop displaying every colour of the rainbow, plus several stacked crates of bottled water. A guy with his back to me is busily sorting through some pallets still in their cellophane.

I ask if he has any beer.

'Are you police?'

'No, I'm here with Richie's sister.'

'Ahhhh,' he says, nodding. 'Anna's a wee star.'

He pulls out a can of Castlemaine XXXX and hands it to me. Hearing him speak of Anna has a curious effect, making me feel legitimate in a way I've not felt since leaving the house, and I'm glad I had the courage to be honest with him rather than trying to pretend to be a proper UTR person.

'This your first UTR?'

'That obvious?'

He laughs. 'I can always tell. How are you finding it?'

'I really enjoyed the guy earlier. The, er, American.'

He says a name. 'Bit of a UTR coup, that one.'

He is somewhat older than most of the crowd. Not *old* old, but his hair is flecked with grey and the lines on his face suggest a man who has seen things and been places, and probably has a few stories to tell.

'Most promoters wouldn't even try,' he continues. '...'s known for saying no. Big players, with pockets a lot deeper than Richie's, get knocked back all the time by this guy. Okay – this could be UTR bollocks talk, but the story going around is that he's a bit of a walker, likes to go hiking in the Rockies when he's not in the studio, and someone told him that the countryside around these parts is worth a visit and, so the story goes, *that's* the reason he said yes.' He chuckles. 'Don't quote me on that, mind. UTR stories tend to have a loose relationship with the truth. If you ask me he just liked the idea of doing something properly underground. Most of the sound systems are gone, the scene is pretty much dead. It's all these shitty clubs now.'

'I know which story I'm going with.'

'Hahaha!' he laughs. 'Me and all, mate! Me and all.'

'What do I owe you?'

'The beer? On the house. Tell you what,' he says, cocking his head. 'Want to earn a tenner?'

'Er...'

'Nah, nah, nah. Nothing like that. I just need someone I can trust to mind the stand while I go for a stomp.'

'Me?'

He shrugs. 'You up for it? There's nothing much to it, this lot will probably only want water, and most people fill up at the tap anyway.'

He shows me where the cashbox goes and where to get more stock should I run out of something. Then he points across to a woman in a hi-vis vest, who may be the same one that let us in at the top, and says: 'There won't be, but any aggro, that's Sasha. She'll look out for you. What's your name, again?'

'Sparky.'

'Well, Sparky, you're a diamond. If you need me, I'll be in there.' He points to the throng of anonymous, gyrating bodies. 'Either that, Sparky, or I'm out the back sucking off our favourite hiking enthusiast.'

And with that, he's off, leaving me alone at the stand, surrounded by colourful sugary pop. I watch him disappear into the crowd.

I get straight to work, familiarising myself with the float and the items on sale, and checking stocks in the way that I've seen people in shops do it.

The prediction that no one would be buying very much proves accurate. Most of the time I don't have to actually do anything. Yet having a role, however small, changes everything, and I soon feel less a fraud and more a member of the crew.

When they finally spot me, working behind the stand, Zee and Anna find it hilarious and Jason puts a sweaty arm around my shoulder.

'Nice one, Sparks,' he says.

They stick about for a bit and buy some fizzy pop, thrilled by the vibrant colours and squabbling over who's having which flavour.

'I'm doing the fucking blue potion,' says Zee, laughing.

'I wanted that one!' protests Anna.

'You can both have blue,' I say, feeling like a parent at a kid's birthday party. 'What about you, Jason, what can I get for you?'

'Pur-ple! Pur-ple! Pur-ple!' shout the girls.

Jason grins. 'Gis a green one, will ya, Chief?'

The girls love this, and go: 'OOOOOOOHHH!'

It crosses my mind to take Jason up on his offer because, seeing them like this, it does look kind of fun, but I don't. Besides, having promised the guy – whose name I failed to get – I can't now let him down.

They go off again to dance and be merry, but soon, one or two or all three of them are back again to say hello, and to check that I'm not getting lonely. And each time it's amusing because I know that none of them are going to remember any of the things they're telling me, or what I say to them, and that makes it all very safe and non-binding, because there is only the moment and once the moment is passed it will be over.

The sky turns from brown to navy blue, and then the sun appears and everyone claps and cheers, and the music shifts to a place we've not been before and gets all floaty, and even I have my hands in the air now

When the music eventually stops, my guy returns, a big grin on his face and sweat all down his T-shirt.

He asks how I've got on.

'Yeah, no bother at all.'

He goes over to the float and pulls out a ten and a five, which is five more than agreed.

'You saved my life,' he says, handing me the notes and planting an unexpected kiss on my cheek.

He spots Anna, chatting with some folk nearby, and calls over.

'Anna, girl, you hang onto this one. He's a prince.'

'I know,' she shouts back. 'We all love him.'

Zee and Jason look as if they are beginning to flag, and I'm reminded that we still haven't secured a ride home.

'Erm,' I say to my new best friend. 'Any chance of a lift?'

He laughs. 'Go on, then.'

And so it is that thanks to my enterprising spirit, we all get back in one piece, and for a brief moment I am everyone's hero.

Anna and I sit up the front, and Zee and Jason climb into the back with the remaining stock.

Once we're safely out of the field, and on the road, a cassette goes on and the volume turned up high.

The sun is shining. The road is clear. I'm with my mates. It's all good.

Anna rests her head on my shoulder and falls asleep after a few minutes. I'm enjoying the music, which is not banging rave or even dance music, really. There are even some songs in there that I know from the radio.

'You like your Balearic stuff, Sparky?'

'Is that what this is called?'

He laughs. 'My, he's green, isn't he? Where did Anna find you?'

He's easy to chat to, and inquisitive, and the rest of the way home I tell him about Folk, how we've known each other forever, apart from Jason who's new.

'The geezer, you mean? Lover Boy back there? That Jason?'

Secretly I'm hoping that they're too wasted to do anything and will just fall asleep, and that Zee will wake up and realise that she doesn't really want to be with Jason.

'Bit of a bad boy, no?'

'I'm not sure. Not really.'

He smiles. 'He's sound, yeah?'

'He's all right, actually.'

Chapter Seven

In the community centre canteen Gerry is outlining the agenda for Survival Night.

'One night, no tent, just a bivvy.'

Someone has opened a window but the room still smells of fish cakes and old fat. We probably know more about what the kids are eating at school than the parents do.

Folk badly needs new premises, it's always being said, but nothing ever changes. Gerry is pally with the manager of the community centre. They have some kind of deal between them. We ask no questions. Since breaking away from the organisation to which Folk used to belong, finances are tight and options are limited. And the canteen is not so bad. Yes, it's a dump, and it smells funny, but it's a space and it's ours.

Folk isn't for everyone. Sometimes protective parents find Gerry's approach too permissive for their delicate offspring. And it is true that Gerry is unapologetically laidback when it comes to things other adults get worked up over: sex, drugs, risk assessments, whatever. Yet such interventions from parents are rare. Usually, when someone leaves, it's because more has been asked of them than they had anticipated. People tend to underestimate Folk, as they underestimate Gerry. They assume that because he (and Folk) appears loose in certain respects – let's call it the Narrow Morality of Authoritarian Society, i.e. the rules-based morality of school and conventional parenting that they're used to – therefore anything goes. This is where it falls down. Yes, you can smoke, you can swear, you can even have consensual sex with your girlfriend or boyfriend (or someone you've just met), and some mild intoxication is, well, *permitted*, isn't the right word: suffice to say, unless there is cause for concern, a blind eye is turned. There are lines that can't be crossed, but these are generated in the most part by consensus.

Likewise, sanctions, if they are required, will in the first instance be set by the group: for if someone steals a packet of custard creams from the camp store in the night or skips their turn to clean the compost loos, it is the group that is wronged and justice must be delivered according to the values and judgement of the group. What I'm saying is that people who are just along for the ride and don't really want to participate in the community won't last long. And for the same reason, someone who expresses values or displays attitudes and behaviours that contradict the basic principles of Folk should expect confrontation, and that may come in the strongest terms, either from Gerry directly or, more often, another member or several members of the group.

With some people, of course, it's clear from the start that it will never work. For instance, the white South African girl, who was brought along to Folk by someone who should have known better. When the subject of Nelson Mandela came up, as it inevitably would, her being from South Africa, she had turned around and said: 'Why are you all taking the side of terrorists?'

According to her, outsiders like us, people who have never been to South Africa and who have no personal experience, are incapable of understanding what it's like, and are therefore in no position to comment or hold a view. She told us a story about waiting at the traffic lights one time and a black man comes out of nowhere and sticks a gun in her father's face and demands money.

'Was it Nelson Mandela?' someone asks.

Now she's really angry, because of course it wasn't, and someone else chimes in: 'One black man robs your family and you blame it on Nelson Mandela? I think that's called racism.'

She repeats her accusation, the terrorist charge, and eventually she refines her position: her problem is not so much with Nelson Mandela himself, but with some of his associates in the ANC, an organisation which she insists has never renounced terrorism and is filled with bullies and criminals.

'She's just parroting the views of her racist Apartheid-loving parents,' someone comments.

'How dare you! You know nothing about me!'

And, only then, does Gerry step in.

'Grace (that's the girl) has a point,' he says, which instantly silences us all because it is unfathomable that Gerry could agree with this bigot. 'There's no such thing as a victimless crime. The thing is, Grace, there's often more than one victim, and very often the aggressor is also a victim.'

Needless to say, the girl never returned to Folk, an outcome that none of us were sorry about. So, yes, on occasions things could get a little heated. But Gerry says without friction there's no fire, and without heat there's no life. We should not fear resistance, he insists, but channel the energy of our feelings into our cause. This is an essential lesson, he says, for anyone who wants to bring real change. He credits his willingness to speak out when decorum appears to demand passivity as the main reason he has managed to remain a thorn in the side of the Establishment for so long.

'A bevvy?' says Jason, putting on a Scottish accent. He mimes taking a swig from a bottle.

'A bivvy.' Merlin corrects him. 'Bivouac,' he adds, slowly, as if talking to a hard-of-hearing person. 'It's a self-erected structure.'

Everyone laughs because, well, Merlin.

'This time,' Gerry continues, ignoring Jason, 'we're doing things properly. No half measures.'

Jason whispers something to Anna, to which she replies, 'Shut up, Jason.'

'Whatever we need, nature will provide,' says Gerry. 'Food, shelter, you name it. We'll bring as little as possible from the outside world. Instead, we'll make use of what we find.'

He launches into a story about the time he ate worms, toasting them on a hot stone beside the fire.

'Once they're dry, you crush them into a powder.' He grins. 'Delicious with a crusty roll! Full of protein.'

Anna chuckles. 'You should be good at that, Jase.'

'Why not just eat the bread?' says Zee.

Anna, wise to Gerry's pranks, and more alert than the rest of us to the indicators, prods her in the ribs. 'He's taking the piss, Zeenah D.'

'Don't worry,' says Gerry, holding up his hands in a guilty-as-charged gesture. 'You won't have to eat worms.' He throws Anna a wink. 'Not this time, anyway.'

Afterwards I find myself alone with Jason outside while we wait for the others to come out. We can hear the clattering of chairs, the scrape of shoes. I smile at him and ask: 'How are you getting on, anyway?'

The question hangs there rather awkwardly. I'm not used to being on my own with Jason. Normally someone else is there to mediate.

'You tell me,' he says, tapping a cigarette out of the pack and putting it in his mouth. Having never started smoking, I've always slightly envied my friends who do smoke, not because I want to get cancer or heart disease, but because they always have a prop to hand, which means they never have to worry about what to do with their hands.

He pulls on his cigarette, holding it in and chewing his lip, which curls in that way of his. And though I'm getting used to this gesture, I'm never sure if he's mocking me or if it's just something his face does from time to time, about which he has little or no control, like me with my Posh Boy Weasel voice or smiling when I don't have anything to smile about.

'So,' he says, releasing a perfectly round ring of smoke, followed up by a second that darts through the first, a feat that I've witnessed a lot of amateur smokers attempt and in almost every case fail. 'What's the deal with Gerry?'

'What do you mean?'

'Is he...' He raises his eyebrows, 'Y'know?'

I can feel myself bristling. 'What do you mean? Of course not. What are you saying?'

Jason doesn't say. He just stands there smoking his cigarette. And immediately I feel bad for snapping at him, because his question might be innocent. In fact, I don't know what those raised eyebrows signify. As someone who has been in the care system it is only natural that Jason would assume that any grown-up that takes an interest in young people must be some kind of monster. Yet he may only mean, is he gay? Or, is he a decent bloke? Or, what's with the jokes about eating worms, etc?

I could ask him. But I don't. Instead, I say, in a conciliatory tone, 'Honestly, Gerry's the real deal. What you see is what you get. He genuinely enjoys being around young people. Really. I think he finds us more interesting than his own generation, or less smug anyway.'

Jason doesn't reply, and if he was going to say something else, the moment is lost because suddenly the canteen door bangs open and everyone is there.

This interruption, on reflection, may be for the best. Baseless speculation can be an ugly and blunt instrument and, well, I want to believe that Jason is better than that.

'There you are!' says Zee. 'We thought you'd done a Merlin!'

It is a running gag that Merlin always leaves without saying goodbye. His Disappearing Act, we call it. Even our parents call it that.

'Cheer up, Mark,' says Anna, ruffling my hair. 'Might never happen.'

* * *

There is heavy rainfall the night before the Survival Overnighter, the rain tap tap tapping against the bedroom window as I lie awake thinking about Folk, about the summer that is almost over, about Zee and about Jason.

Already it is hard to imagine a time before him, yet I do not feel I really know him at all. What we've shared are experiences, sensations. Of his thoughts and feelings, fears, disappointments, dreams; of his past, of the future he pictures for himself and the world he imagines, of the regrets he harbours and the hopes he carries – I know nothing.

I envy his mystery. I know it is preferable, admirable and more honest to inhabit a world of sensation and renounce the intellect. I've read *L'Etranger* (only in translation, mind; Zee's read it in French and English). I feel I know what the sun stands for for Camus. I, too, long to give myself over to the moment, not by murdering someone like Mersault does, but by being more... what? More *Jason Templar* in my approach. How I wish that I could stop analysing life and start actually living!

My brain, of course, has other ideas.

And so I lie awake, hour after hour, listening to the rain, knowing that I should be sleeping, frustrated by my inability to locate the off switch to my thoughts.

It is important to be refreshed and on good form for the Overnighter, an event which has, I must admit, taken on far too much significance following the rift with Council and the decision to break away. The endless hours spent discussing and debating the rights and wrongs of this or that policy has piled on such pressure that, in truth, no Survival Overnighter could ever live up to the expectation heaped upon it. And yet I am, notwithstanding, excited.

To get out on that moor and breathe! My life, I fear, has become small and insignificant. How I crave the gravity and... epic... Truth of Nature! Zee has a word for it: sublime. Top of the World may be a good place to get stoned, but it will never be sublime.

As for the rain, it doesn't matter one jot. Cancellation or postponement is clearly out of the question. No, no, no. As Gerry says, *Weather-beaten? Yeah yeah yeah! Beaten by the weather? Never!* We'd chant this mantra while hailstones pummelled our faces and thunder shook the trees. Hell, we've bivvied in gale force winds and sub-zero temperatures. A little summer rain? Nothing. Bring it on. Good for the hedgerows. The worms will be happy.

I wake too early. It's still raining.

I go over to the window and open the curtains. I watch the puddles on the patio, the little whirlpools when a drop lands, spraying and bouncing over the water, like a miniature ballet.

My room, with its Sapphire Salute walls, seems childish and abandoned, as if I had died and my parents had kept it as it was, a shrine to the child they lost. Model boats and Airfix planes, painstakingly constructed in prepubescent fervour, are still on display.

The posters depict a hopelessly out of date version of me. Why, for instance, do I have a picture of Bob Marley above my bed? I don't even like reggae. I just got the poster because... I can't even remember why.

I make a vow to do something about the state of this room after I return from the Survival Overnighter. Then I tiptoe out to the hall, careful to avoid the creaky floorboard that is just outside my door.

The door to the spare room is closed. One of my parents will be sleeping in there. They're still pretending to be together.

In the kitchen, over a bowl of cornflakes, I get out my Survival Checklist to check in case I've overlooked an essential item. This is more a ritual than a serious anxiety. I've already been packed for a couple of days.

I shower, brush my teeth, cut my nails. I check my stubble. There's a bit of growth above the lips. Nothing to write home about.

Mum waves me off. She has a session in the evening at the Dog, she says. She's planning to debut some new material she has been working on with *Adrian*, whose name has popped up a few times of late. *Adrian* – that first A is very long when she says his name – plays double bass. The biggest instrument in the band. The biggest instrument in the orchestra.

* * *

Outside the community centre canteen the mood is buoyant. Everyone is kitted up in waterproofs. Zee has on her new Gore-Tex jacket, which I know – because I've checked out similar ones for myself – will have set her back a fair bit. Lightweight yet substantial, with a really good cut and a great yellow/grey colourway. She looks hot. Jason has borrowed one of Gerry's old anoraks and waterproof trousers. It's funny seeing him in these clothes because I'm used to seeing them in the back of Gerry's car and I'm pretty sure at some point we've all worn these items as back-up options when ours have got wet or dirty or we've failed to anticipate wet conditions and packed inappropriately.

Gerry has also lent Jason his old rucksack. Everyone knows it's Gerry's rucksack because a couple of camps back, Merlin turned up with the same one – not just the same make and model, the same colour, everything – and everyone had laughed because Merlin does really look up to Gerry, like, a bit too much.

The minibus Gerry has secured for the trip is an old German ambulance. Some joker has stuck a peace logo over the Mercedes badge. In big letters along one side it says CAPITALISM ISN'T WORKING!

This is not the first time Gerry's borrowed this vehicle for Folk trips.

Someone referred to it once as the *Battle Bus* and the name stuck.

There are no seatbelts.

There's a bit of a tussle over seating. In the end I give in and let Jason and Zee go at the back, even though the back has always been my spot.

I squeeze in beside Seb and Anna, our backpacks wedged in at our feet. In front of us are the Three Kats – Kathia, Katie and Kath – who, as well as sharing the same name, attend the same private all-girls school rather than the local sixth-form college. Merlin, who is still home educated, sits up in the cab with Gerry.

Gerry revs the engine, and we all whoop, as per the ritual.

He spins around in the driver's seat, grinning like a flashy game show host. 'Fit?' he asks, and revs the engine again and everyone cheers some more and Merlin makes a thumbs up sign.

'Everybody in the place!' shouts Zee.

'LET'S GO!' Anna and Seb yell back.

They repeat the call and response again and again, the rest of us joining in after the third or fourth time. It's a new chant for Folk, but it does the job, and we enthusiastically bang the palms of our hands against the roof of the bus while we crawl along the lane behind the community centre, squeezing by the cars that have been left there over the weekend. The rain continues to patter on the roof, the windscreen wipers beating like a metronome.

At the end of the lane Gerry pushes a tape into the slot. Nine out of the ten people on the bus know what's coming and there are a few groans as the opening chords of Terry Jacks' Seasons in the Sun spill from the tinny speakers.

Goodbye to you my trusted friend...

Gerry's Guilt Mix has soundtracked so many Folk trips that the songs, which even Gerry refers to as his 'stinky old cheese', have become core to the ritual, as much Folk as bonfires, long drops and the smell of insect repellent.

'Here, Gerry,' Jason calls from the back. A C90 cassette is thrust forward. Merlin takes it, tentatively, as if it might be infected, and waves the object in front of Gerry.

'Sorry, buddy,' Gerry says into the rear-view mirror. 'My mix today.'

It's the first time I've seen someone say no to Jason.

The location for this year's Survival Overnighter has been kept secret until this point. Now Gerry reveals that we're heading north to the wilder, less populated part of the moor, and a site called Ricketts Drop.

'It's a magnificent spot,' he says, adding that there is a fresh water source, ancient as well as younger woodland, and plenty of material for building shelters.

'You're going to love it,' he shouts over the music.

We've heard both sides of Gerry's Guilt Mix by the time we reach the drop-off point, and any reservations anyone might have had about Gerry's selections have retreated. Even Jason's joining in. The Fleetwood Mac shout-a-long (PLAYers only LOVE YOU when they're PLAY-ing!) followed by Gypsies, Tramps and Thieves are particularly raucous that day, and the bus shakes as you speed around the lanes, water flying up at every bend and spraying pools across the open road. At last Gerry turns off the road and into a desolate carpark facing onto the moor, a grey-brown desert dotted with dark patches, which are either trees or rocks.

Carpark is a bit of stretch, for in truth it is more a patch of level-ish ground where parking is permitted, although on this day there are no other vehicles, because most people are fair-weather walkers, even if they don't admit it. These are the perfect conditions for the Survival Overnighter as far as I'm concerned. Just us, the wind and the rain.

We all clamber down from the Battle Bus and the gear is unloaded into a big heap on the dirt floor. Jason, who has no experience of Folk trips, is keen to locate his rucksack immediately, but we tell him to leave it for now. Because the first task of the Survival Overnighter is to figure out where the hell we are.

Gerry never reveals this information. We have to 'ground ourselves', he always says. 'Engage with land.' It's the best way to get going. And he's right. Forced to rely on the map, we immediately start to pay attention to the features and shape of the land.

Someone suggests that Jason, since this is his first Survival Overnighter, should set the first compass bearing. A map is spread on the bonnet of the Battle Bus and Zee passes Jason a compass.

'Do you think you can find north?'

He looks at her as if he thinks she's taken leave of her senses. Without going anywhere near the map, he turns the dial so that it points to the N. Then he hands it back to Zee.

She smiles. 'Jase, you have to use the map.'

His face colours. 'Yeah, I know. Safe.'

'Here,' she says. 'I'll show you.'

Everyone gathers around as Zee takes charge, explaining what she's doing and the principles behind it. She's a confident and generous teacher and she gets Jason too involved, careful not to embarrass him because (it's plain for everyone to see) he's completely clueless. But we all had to learn sometime, and some people never learn at all.

Merlin keeps out of the orientation discussion. I'm not sure how many of the others know it, but I know (and he knows that I know) that he lives nearby and could easily tell us where we are and which way to go without needing to consult the map at all.

We catch each other's eye, Merlin and I, and he looks nervous as if he thinks I might be about to reveal this fact to the others and thus effectively disqualify him from the trip, since it is hardly a Survival Overnighter if he already knows the area.

Once our location has been established and compass bearings set, the Three Kats push off towards the open moor.

Anna and Jason must stop to roll cigarettes for the road.

'Couldn't you have done that before?' says Zee, who is as keen as me to get going.

Gerry comes over and asks if we all have our Survival Bags.

'Whaaa—?' says Jason.

'Someone didn't read the memo,' says Anna.

This is met with a wry shake of the head from Gerry, who turns and goes back to the bus.

Gerry returns with a folded square of orange plastic and hands it to Jason. 'You're in luck,' he says.

The colour is faded from years of use. Jason holds the Survival Bag up between his thumb and forefinger and grimaces.

'I'm s'pose to get in this?'

We all laugh, because Jason can be pretty witty, and also because he's so new to everything and so clueless.

Chapter Eight

By the time we get going, the rain has eased off, the wind has died down and the sun is trying to poke through the clouds. I let the others go on ahead, savouring the moment. After a short stomp across open moorland, we reach a track that runs beside a hedgerow that is teeming with life. The leaves, beaded with raindrops, sparkle in the defiant sunlight that feels all the more magnificent for having broken through what had been a thick carpet of dark cloud. I inhale the smells of hawthorn and fresh rain, holding the air in my lungs and feeling my soul revive, while chirps and clicks and taps and chatter spill out. *The Wildlife Tape* Zee once named it, and this became a running gag between us.

'Listen! They turned on the tape for us!' we'd say.

I can see Zee ahead, walking with Jason, and I want to run up and say something about the Tape, but I worry that it will seem too forced. Besides, Jason won't understand, and Zee might be embarrassed and that will be the end of the joke, which is just a silly thing we have, but it is ours and I don't want it to be lost, and so I say nothing and just keep following the bumpy track, quickening my step so as not to be left behind.

I've almost caught up with them when I hear Zee say, 'Does that mean you're on probation?'

I don't catch Jason's answer. I consider coughing, or saying something, even whistling a little tune to let them know I'm there, because I don't like being sneaky but, before I can decide how to alert them to my presence, Zee has asked him another question.

'What are those places like?'

This time I do hear Jason's reply.

'Tough.'

'How did you, you know, survive?'

'I dunno I did.'

'Do you make, like, friends?'

'Friends? You think you make friends in those places? You think it's like this?'

'Well, no, I just...'

'You do what you got to do. You keep your head down. You learn who's in charge. You get through it. That's it. Right? Can we fucking drop it now?'

I'm suddenly highly conscious that I'm listening into a conversation that I am not supposed to hear. I didn't intend to eavesdrop, it just sort of happened. And now I'm faced with a dilemma. Do I reveal myself (and what I've overheard), or do I drop back and hope that they don't realise I was listening? In the end I do neither because, distracted by what I've just heard, I fail to notice in the path ahead of me a stray root that has sprung loose from the ground, and before I can stop myself I've lost my footing and I am tumbling forwards, the weight of my backpack making it impossible to regain my balance, and for a moment I'm stranded in the dirt like a capsized beetle or a cockroach, unable to get back up.

Zee and Jason stare down at me.

'Careful there, Sparky.'

Zee shakes her head. 'Fuck's sake, Mark.'

Jason gives me a hand up.

'I'm sorry. I didn't mean...'

'You were listening to us,' says Zee. 'Weren't you?

'I might have heard something.'

He waves his hand to calm Zee, who I sense is about to give me an earful for snooping on their conversation.

'Does Gerry know?' I ask.

'Yeah, big G knows.'

This new piece of information, that Jason was in some kind of prison or Young Offenders Institution before Gerry decided to take him under his wing, goes a long way to explaining for me at least why Jason has come into our lives.

Gerry has strong views about incarceration, particularly the incarceration of children. And while it was often the case that when he spoke of society *locking up children* he meant it in relation to over-protective parents and risk-averse youth organisations, he also holds opinions about the ethics and efficacy of punishment in general and Britain's failing penal system in particular. So it is easy to see why the opportunity to give a kid like Jason a fresh start and chance to start over would appeal to Gerry, a man for whom there is no such thing as a lost cause.

I smile and say, 'How is it at Gerry's?'

'Yeah,' he replies, 'pretty tidy.'

'Tidy? Gerry's house?'

He laughs, a little nervously, but with enough warmth to make me feel my intrusion has been forgiven.

Zee, however, does not react. This may be because she's still pissed off with me for eavesdropping. Although, later, it occurs to me that she might not have known about Jason living at Gerry's.

* * *

The track ends, opening out again onto the moor, which is marked on the map as a military training zone. A sign warns that when a red flag is flying the area may not be entered by civilians, as live rounds may be in use. There are a few of these areas dotted around the moor and, alarming though it may sound, the idea of being accidentally shot, they generally pose no threat to ramblers. The knowledge, however, that we are on army training ground makes me think of the barracks I used to pass on the way to my old school. With its razor-wire fences and squat single-story buildings dotted around like plastic houses on a Monopoly board, the place had an unreality to it that was both sinister and intriguing. I used to watch the barrier that went up and down to let cars in and out. No one ever seemed to enter or leave on foot. I knew it was a training facility because of the sign, but what went on beyond the fences was a total mystery.

My parents and their friends call them *squaddies*, and at weekends they are often seen roaming the streets in packs, hitting up the city centre bars and nightclubs, where they consume vast quantities of lager before spilling out onto the pretty cobbled streets. Dressed in their pressed chinos and polo shirts, bulging with arms as thick as tree trunks, they are easy to spot. When things get fisty, as it sometimes does, when drunk squaddies clash with equally drunk local lads, police are called, and then, as suddenly as they arrived, they are gone, piled onto a train, shouting and rocking the seats, whisked back to a single bed in a crowded dorm in their home behind the razor wire.

A story circulated for a while about this one time when a squaddie got separated from his squad and missed the last train of the day. Seized by rage and panic, the squaddie – a young guy, nineteen years old and not long at base – climbed over the ticket office barrier and proceeded to beat the living shit out of the guy working behind the ticket desk that evening, who endured serious injuries. After that they brought in more security measures to protect railway staff.

We skirt around a bog, then criss-cross through thick gorse dotted with yellow flowers, following the tracks of animals.

At last, in the distance, we see a line of trees on the hillside. We check the map, set a new compass bearing. Yes, we conclude. That must be it. Those trees ahead must be Ricketts Drop.

We arrive at a fence where a large wooden sign warns:

PRIVATE PROPERTY KEEP OUT.

'You sure about this?' says Jason, panting because he is not used to the terrain.

We assure him that Gerry will have secured permission from the landowner.

The fence, it must be said, is more symbolic than defensive. It is easy enough to climb over, even with backpacks. Yet the symbolism of this act suddenly gives the expedition an exhilarating quality, as if we are entering forbidden territory.

The moment we're safely over the fence and walking among the birch trees, their limbs naked and marked with what look to be scars, an eerie silence falls. We stop, briefly, to drink some water and toast our achievement. But we are all keen to press on.

Zee picks up a delicate flap of bark that has fallen from one of the trees. It is white and as thin as silk, and speckled like a Disney deer. She places it carefully inside the pocket of her anorak.

I decide to do the same and I look around for the perfect piece. I will write a few lines on it, nothing soppy, just a small memento of a time, and I will give it to Zee and she will know exactly where it came from and that I was thinking of her.

'You love birds coming?' Anna calls back.

All three of us look up.

After a while walking we emerge into a clearing and it is decided that this is a suitable spot to set up camp.

'We'll need branches and twigs and shit if we're going to build this Bivvy-bevvy-self-erected thingamajig,' says Anna, going into Boy Scout mode.

Seb crouches down beside his rucksack and pulls out a camping stove and four packets of instant noodles.

'You fucking diamond, Sebastian,' says Anna. ''Cause, dunno about you lot, but I'm not eating Gerry's worms.'

'Er,' I say, shaking my head. 'What happened to Survival Conditions?'

'Tell you what, Cottontail,' she says, ruffling my hair. 'You can be a good little rabbit and gather berries and nuts. Me, *I'm* having Super Noodles.'

Everyone laughs.

Even I have to smile. 'So, erm, we're taking Gerry's rules with a pinch of salt?'

The ground is soggy after all the rain, so we lay out the survival bags to form a large groundsheet, and sit around doing nothing. The smokers smoke some cigarettes. Zee and Jason attempt to hang the ghetto blaster from a tree.

Slowly a general consensus forms that, it being Gerry's Famous Survival Overnighter and all, we should do something. More pressingly, we have nowhere to take shelter should the rain start again or a storm come in. So we get busy – levelling ground, selecting trees, securing ropes.

Anna goes off on a recce, returning after a while, jubilant because she's found something, and she needs *some muscle* to bring it back to base camp. Jason and I offer our services.

'There's this big fuck-off wooden frame,' she explains enroute. 'I mean, fucking top notch, boys. This is like premium building supplies we're talking.'

'Erm, isn't that rather against the Spirit of Survival?'

She shrugs and I'm struck by how quickly we each fall into our standard patterns. I've always been the anxious one, worrying about sticking to the rules, rules which Anna, almost by reflex, pushes against.

'Just being resourceful,' she replies. 'Gerry said we should use whatever we find. I found this. We're using it.'

'I'm not sure that's quite what he meant.'

'Yeah, whatever, Mark.'

We come upon a narrow and fast flowing stream. It's easy enough to jump. I pause for a moment, bend down and dip my finger in the water. I lick my finger.

'You know what,' I call after them because they've gone on a little. 'It's good. We can fill our bottles here. We've found water!'

'We're saved!' yells Anna. 'We're saved!'

The frame is leaning against a shed-like structure. A squat, lumpy sort of hut that appears to have been constructed out of the same wood that grows around it, it might as well have sprouted from the earth or been made of gingerbread, so far removed it seems from the kind of shed my parents would buy at the local garden centre. The door is secured by a heavy padlock.

The frame is an old window. Most of the glass panels are missing but the wood itself feels solid.

'You reckon we can take it?' I say, glancing around.

Anna shrugs. 'Who's gonna stop us?'

It requires all three of us to disentangle the frame from the weeds and creepers that have attached themselves to the wood, and which suggest the object has been there undisturbed for some time.

At last we manage to free it, and we haul our discovery back to what we've begun calling Base Camp, Anna marching on ahead, leaving me and Jason struggling with the frame. By the time we get back to the others we're panting and sweating like a couple of knackered race horses.

Zee, at least, is impressed.

'Nice one, lads,' she says.

We lean our find against a couple of trees, and everyone stands around admiring it. It's the perfect frame for a structure, someone says.

'Right,' says Anna, putting her arm around Zee. 'This will do us just fine. Where are *you* going to sleep?'

I stare at them. 'Nah, nah, nah. That's not how it works.'

Anna grins. 'Your face, Mark.'

'We carried it, Anna. We did all the work.'

'So?'

'So we should benefit.'

'Why?'

'Because.'

'Because what?'

'Because that's fair,' I say, before I can stop myself.

'Fair? What's that got to do with anything? You think the world is fair?'

'She's got a point,' says Seb.

I look at Jason. His lip twitches. I shake my head, because I know we've been had, and because this is classic Anna. I know, too, that I shouldn't give her the satisfaction, shouldn't let on that I care, but I can't seem to let it go.

My arms still ache from carrying the damn thing and my wrists feel sore from where the wood was digging into my skin. But it's not this that bothers me. I don't really care about the frame. It's the principle. Of course, I realise, that's why she's doing it. She doesn't care about the frame either. She's making a point. At my expense. Classic Anna.

'You do realise,' I say, 'you're totally cheating with that thing.'

* * *

Jason is quite handy when it comes to constructing a shelter. He goes off to look for material and returns with an excellent selection of branches that can be arranged into a frame, leaves and stringy roots. The latter we apply as a bind to fix the main elements in place. It's the sort of innovation that even Seb and I might not have thought of had we been alone.

An hour later, two (semi-) self-erected structures stand facing off against each other across the clearing, as if preparing for a duel.

'Dream team,' says Zee, coming up to me and Jason, and putting an arm around each of us. 'Sorry about the wind up earlier.'

I'm about to say it doesn't matter when I am suddenly interrupted by a loud hooting sound from the bushes. An owl? I think. Surely not?

'Huh?' says Seb. 'Bit early for that, isn't it?'

'I'd say so,' says Anna cooly, looking directly at Zee, and I wonder if she is really referring to the sound we just heard or making some other point that I don't understand.

The hoot comes again, closer this time, and we all look around trying to locate the source of the sound. Finally, we see Gerry emerge. Anna lets out a loud groan, to which Gerry answers with another hoot. Then he turns his attention to our structures.

'Nice idea that,' he says of ours. 'Using the roots as bind.'

When he gets to the girls' frame-assisted shelter, he sucks his teeth in, in the exaggerated way people do when doing an impression of a negotiating builder. 'I'm not sure I approve of this.'

'What?' says Anna, flicking her hair. 'We were being resourceful.'

'Hmmm.'

Everyone laughs at the routine. It is shaping up to be a vintage Gerry trip. After everything we have been through – the spat with District, breaking away from the Organisation, standing up to the haters and the doubters and laws makers and dreaded Health & Safety brigade – the victory of just making it this far feels all the sweeter. And all because Gerry refuses to give up, refuses to accept no for an answer, and was prepared to go out on a limb for us to bring us this experience.

He frowns suddenly. 'Where's Merlin?'

It is a straightforward question. Yet the effect is quietly devastating. For we have no answer, obviously, and it is as if someone has come in and turned on the lights and silenced the music at a party which had hitherto been in full flow.

Gerry's enquiry hangs in the air.

'Isn't he with you?' says Seb.

'Oops,' says Anna.

'Honestly,' says Zee. 'We had no idea.'

I say nothing, for I know he has every right to be angry, I lament how we were all too distracted by Jason – teaching him how to read a map, laughing at his jokes, listening to his stories. I didn't once think of Merlin.

'Not cool, guys. Not cool.'

He starts walking away, still shaking his head. On the other side of the clearing he stops and turns. 'I'll be back,' he calls. 'I'll be back.'

His footsteps fade into the swish of leaves swaying on the trees, which seem to tut and chastise us for our transgression, the cold reality kicking in that we have messed up big time. Indeed, the whole Survival Overnighter is now in jeopardy because of our negligence. And I can't help but feel a little angry with Merlin for putting us in this position, because it is so typical of him to do something like this. And I then feel doubly guilty for thinking that.

'I'll be back,' repeats Jason in a silly voice, but no one is laughing now.

Jason Templar, the Terminator, the clown.

Chapter Nine

Jason, in his innocence, seems genuinely anxious for Merlin. Shouldn't a few of us go looking for him, he suggests? His concern is sweet, and understandable given that this is his first proper Folk trip. So we put the kettle on and try to bring him up to speed on the enigma that is Merlin Cooper-Clarke. Because this isn't exactly the first time Merlin has gone AWOL on a Folk trip.

'We call it his Disappearing Act,' I explain, 'I mean, everyone calls it that.'

This does not reassure Jason.

'We should still find him, like?'

'The thing about Merlin,' says Zee, gently, because it's quite touching that Jason is upset about this, 'he's very... particular... very definite about how things should be done and if he disapproves... which is quite often... sometimes he'll just, well, take off.'

'He might not want to be found,' Seb adds.

'Also,' I say, scrunching my face, conscious that what I am about to say may disclose classified information, 'Merlin lives really close to here. He probably knows this area better than anyone.'

My revelation is met with knowing looks and nods, for it turns out that, with the exception of Jason, we all knew this and for similar reasons had kept quiet, not wishing to draw attention to a detail that somewhat undermined the legitimacy of Gerry's Famous Survival Overnighter.

'Knowing Merlin,' Zee continues, 'he's probably abandoned us and is doing his own ultra Survival Overnighter. He's a total purist.' She gestures towards our setup. 'He wouldn't approve of any of this.'

'That,' Anna agrees, 'Or he's already home, and this is Star Cross Part Two.'

Jason doesn't know about Star Cross Part One, so we fill him in. The incident had occurred the previous summer on a particularly hot day. On account of the fine weather, instead of staying at the community centre, we had spontaneously decided to pile onto the Battle Bus for a day of wholesome sailing. Gerry had a chum who kept a little skiff over at Star Cross Sailing Club. Two of the Three Kats had done a little bit of sailing in the past. The rest of us were utterly clueless, a detail that only added to the tomfoolery. We would pose as the wealthy people, off on a jolly boating trip, and quote lines from Jerome K. Jerome and PG Wodehouse or at least Enid Blyton. It would be spiffing! Unfortunately, we never even made it onto water because, at some point we lost a member of the party. Merlin. (Who else?) For almost two hours we searched the area, recruiting random members of the sailing club in the search. We even considered calling out the coast guard. Until someone at the club remembered seeing a red van, and a kid about our age, climbing in, shortly after we had arrived. Sure enough, when Gerry telephoned the house it was confirmed that Merlin had gone home. By this point it was too late to do any sailing, so we all just got back in the Battle Bus with our lashings of ginger beer and sandwiches, and that was the end of that.

'Where were you?' Jason asks, once I've finished recounting the tale.

I'm slightly thrown by his question. 'Er, we were looking for him.'

'Yeah, but why weren't he with you?'

Zee looks up. 'Are you saying it's our fault?'

He shrugs. 'What do I know?'

The water finally begins to boil, and we turn our attention to the serious business of finding cups and fixing tea for everyone, diverting the conversation away from what was turning into a tetchy situation. But Jason's response is troubling, and I wonder if the problem was in the way I had told the story or the story itself, which in my head had been quite a funny story.

'So,' says Seb. 'What's our tipple?'

It is a running gag in our little gang that I always carry a substantial stash of tea with me on Folk trips. 'Okay,' I call, rummaging inside the roof of my backpack. 'We've got Rooibos, Green, Peppermint, Fruit Medley, Lemon and Ginger and, erm, Sleepy Dreams.'

Jason's top lip curls. 'How about Wakey-Wakey?'

He goes over to his rucksack. Not immediately finding what he is looking for, he opens a side pocket. A pack of water purification tablets falls out. Next he pulls out a first aid kit, a whistle and some diarrhoea medication.

Panic spreading through him, he returns to the main compartment, emptying the contents onto the ground. Good quality lightweight trousers. Base layers wrapped in waterproof casing. Trangia, couple of mess tins, fuel. An ultralight 3S down-synthetic mix sleeping bag. All neatly packed. All pristine.

'Well,' says Anna, drily, 'aren't you full of surprises?'

'It ain't mine,' he murmurs.

'No shit,' says Anna. 'You been shoplifting, Mr T?'

And before anyone can stop him, he's off, tearing across the clearing, back the way we had come, his pockets rattling with whatever is inside. He stumbles on the uneven ground, but recovers, his puffer jacket twinkling in the distance.

'Jase!' yells Zee, running after him. 'Jase!'

We stare at the offending rucksack, the abandoned kit lying on the ground. It is fairly obvious what has occurred, for we all know there is only one person who owns such gear and packs with such anal precision.

The bags must have got switched when we were unloading them from the Battle Bus.

'So we know what Merlin's missing,' observes Anna cooly. 'I wonder what surprises he found in Jason's?'

'Poor Merlin,' says Seb, gathering the stuff and packing it away again. 'He'll be upset when he realises.'

'One thing's for sure,' I say, picking up the sleeping bag and reading the specs printed on the side. I'd had my eye on several pieces of the new Ultralight multi-season range. 'Jason sure got the better end of the deal, I mean kit-wise.'

Anna frowns, her expression suddenly serious. 'Jay will be devastated if he's lost his Spiral Tribe shirt. It's from his brother.'

We fall into silence, none of us sure how to continue. It had all been going so well. Until suddenly it wasn't, and now everything was going wrong.

'I hope Merlin *is* all right,' says Seb at last. 'I mean, I hope it *is* just the usual.'

'Tell you what,' says Anna, taking out her tobacco kit. 'If something has happened, Gerry's screwed.'

Seb and I cannot disagree. The decision to go ahead with the Survival Overnighter, despite the warnings from Council, had already raised eyebrows, and while parental consent had been gained, there had been doubts and murmurings even among the parents who had hitherto fully supported Gerry in his battles with the powers that be. Should an incident occur, even a fairly minor one like a broken ankle or a head injury, Gerry's position would be hard to defend.

There is a movement in the trees, followed by the sound of someone approaching from the opposite side of the clearing. I look up to see Gerry coming towards us, and I wonder if he heard our conversation.

'Ah,' he says, spotting the rucksack. 'Merlin back?'

Anna shakes her head. 'Just the bag.'

We explain the muddle.

'I see,' says Gerry, pursing his lips. 'And the others, where are they?'

We tell him they are off looking for Merlin, which seems to placate him.

'Together?'

Anna chuckles. 'For now.'

Gerry nods. 'Young hearts, eh?'

Perhaps it's the knowledge that we are at least trying to make amends, or maybe he's just had time to calm down, but Gerry's mood seems brighter. Meanwhile, the clouds too have lifted. Sunlight pokes through the leaves, which seem to whisper in the breeze, swaying and shimmying like the chorus line in a West End musical. More tea is poured and Gerry tells us about the trees, which he explains are a rare species of silver birch, native to the area.

I remark that the branches look almost human, like arms reaching up to the sky.

'They look fucking predatory,' says Anna. 'Like, they might grab you, like...' she thinks for a moment. 'Like creep hands at the school disco.'

'That's dark, Anna.'

She shrugs. 'That's school discos.'

Gerry drains his cup and gets slowly to his feet. 'Well,' he says, adopting his camp master voice. 'It appears the time has come, comrades, for us to part. You know the drill by now. I'll be nearby, but I'll be keeping a low profile. Be strong, people! Love the sun! Follow the trail!'

He glances again at the rucksack.

'I better take this,' he says, picking it up and slinging it over his shoulder. 'Merlin will be needing it.'

* * *

The sun has sunk behind the trees by the time Zee and Jason return. They are without Merlin. They have been gone nearly two hours. Were they really looking for Merlin, I ask myself, or did they use the time for other purposes?

But even as I torture myself with such dark musings, I know, as clearly as I know that day will follow night, that Zee will, sooner or later, tire of Jason. Does he realise, I wonder, as we all do, that he is just a plaything to her, a summer fuck; and that summer is almost over?

Can he not see that once she's back at college she will want someone bright, her intellectual equal; someone who reads books and has ideas about the world, someone who can sustain a conversation with her about weighty topics that, you know, Actually Matter rather than – what, Spiral Tribe? Sure, I tell myself, Jason might be fun to bed, but serious boyfriend material? I don't think so.

In any case, in the interim, while Zee and Jason had been off doing what they needed to do, the rest of us had got creative, fixing up base camp ready for the night ahead, including lighting in the form of paper lanterns hanging from well-placed branches, and seating in the form of a simple yet sturdy bench.

Jason comes over and sits down next to me.

'Gerry took Merlin's rucksack. In case you were wondering.'

He does not respond.

'If you need to borrow something, I'm sure we can spare you a few things. You just have to ask.'

'Yeah, safe.'

'Are you sure you're all right?' I ask, because he seems very subdued. 'Was it something in particular? What were you looking for earlier? Is it something precious?'

He glances around, then puts his finger to his lips and whispers: 'Doves.'

'Doves?'

'E,' he hisses.

Anna looks up. 'Jason Templar,' she says loudly. 'Did you bring ecstasy to the Survival Overnighter?'

We all stare at him. Even Zee, judging by the expression on her face, is astonished by her boyfriend's behaviour. After all, it is one thing at a UTR rave, but this is Gerry's Famous Survival Overnighter.

Anna holds out her hand. 'Go on then.'

His lip wobbles. He looks as if he might be about to cry.

'Come on, Mr T. Gis' a pill.'

He shakes his head. 'You lot are fucking mental.'

Anna laughs.

'Naw, Sparky's right. Forget I said nothing.'

But Anna won't let it drop. She can be ruthless when she wants to be.

'What?' she demands. 'Saving them for you and Zeenah D, are we? Well, Romeo, welcome to the People's Republic of Folk where we share everything – food, secrets, STDs, you name it. So get your eccies out and we'll divvy them up like nice little campers. Yes?'

He tries to smile, but it's pitiful, and I want to say to him: *Dude, just stop digging, and come clean. She knows your game. She's marked your card.*

'Sorry, love,' he tries, exaggerating his accent rather awkwardly. 'Ain't got none.'

This is met with a cackle from Anna, who then goes over to her own rucksack and pulls out a large bottle of White Pearl.

'Just teasing you,' she says, in a gentler tone. 'Mr Raindance *I-brought-a-bag-of-fuckin'-eccies-on-Survival-Night* Templar. You know, Jay,' she continues, 'the thing you need to know about us is we're absolute sticklers for tradition.'

The cider erupts, like a magnum of champagne at the end of a Grand Prix, and she uses her mouth to catch the liquid, rubbing the sides of the bottle with both hands as if she's giving it a blow job.

('Anna!')

'Shall I be mother?'

She gathers up all the cups she can find, tipping out the dregs of tea left in the bottom of some of them. She is meticulous about fair and equal distribution. And, with this strangely ceremonial gesture of hospitality, peace is restored.

'Maybe it's for the best,' says Seb, sipping his cider. 'I'm not sure it's the time or the place for that sort of party.'

After that Zee fires up the boombox, and Jason's tape finally gets played, and it's not the nosebleed stuff I had expected but the stretchy floaty kind, like we heard in the quarry, and I ask: 'Is it the DJ who likes rambling?' And because no one has a slightest idea what I'm talking about, I recount the story, the one my drinks stand guy told me, and when I've finished Jason puts his arm around me and says: 'Sparky. What a legend!'

I'm not sure if it's the DJ or me that has earned 'legendary' status, but either way I'm chuffed with this reaction to my tale after my account of the Star Cross Incident had gone down so badly.

* * *

As day turns into evening, more stories are shared, and Merlin's name comes up frequently. It's great having a fresh audience, someone who wasn't there to witness the mishaps and the messy situations that made these memories so vivid. For instance, Jason has never heard the tale of Merlin and the Didgeridoo Player!

On this particular occasion we were attending one of the unofficial camps that two or more districts would sometimes hold on the fallow years in which no national or international event was scheduled. It was evening and we were gathered around the fire. People were taking it in turns to do little performances – skits and stand-up comedy routines, songs, circus skills, all sorts.

Merlin, being Merlin, decided to do a classical guitar recital. It started off fine, but it was a rather long-winded, rather complicated piece he had selected, and no one – like, no one – was interested.

So the performance was going on and on and on and, understandably, people were starting to get restless. They weren't there for a classical recital. They wanted to laugh, drink, be entertained, and maybe get a snog at the end of the night.

It was clear, therefore, to everyone that he needs to stop now, bring it to a close, like really right now. And had he done so, we all would have clapped politely and the rest of the evening would have gone on just fine. But Merlin, out of belligerence or complete inability to pick up on the social cues that were getting louder and less subtle by the minute, didn't stop. Instead, he ploughed on, and there was no end in sight.

Suddenly, without warning, fart-like sounds began to emanate from the other side of the circle. This provoked a few stifled giggles. Merlin kept going. The sounds got louder. They became more frequent. Eventually, we realised it was coming from a didgeridoo, which had featured earlier in the evening and belonged to one of the guys we had been hanging out with the previous evening.

And still Merlin kept going. People were now openly laughing. Then the fart noises stopped and the didgeridoo player burst into a blistering rhythmic attack, that in hindsight wouldn't have sounded out of place on one of Jason's tapes, drawing applause and cheers from many of those gathered.

This would have been the perfect moment for Merlin to bow out gracefully. What had been a toe-curling solo performance had become a jam. Other people might even be grateful to the didge guy for the rescue.

Not our Merlin.

When at last he stopped, his face was pale, and his eyes were bulging with rage. What followed shocked everyone. Getting up from his stool, he hurled the music stand to the ground, sending his sheet music flying and, guitar in hand, marched over to his nemesis accompanist, going right up to his face.

'I WAS PLAYING.'

The didgeridoo player was cowering now, but also trying not to laugh, while the rest of us gazed on in bewilderment.

'Easy, brother,' he said with a smirk.

Voices called out:

'Leave it, Merlin!'

'Is he going to hit him?'

'Who is this loser?'

Even then, having made his point, Merlin could have walked away with some dignity. Sure, it was an overreaction, but to be fair he was interrupted. It could have been explained and the two of them may even have been able to put the whole thing behind them.

Unfortunately, Merlin was not ready to let it go. Without warning, he made a frankly pathetic attempt to grab the didgeridoo from its owner, and in the tussle Merlin lost his balance and went tumbling to the ground, knocking over several drinks in the process, which didn't ingratiate him to those in the vicinity. Eventually, Anna and I succeeded in helping him to his feet, which earned us an earful from Merlin, who by this point was just raging incoherently at the world. Then he stormed off into the darkness, his guitar slung over his shoulder, like a murderous freewheelin' Bob Dylan.

After that, everyone knew Merlin's name. Indeed, people who had never met Merlin, and who weren't even at that event, began using the phrase 'doing a Merlin'. For a while, the phrase became a kind of Folk slang, used as a reprimand when someone seemed to be getting worked up over small and trivial matters.

There is silence. In the telling, it does sound rather worse than I remembered it. For instance, it occurs to me that we could have come to his aid sooner than we did. Also, it was a bit mean, the fart noises and everything.

'Harsh,' says Jason, quietly. 'Don't he got no one?'

'He's got us,' says Zee.

Jason's lip curls. 'Right.'

'Yeah,' says Anna. 'Quite.'

'Used to know a lad,' he continues, reaching for the bottle of White Pearl. 'Bit like your Merlin.'

Finally, I think, a story from Jason! And I notice we are all leaning in, eager for him to share some personal history of his own.

'Yeah?' I prompt, realising that maybe he is waiting for permission from us. 'Go on.'

We all wait. He has the floor. We are eating out of his hands, hanging on his every word, because Jason almost never shares anything. It's always us on the confessional.

But the story never comes. Instead, he just shakes his head.

'Kid needs friends,' he says at last. 'Kid needs friends.'

Then he picks up his cup and we watch him raise it to his lips and drink the contents, downing it all in one gulp, before clicking his cheek and letting out a lengthy and very noisy burp.

* * *

As the evening rolls on, and the White Pearl keeps flowing, I become more and more conscious of the noise we are making. It's not just the music. It's the chatter, the shrieks of laughter, the cheers and shouts. While it may not break the letter of the law, as stated in Gerry's Survival Guide, it is not in the spirit of the Survival Overnighter to behave like common louts.

There are no houses around, so the chance of someone making a complaint is slim, yet it feels a shame we can't appreciate the nature. Part of me longs for Gerry, just this once, to break his own rules and come over. But I know he won't do that. He refuses to police us. We have to govern ourselves, that's part of the code.

I need to pee, so I get up from the bench. My legs feel wobbly. I have been sitting in the same position too long. I mumble something about answering nature's call. I walk a short distance from our camp, further than is necessary, for the woods seem to beckon me in, the ancient trees murmuring their secret song, their delicate white skin and silver leaves bathed in moonlight.

I have a torch in my pocket, but I will not use it. We have already polluted this spot enough. I keep going, and the voices grow faint, their shrieks and drunken whoops merging with the sonic smorgasbord of the forest and the night. Onwards I go, deeper and deeper, breathing in the sap, the sweet hawthorn and the silence. With every step I feel more alert, lucid suddenly, my eyes keen, my movements sure. At the stream I dip my hands into the dark flow, scooping up water, which spills down my chin, my neck, my breast. I have a strong urge to take off all my clothes, to let the cool, clear water roll over me. To submerge myself fully.

I am running.

Through the bracken and ferns I crash, dry leaves crunching beneath my feet. I run and I run and I run, oblivious to the commotion, reckless in my pursuit of nothing, at least nothing I can name, nothing for which I have language. At the top of a verge I throw myself to the ground, and lie there on my back panting, exhilarated by the chase. The fallen leaves tickle my face, my wrists, my ankles, my palms, and through the cracks in the canopy I see a full moon shining, and I think of my younger self gazing up at these same stars, full of wonder and questions, and though I know the stars are as bright as they always were, I cannot shake the feeling that my ability to see them as I did has already begun to fade.

Gradually, I return to this planet, and to my immediate surroundings. The trees here are densely packed together, so that almost no light can break through. Shadows and shapes shift, darting this way and that in a kind of cosmic dance. My eyes become drawn to a dark mass, right at the bottom of the hill. It seems different to everything around it. Suddenly, I see a small rectangle of light. It appears for just a blink of an eye and then it is gone.

Clasping the torch that remains switched off inside my pocket, I creep closer, imagining myself a fox or a deer, zigzagging down the hillside, elegant and swift and sure-footed.

When I reach the bottom I recognise the dark mass as the same structure that we found earlier in the day, where we had picked up the frame. My body must have taken me back to the spot, for I thought I was going in a random direction. Gently, I touch the wood with the inside of my palm. It feels smooth and cold. The moon's light suddenly catches the metal hinges on the door, where a small, rectangular window has been cut, and I try to look through the glass, but all I see is my own reflection.

* * *

On my return to Base Camp, I discover the music has degenerated into a repetitive dirge and my friends are practically comatose. Jason and Zee are still under the blanket.

'There you are!' Anna slurs when she spots me. 'We thought you'd been eaten by the beast!' She puts a drunk arm around me. 'Would you like a glass of cider, Mark?'

Without waiting for an answer, she picks up an empty bottle of White Pearl and pours the dregs into a plastic cup that's lying around.

'We solved the mystery of the doves anyway.'

'Sorry?'

'Me bro was down,' Jason calls from the darkness. 'He must've nabbed 'em.'

'And there's you worrying Merlin might have caned them! Ha ha, imagine that!'

Zee, I notice, stays silent. She is still sitting next to Jason but I sense a distance between the two that wasn't there earlier, and I wonder if this is the bit where she drops him, and whether that means I might still be in with a chance and whether the chances are better if I was to try to get an invite into the girls' shelter or persuade her into mine, but then what about Jason? I am weighing up these complicated practical matters when I realise that I am, actually, quite drunk as well.

We are all completely mullered.

I glance at Anna again. She has fallen asleep, still cradling her bottle of White Pearl to her breast, like a teddy bear, with a joint between her fingers that is no longer alight. Seb and I unsteadily help her into the shelter, which wakes her up briefly, whereby she declares her love for at least one of us, which is quite sweet really, although she'll have no recollection of any of it in the morning.

'I'm going to hit the sack too,' says Seb, lying down next to her. 'You burning the midnight oil much longer, Big Man?'

I think about Zee and Jason, sitting morose on the bench outside. If they are breaking up, I feel no great desire to have to witness it. If she wants to climb into my shelter and seek comfort afterwards then obviously I would be amenable to that. But I know, even in my drunk state, that this is not likely.

'Nah,' I say, and I bid Seb goodnight.

Alone inside the shelter that Jason, Seb and I built, but which I seem to have acquired all for myself, I undress and get into my sleeping bag inside my bivvy bag.

I am beginning to drop off when it occurs to me that Jason, after we gave Gerry Merlin's rucksack, is without a sleeping bag, and in fact has no kit at all, and I wonder if I should get up again and offer him something or maybe insist that he comes inside the shelter, but it is so cosy in my sleeping bag and my eyes feel wonderfully heavy, like I could sleep for a thousand years, and besides I remind myself, the bastard's got Zee, what more does he need? Even if she is going to dump him. He got to sleep with Zee! He got to sleep with her all summer! No, I think, fuck him. He can be cold.

Just make him feel included.

Oh, Gerry, no fear there.

Chapter Ten

My sleeping bag inside my plastic bivvy bag is sodden. My mouth is dry, my face aches. I am awake, though I wish I wasn't. It is light outside. I am alone. I climb out of the shelter, squinting in the morning sun. Seb is up and about, being active and outdoorsy. I watch him roll up his carry mat and pack away the stove. In the cold light of day the shelters appear childish, more like a kid's den than the architectural miracles of yesterday. I groan.

'Afternoon, Mark.'

'Fuck off, Seb.'

I check my watch. It is only eight-thirty, but it's true, it feels late. The sun is already high in the sky and the birds this morning are going at it with proper gusto.

'Jay's gone,' he says, shaking out the leaves from his bivvy bag.

'Excuse me?'

The girls return from wherever they have been, carrying towels and severe expressions on their faces, their hair wet.

'Hello, ladies!' I call out, jovially.

The remark is intended to be ironically sexist and cheap, but I realise as soon as it is out that it just sounds sexist and cheap.

We set about breaking up the shelters. After all our efforts the previous day, the ritual of destruction feels brutal, though of course it is one of our tenets that no trace should be left. Without the additional muscle of Jason, it's even harder to drag the window frame back to the shed, but between us we manage it.

'Better get a move on,' suggests Seb after we are finished restoring the site to its original state. 'Don't want to keep Gerry waiting.'

Zee and Anna lag behind the whole way back to the bus, talking in low voices and going silent every time I slow down to let them catch up. My hangover is kicking in and I want to be home with a hot bath, a high tog duvet and some trashy telly. Nature, it turns out, is all well and good, but let's also hear for it fluffy towels, quality bedding and the latest home entertainment.

We find Gerry leaning against the side of the Battle Bus. The Three Kats are already on and in their seats. We climb in too. There is no argument about seating.

'I imagine you all know by now,' says Gerry. 'We found Merlin.'

He offers no further explanation. Something in his tone warns us not to demand one, for the failure is clear. In failing Merlin we have failed Survival, failed Folk, failed Gerry, failed ourselves.

'Where's Jason?' asks one of the Three Kats.

Gerry starts the engine.

'Jason decided to make his own way home.'

He does not elaborate, and again no one presses him. Another failure. There is no Guilt Mix this morning; the stereo is silent. Some sleep. I stare out of the window. We pass farms and agricultural warehouses, fields, factories and large houses with driveways and shiny four-by-fours parked behind security gates. In the lost years, before we were reunited by Folk, Zee had lived in a village way out like this. That was back when she had a dad, meaning before he took the Big Job at the Prestigious American University. Zee rarely speaks of this time, but she told me the cottage had roses around the door, a wood burner and a stream running through the garden. It even had a thatched roof. The plan had been for Zee's parents to write important books while Zee and the girls cavorted gaily in all that nature, while getting a more intimate educational experience at the village school where class sizes were half what they were in the city, and no one locked their doors. Zee recalls that it didn't matter at first to them not knowing anyone. After all, they were busy building dens, riding ponies etc. But when the summer ended and they had to start at the school everything had changed, and while she had never gone into details, I could guess. To make matters worse, the marriage fell apart, which led to Zee's dad, who is white, moving to America.

A year into village life they had left, or as Zee put it: 'We went back to where we came from.'

Of course, I tell myself, they could have been unhappy anywhere.

My mouth feels furry, as if an animal has died in there, and my brain is a few beats behind the world. I'm tired. I don't know what is going on with Zee or why she's not talking to me. And I wonder why it matters to me so much, her good regard. People always tell me I have my whole life to fall in love. 'Experiment! Live!' says my mother. Her friends, most of whom are splitting up with their partners or already on to marriage number two or three, are only just learning this lesson, she says, 'So you're already well ahead!'

She says she didn't do nearly enough *living* before she got together with my father.

I get the impression that Mum really hates Zee. She claims she 'admires' Zee, that's the word she uses, like she admires Yolanda and Polly.

Is my mother racist? Or jealous? Or is she merely protective of me, knowing that Zee will always break my heart, that I will never be good enough, not for Zee and not for her family either?

The fields and hedges and cottages morph into a generic sprawl of new-build estates and dinky starter homes, and I think of the song about the Little Boxes on the hillside, the ones made out of *ticky-tacky*, and I wonder how I would feel if I lived in one of them and heard a bunch of kids like us singing this song that is meant to be funny but maybe isn't that funny after all.

Chapter Eleven

It is raining. The lights in the community centre canteen are off. A hand-written note has been taped to the door:

FOLK OFF

The ink has run in the rain, so that the O looks more like a U and the L could be a C – but none of us are in the mood for jokes.

We huddle under the porch and talk, in a vague sort of way, about college, the classes we are taking and not taking. Schedules and timetables. And it is as if we don't really know each other at all. No one makes direct reference to the Survival Overnighter. No one makes direct reference to Merlin's and Jason's absences.

'It's not like Gerry to miss Folk,' says Zee.

There's a suggestion of going round the corner to the Last Stand, but Zee's not up for it, which is a relief because they'd probably ID me, and then I would have the humiliation of drinking children's drinks while the others drink cider or vodka with lemonade.

We part without ceremony, because we'll see each other next week, if not before. There is no reason to think otherwise.

When, after a few more days, there is no word from Gerry – nothing, in fact, since he dropped us back after the Survival Overnighter – I decide to take matters into my own hands and go round to see him.

I will tell him everything, I decide. Jason, his *Doves*, my fear that Merlin may have taken them. I will even, I think, mention the strange noises and light coming from the shed.

Gerry's lodger, Kay, answers the door. With her henna'd hair and nose ring through the centre of her nose rather than the conventional side piercing, she fits closely with what my parents would describe as *a Gerry person.*

She comes from somewhere in the north of England and her voice, as well as having a strong regional accent, has a hoarse, throaty quality that sounds as if she has been shouting all night.

'Hello, chicken,' she says with a smile. She has invented many names for me over the years.

As usual, I have to wade through piles of unopened mail, as well as several cardboard boxes and a toaster that's missing a plug, to get down the hall.

'I'm not sure he's here,' she says. 'Is he expecting you?'

'No,' I say, squeezing past the bikes blocking the entrance to the kitchen. 'I was just in the area.'

Kay has made tea, a concoction of fauna and flora and God knows what, cooked up in a big cast-iron pan. She uses a ladle to transfer a serving of it into a chipped mug commemorating the Battle of Orgreave.

'Hardly seen him this last week, Chuck,' she says, handing me a steaming mug of twigs. 'But take a look, by all means. You know Gerry, he's probably up there plotting the revolution.'

I go upstairs to look for him. The carpet is worn and frayed. In some places the boards have come through. I am charmed by these blemishes, which seem more authentic and more desirable than the fussy attempts of my parents to replicate the fashionable interior design ideas they've seen on the telly.

Most of the walls at Mount Pleasant Road are in a state of profound neglect, with holes and marks from hangings that have been put up and removed, and telltale brown stains in corners suggesting damp. My father would be appalled. He would be straight down to B&Q for de-moulder and tins of emulsion. But in Gerry's house, these idiosyncrasies feel part of the natural order of a place where life is allowed to play out, and where there are more important things to worry about than the state of the carpet.

On the first floor, a whole wall is taken up with a mural depicting a group of protesters and police. There's a guy with a megaphone who is probably supposed to be Gerry. It's all very cartoonish.

I can smell the incense from Kay's room. I keep going up.

'Gerry!'

There's no answer. The doors to Gerry's two rooms at the end of the landing are closed. There is light coming from the other end of the landing, where the door to the small room is slightly ajar.

I peek in. There's just a bed, a wardrobe, a desk and a chair. There is no evidence that anyone has been living there. It's not a particularly sunny day, but the room is bright. I enter and sit down on the mattress, which is firm and warm from where the sun has been shining on it.

While it is considerably smaller than my room at home, it feels spacious and airy and open and light. It is not a child's room. It is not weighed down by relics of a life that never was.

I like the flecks of paint on the legs of the desk. I like the mismatched quality of the furniture, as if it has been chanced upon rather than chosen, picked up here and there and salvaged rather than planned from the dull selections of a catalogue.

I hear Kay on the stairs, and hurriedly get up from the bed, but she is already standing at the door.

'Such a shame,' she says.

'Shame?'

'About Jason.'

I nod, as if I knew already.

'So, er, what happened?'

'Buggered if I know. One minute he's taking him camping. The next, the kid's gone, and Gerry's not saying a word.' She looks at me, squinting. 'You were there, right? What happened? Did they have a row or something?'

I'm hesitant, unsure how much I should tell her. It would be prudent, I decide, to speak to Gerry before unwittingly blurting out something that we might later come to regret. I don't want to be the sort of person who spreads rumours and gossip.

'I don't really know.'

'It's a shame,' she says again, shaking her head. 'Seemed to be getting his head together. College, friends – lovely girlfriend. I suppose you never really know what's going on inside someone's head, do you?'

I nod and, remembering something Jason had said, enquire: 'Do you think it has something to do with his brother's visit?'

'His brother visited?'

'He didn't?'

'News to me.'

'Oh,' I say. 'Right.'

I'm saddened that Jason lied to us but not that surprised. The story about the mysterious brother coming to visit had not rung true at the time. Indeed, Jason himself seemed to be having trouble believing it. He probably didn't even come up with the explanation himself.

'Poor kid,' she adds. 'Jay was my guy.'

* * *

The following evening our doorbell rings. It's a ridiculous doorbell, the most ridiculous doorbell ever: a bleepy rendering of Greensleeves that goes on and on and on, so that by the end you can't help but loathe the person who rang it. And the worst thing? It's my fault. I chose it. And for reasons that they would have to explain, my parents – who never listen to me on anything that actually matters, such as which school I attend, or the decision to put the piano in the most public place in the house so that every practice becomes a performance for my parents and their friends – on this one stupid thing – the doorbell – my vote, it seems, is binding; my power absolute.

It is unusual during the week for us to get visitors, so I assume it is a cold caller. A lot of people are rude about these desperate individuals, but I pity them, for I can see that, compelled by poverty, they are forced to spend their evenings and weekends trying to sell plastic windows and shit conservatories and timeshares and whatever other newfangled pyramid scheme and whatnot that someone, somewhere has concocted in order to swindle people out of their savings or their kid's future happiness. In other words, it is the devil's work they are doing, and they are universally hated by people (like my parents) for whom wealth and privilege makes them immune to the suffering of those less fortunate than themselves. It is a topic that Zee and I (me and Zee) have discussed extensively.

I hear my mother getting up from in front of the telly and going out to the hall. Perhaps it is someone canvassing for a politician or, God forbid, the church. *God Squad* is the name my parents call the latter subgroup. They are obviously the lowest of the low, the real untouchables, for their motivation is not even strictly financial, and so cannot be excused by poverty.

'Gerry! This is a surprise!'

'Hope I'm not disturbing anything, June.'

I hurry out of my room and down the stairs, conscious that I should avoid leaving my mother alone with Gerry for too long, for she will only embarrass herself. I know what she's like.

'Ah, Mark,' says Gerry, when he sees me.

We go through to the living room. Gerry sits in the corner in the rocking chair that's not as comfortable as it looks. He smiles his parent-friendly Gerry smile.

'David not around?'

Mum smiles back and shakes her head. 'Just us, I'm afraid!'

This makes Gerry chuckle. It has never been confirmed, but I am pretty sure Mum and Gerry have a history that goes beyond friendship.

She gets up and goes into the kitchen. There is a sound of the kettle being filled. 'Rooibos?' she calls, in a sing-song voice.

'Oooh,' Gerry returns. 'June, you know how to spoil me!'

He's trying too hard, I think. He's all over the place this evening. I watch him cross his legs, then uncross them, then re-cross. It's quite excruciating.

Something else that's odd: I cannot recall Gerry ever having visited the house before. Not once, in all the years, has he come for tea.

'How's college?' he says, awkwardly.

'Yeah,' I reply, relieved that the silence has been broken, even if the question feels formal and far too impersonal for Gerry. 'Not too bad, really.'

'Good. Great.'

I know Mum is listening. I can feel her judgement on the quality of our conversation all the way from the kitchen.

'Sorry I missed you, Mark.'

'Oh, yeah, I was, er... passing.'

'Hmmm, Kay said. Sorry about that.'

It must be stated that I am not doing any better at this than Gerry.

Everything feels slightly off. Gerry sitting in my parents' front room. Mum, not just present, but involved. This is not the way we do things. It's just not Folk.

It's as if a bad Gerry impersonator has turned up, and we're all carrying on, pretending it's normal when clearly it's all wrong.

Gerry clears his throat, somewhat theatrically. 'So, Mark,' he begins. 'You're probably wondering what's going on?'

Mum comes through carrying a tray, which she sets down on the coffee table, with a self-satisfied, '*There.*'

Jesus, I realise, she's doing the 1950s housewife routine. It's a joke she does, obviously, at least that's how it started.

'Oooh,' Gerry coos. 'June!'

She sits down beside me on the horrible cream-coloured sofa that cost them an arm and a leg, and is just waiting for someone to spill something liquidy and staining it. The clock in the hallway ticks.

Gerry puts his hands together in a gesture that looks as if he's about to lead us in prayer.

'Well,' he says. 'I'll get straight to it.' He shuffles in his seat. 'I don't know how much Mark has told you?'

He smiles at me in a way that indicates that this is not a question to which he expects an answer, that even though he says it in a questioning sort of way, it is not so much a question as a lead in to what he's about to say next.

'About the trip?' asks my 1950s-esque housewife-mother. 'Oh, you know, I don't think it's considered very *cool* to tell your parents about these things.'

Gerry nods. He's not really listening. Mum leans in, lowering her voice in that way she does when she's feeling flirty. 'It's not Merlin again, is it? I do hope it's not another of his Disappearing Acts?'

'Well, June, the thing is...' He scrunches his face into a grimace. 'There has been an allegation. Quite a serious one.'

Mum's eyes widen at the word 'allegation'.

'Oh?' she says, carefully.

'Yes,' Gerry continues. 'It seems someone – not Mark, I may add – brought along something they shouldn't have.'

'Oh?'

'Let's just say, things escalated.'

'Oh, Gerry, I am sorry.'

The relief in her voice confirms the shift in her from anxious parent to trusted confidante and wise citizen.

'Is it drugs?'

Mum has always prided herself on her relaxed attitude to such things. 'I'm a Child ff the Sixties!' she would boast, casually, whenever the subject came up, and then her and her friends would wax lyrical about the glory days. 'I tell you,' someone might say, 'young people today are so sensible! So much better behaved than we ever were!'

Whenever I heard this talk it made me want to go straight out and score some heroin, just to wipe the smug smiles off their faces, but of course I didn't because I'm terrified of getting AIDS.

Gerry looks away, his face grave.

'You shouldn't blame yourself, Gerry,' she continues, laying her hand on his corduroy-clad leg in a gesture that I will later consider overly intimate for a parent and their child's youth leader.

But for now I am focused on the words, which confirm to me that everyone in my parents' friendship circle had known about Jason, that they all knew Gerry had taken him in, and that they had probably discussed the matter extensively at their dinner parties, etc.

'I don't know, June. I just don't know anymore.'

Mum picks up the teapot and smiles. 'Shall I be mother?' She sighs, because it is, of course, very regrettable, very sad. 'Look,' she says. 'Gerry, you tried. You really did. I mean, how many people would have even given him a chance? You know you always think the best of people, and it is a wonderful quality, I don't want to do it down, but you know yourself you can sometimes be too trusting, too generous in your nature.'

'I just wanted to give the lad a chance. You know?'

'Of course you did,' says Mum. 'But people have to want to help themselves.'

I stare at the floral swirls on the hand-made rug – handmade by child slaves, mostly likely. Most of the things in this house are products of exploitation. And I wish that the ground would swallow me up.

'Fact is, June, a line has been crossed. And that's a problem.'

'Oh, I know, Gerry.'

'I can't ignore it.'

'No, I suppose not. Will the, er, boy, be sent away?'

Gerry lets out a long sigh. He glances at me, then at Mum, then back at me. 'Unfortunately, and I wish it wasn't so, but this has wider consequences. It doesn't just concern the person or persons in question. This affects the whole group.'

'Oh?'

'The fact is I went out on a limb to make this year's Survival Overnighter happen. You understand that, Mark, right? I took a risk. There are a lot of people who told me I was making a mistake but I trusted the group, and I trusted my instincts. But we are fallible, June, and our instincts can send us the wrong way.

'Folk needs trust,' Gerry continues. 'Trust on all sides. Without this, there is no Folk, I've always said that. So, I'm sorry, Mark. I wish it didn't have to be like this, but you understand why I have to take this decision, why we can't carry on as if nothing has happened?'

I try to tell him that we can change, that we know we did wrong and that it will never happen again; that next time we will be more considerate, more *Folk*. But Gerry just shakes his head sadly.

'It's a little late for that, Mark, I'm afraid.'

He gets up from the chair and goes over to the French-style windows.

'Believe me, Mark. I hate this as much as you do, but there really is no way we can continue after this. I just don't have the energy for it any more.'

He goes back out to the hall and Mum helps him into his jacket. I can hear them whispering to each other but I do not catch what is said and, frankly, I no longer care. I am stunned by the suddenness of the decision. But something else is bothering me even more. The way it has all been pinned on Jason, as if him bringing ecstasy was the only thing that went wrong on the trip, as if the rest of us were blameless.

'Jason didn't do anything,' I say, joining them at the door.

My words are met with kind smiles.

'I think we all know that's not quite true,' says Gerry. 'But I appreciate you want to stick up for your friend, Mark.'

'He didn't, though! He wouldn't! He's not like that. He just isn't.'

Gerry nods.

'I'm shocked as well, Mark.'

'He didn't do it.'

'You're very loyal, darling.' Mum this time. 'It's an excellent quality in you.'

'But it wasn't Jason's fault.' I am pleading with them, but I know my efforts are futile, that the case is already closed and no matter what I say no one is going to change their minds about what happened, and I think about the empty room and the stripped bed at Mount Pleasant Road, and Kay's words: *Poor kid*.

The worst part of it is that Jason's departure is what I wanted, at least it is what I wished for, and not just because of Zee, but because of Folk. Because of the influence he had on the group and, perhaps, because of what Jason revealed in us.

We watch Gerry leave, making his way slowly down the garden path, past the wisteria, the pond, the 'crazy' paving they installed, Mum's azaleas. At one point he stoops and bends down, as if to retrieve something off the ground, before straightening again and continuing on. He does not look back. At the gate he pauses, and I will him to turn around and say it isn't so, tell us there is still something we can do, that Folk is not beyond saving. But he doesn't. Instead, he reaches for the latch.

The gate is stiff at this time of year. The warping of the wood causes it to jam and visitors often struggle to get it open. Dad tells every visitor we receive that it is 'like the Hotel California' in that '*You can check out any time you like, but you can never leave!*' There's a trick to it, he says. Gerry opens the gate without difficulty.

Then the sound of footsteps on the pavement. The sound of a car door being opened, closed, an engine stuttering to life. The sound of silence.

PART 2

NESTS

Chapter Twelve

Without Folk I'm lost. It is as if everything is moving and I am rooted to the spot, mute, like a statue in a public square. There but not there.

I still exchange words – with my parents, with acquaintances at college, with teachers, with people in shops – but I come away from these encounters empty and unable to recall what has just taken place. I begin to comprehend how it must have been for Merlin. Present yet not. Absent in plain sight.

Mum says Folk has run its course, that I should see this as an opportunity to branch out, find new things, expand my horizons. She always hated Folk. I should try the Thursday session at the Dog, she says. Lots of young people. It's not all *wrinklies* like her. I might like it.

I say I'll think about it.

My father tries to downplay the whole thing. 'Does it really change anything? You are all friends,' he says. 'With or without the Folk badge. Why do you need Gerry's blessing?' Dad has always felt threatened by Gerry.

Meanwhile, they are making moves, what's called a *concerted* effort, to repair their shit marriage. They drive to B&Q and pick out wallpaper. The hallway is a bit dingy, they agree. It needs cheering up.

A presenter on a television show they like says that citrus colours and florals are back. That whole 1970s vibe is apparently the big thing right now in interior design. This pleases my parents because they feel they were at their happiest in that decade.

Further home improvements are discussed. They are more united, more attentive to each other's needs, than they have been in years. They are actually communicating, even if only through the medium of dado rails, floor coverings and wall hangings.

The leaves on the Dutch lime trees at the end of our street turn red, orange, brown, their flaky forms fluttering, floating, falling in the wind and blocking the drains. The temperature drops and the days get shorter. And then it is Christmas, at least in the shops, and the town centre fills with giant Santas and Rudolphs and sleighs with flashing lights. It is all canned cheer and forced camaraderie and I loathe it.

One day, at the end of November, I get home earlier than usual. A class has been cancelled and no one is hanging around. I'll sit in my room, I think. Maybe put on some music; read a book. Do nothing.

It is the smell I pick up first. I cannot place it. Musty. A bit *barnyard*. My glance falls on a pair of shoes that have been placed in the rack. They are red and quite enormous, far too big for Dad. The leather looks handmade. Rustic. I know a shop in town that sells shoes like that. It is not a shop my father frequents.

And then I hear the scrape of wood on wood, followed by a grunt, and a groan, and more scraping, and more wood, and more sighs. Jesus, I'm thinking – they're really going for it.

I stand there in the hallway, clutching my key, unsure what to do. I have not yet removed my jacket.

Later I will try to laugh it off. I will say it was like one of those call and response songs, the ones we'd do at Folk. But my response at this moment is pure, physical, repulsion. I stare at the shoes. They really are enormous.

There is another groan. More banging and scraping. I've heard enough.

I go back outside, allowing the door to close behind me. If they hear me I don't care. But I doubt they will hear anything.

I retrace my steps down the dinky path my parents installed. The flowers in the garden are all dead. The bird table stands there forgotten and neglected. The pond is silent and dead. To the gate. Out onto the street.

And I walk. I walk without a plan, only a need to put as much distance between myself and my mother's sex nest. And when I feel one, two, three drops on the back of my neck, it feels as if the rain has been sent to cleanse my soul.

I regret my failure to pick up a proper jacket on the way out. I am dressed in a preposterous flimsy sort of anorak that I chose based on what other people at college seemed to wear. It had cost a fortune. It has not been designed for weather of any kind.

At St Bart's, the local parish church, I consider going in. I've done it before, just walked in off the street and sat down at a pew! But then the vicar or priest or whatever had come in, and he had had that look about him, like he was going to try to convert me, so I had to make a dash for it.

In almost every story I know, the church represents oppression, and obviously I am against that. But I am rather drawn to the buildings. In my mind they are exotic, forbidden spaces that may only be entered for the purposes of marriage, death, Christening or at Christmas. Maybe I am intrigued by churches because they are so markedly different to all the other buildings I know, none of which have spires, doors made for giants or colourful depictions of torture, salvation and the eternal. Zee (also an atheist) likes churches, too.

My main association with organised religion is the annual community carol concert, which Mum and Dad and some of the neighbours attend because it makes them feel Christmassy. A few people we know do go to church, on a semi-regular basis, but their motivation is ambition (for their children in this case) rather than spiritual, regular church attendance being an admissions requirement for one of the better schools on the other side of town.

The rain is biblical. It runs down my face, down my neck, down my back, down my jeans, down my ankles and into my shoes. There is no way on God's earth that I am going back to that house now.

I look through the railings at the churchyard, and at graves so weather-beaten that the names are no longer legible. The lost souls buried here lived and died in the parish back when people still called it *the parish*, passing before death and grieving had become the industry it is today.

Zee and I have discussed what will happen to us when we die. Our bodies, what's left of them, will go to medical science, every last bit, or whatever parts can be of use to the next generation of scientists and researchers. We both carry donor cards.

Onwards I trudge, leaving the church and its neglected graves behind, rain pounding on the pavement. The streets are eerily quiet. Large puddles have already formed in places.

I enter the park. Even the dog walkers have stayed home.

I keep going: through the heavy gates and into John Locke Place, behind the Firs, up Hobbes Hill, and I think about the day we first took Jason to Top of the World. Zee in her paint-flecked jeans, ghetto blaster tucked under her arm, impervious to the disapproving looks of residents with their prim and tidy gardens and their net curtains twitching away. How beguiling she is! The way she doesn't give a fuck.

If one didn't know, one could easily miss the entrance to the narrow lane that runs behind the gardens at the far end of the crescent.

The gate at the end of the path is locked, as usual, yet something feels different today. I put it down to being on my own. Places, even very familiar ones, can take on a different quality in different company or, in this case, in no company at all.

Going up Top of the World, the joke went, is rather like entering another realm. That's stoner talk, obviously, but there is something *otherworldly* about the place. In the same spirit, it is often said that the air up here tastes different, the gag being that this is Top of the World not the Himalayas or the Andes or the other places people we know boast about. Top of the World is about ten minutes from Littlewoods.

Joking aside, it is refreshing to be somewhere that, so far, nobody has managed to turn into a carpark, a shopping centre, a leisure park or yuppy homes – though it is surely only a matter of time.

Unsurprisingly, it is a hotspot for fly-tipping, and the gap between the fence that runs behind the backs of the houses and the brambles and nettles, behind which lies what we like to call the *meadow*, is littered with all manner of refuse and abandoned goods.

I pass bags of building materials and the drum of a washing machine. A chair, missing one of its legs and most of the seat, has been placed on top of all the rubbish in such a way that it looks like a throne. I imagine the ruler of this apocalyptic kingdom sitting up there presiding over our provincial concerns, arguments and infidelities. Leaning against the railing is a filthy mattress on which someone has written the words:

NOTHING MATTRESS

It is getting dark. The nights drawing in. Days getting shorter. One by one lights come on in the windows of the houses behind the fence. The rain shows no sign of abating. The sky is a heavy thick grey.

At last I reach the secret hole in the hedge. Nature here has been left to its own devices and there is considerably less rubbish at this end. People can't be bothered to go down this far.

I glance around, checking that no one is watching, and squeeze my body through the gap in the hedge. The wet branches and leaves are cold against my face.

Top of the World opens out before me, stretching into the distance to where the railway meets the road and rows of houses back onto industrial units, like a scale model at a museum. Across the valley, the grand spires and towers of the university gaze down on the little people going about their little lives.

It seems no one has heard from Gerry since the evening he broke the news, a task he conducted in a rather ceremonial way, beginning with Anna and working his way through to Zee, each one of us given the same speech. Eight visits, eight speeches, until there was no one left to tell.

Evening has come, and soon it will be completely dark, with only the windows of the houses, partially obscured by the fence, and the orange glow of the town below to guide the way.

I shiver, aware suddenly of the cold. The rain has worked its way into my skin, into my bones. It occurs to me that no one knows where I am, and I am scared, scared that I will die in this desolate spot that we used to think of as ours.

I hurry through the hole in the hedge and back along the junk-lined track that runs in front of the fence. In this light, every shape looks like a threat, and I start to plan my escape route in the event that someone, or more than one person, were to appear on the path ahead.

And I know that either way I will not be coming back to this place again.

* * *

Christmas finally arrives, not just in the shops but in the calendar, and it is excruciating. My parents, who are avoiding each other, channel everything through me, making a great display of trying, in spite of the other's failings as a human being, to *at least give Mark a nice Christmas*.

Dad brings home a tree that's too big to fit through the front door, and has to get the saw out of the shed to chop a few inches off the stump.

On the day, there are too many gifts for me and not enough for them because I only got them one each.

Christmas is always a bit like this, but in previous years I have been able to escape to Zee's for some or (once) all of it. This year, however, they've gone away. Somewhere up north. Zee's being a bit distant with me. I think it's connected with the new boyfriend.

The fridge is crammed full of food that no one is really eating. We receive no visitors, just a few calls on Christmas Day, none of which last very long.

The television stays on at all times. We develop a sudden interest in Christmas specials of soap operas and sitcoms. We even watch the Queen's speech.

And then, on Boxing Day evening, the phone rings and it's not some distant blood relative that my parents must pretend to be pleased to hear from, and then complain about after they've hung up – it's for me.

It is Gerry.

He's sorry for being such a stranger. He was away, he explains, and then it was hectic, but he's back now and he wants to see me. In fact, he wants me to come over to the house. He wants to cook me dinner. He asks me how I'm fixed, whether I have time this week, which I do. Obviously.

The following evening I spend a ridiculous amount of time in front of the mirror deciding what to wear. I don't want to seem too dressed up, yet I'm conscious that Gerry's various waifs and strays will be there and I don't want to come across to them as a kid in my teenager clothes. In books and the sorts of films that Zee and I watch, it seems much easier, because men wear shirts and blazers, ties even. Not in a school uniform way, or like my Dad when he's going to meet with some corporate types to talk about money or health and safety or whatever, but in a cultivated, refined way. I don't own such clothes and if I dared to dress like that I'm quite sure everyone would think I am trying too hard, or else that I went to a posh school and I call Dad 'Father' and Mum 'Mother'. So, in the end, I just plump for some blue jeans, a plain long sleeve T-shirt and a nondescript jumper over the top.

Whatever.

At least it's not raining. It's not particularly cold either. I don't think I recall ever getting snow at Christmas. The closest to a White Christmas I've experienced is the snow machine in the high street outside Dingles.

Of course, I've been avoiding town for the last few weeks, but sometimes it can't be helped, and then it's fighting it out among the hordes of shoppers, collectively urged to approach the countdown to the big event in a state of profound delirium.

Only six more shopping days before Christmas!

At the corner of Paris Street some intrepid souls are camped outside one of the larger furniture shops, cheerfully huddled together with their thermos flasks and their deck chairs and their sleeping bags. These people are not homeless, or raising awareness about the plight of the homeless with a sponsored Sleep Out, as a few of us have done over the years; no, these people are here for the bargains when the shops open in the morning, for the SALES are NOW ON and MASSIVE further reductions are promised.

Mount Pleasant Road is as unpleasant as ever. The pavement is littered with dog shit and fast food boxes. The street lamps give off a dirty orange glow and in the houses television sets flicker. There are plastic Santas in some windows.

Chained to the railings outside Gerry's is a rusty old bike that's missing a front wheel, handlebars and saddle.

The lights are on in the front room and I can hear droning whirring music coming from inside. I press the bell, but no sound comes, so I knock on the window.

Kay answers the door. She has done something to her hair and there is glitter around her eyes.

'Here he is!' she exclaims.

'Merry Christmas!'

'You too, chicken,' she says, taking my fleece and hanging it on one of the hooks in the hallway. 'Gerry's fixing the feast, so me and Badge have been banished from the kitchen. Can I interest you in an aperitif?'

I spot Badger on the couch, joint in one hand, glass in the other. When he sees me he nods and raises his glass. 'Very nice to see you, Mark.'

Kay returns with a glass, an old-fashioned pint mug with a handle, stolen from a pub during a drunken escapade no doubt. She holds it up to the light to assess its cleanliness. Then she goes over to the table in the corner on which a demijohn of cloudy yellow liquid has been set up. She turns the little tap, the demijohn emits a low gurgling sound, as if something is alive in there.

'Here,' she says, handing me the glass. 'Badger's Festive Scrumpy!'

We clink glasses ('Cheers!') and I sit down in a battered armchair opposite Badger. The cider tastes sweet and flowery, and very alcoholic.

'Delicious,' I say, and they laugh.

'Tastes of old pants to me,' says Kay.

'Well, you'd know, darling,' Badger replies, getting up from the couch and going over to the record player. He flicks through the records in the shelf above. Having never owned a record player, records retain a certain mystery to me. Zee has one, though her collection is tiny in comparison with the bulging shelf of records that Badger is now sifting through. Mostly we play tapes. Tapes are good because you can record stuff as well as play stuff, so it's like both. But vinyl is sexy. That's what Zee says and I think she is probably right. My parents used to have a record player, but they got rid of it, and most of their vinyls, when they upgraded to CDs. Maybe there are still a few LPs in a box somewhere.

Gerry appears in the doorway, grinning and wiping his hands on a tea towel, and we go through to the kitchen where the table has been cleared, wiped and set. There is a steaming cauldron of veggie curry in the middle.

Food is served and glasses are replenished. Everyone digs in. We're all hungry. Everything, the food especially, reminds me of Folk. And even though Kay and Badger are a bit too old and never actually went to Folk, they are one-hundred per cent Folk people.

Badger tells us about the recording studio and practice rooms he's setting up. He's on the hunt for premises. Gerry thinks he might know somewhere. Badger says we can all have Mates Rates. I confess that I don't actually play anything, that I'm not very musical, but that I know plenty of folk who are and I will definitely mention it to them.

He grins and says, 'Since when did you need to be musical to be in a band?'

Most of the bands he knows – most of the bands he *likes* – can't play an instrument between them. Kay agrees. She says she knows loads of people in bands who are completely devoid of talent, and she looks at Badger in an exaggerated way and we all laugh, Badger too, and I am reminded what it's like when people just get along and can banter with each other without someone taking it the wrong way or trying to score points or anything.

It isn't until pudding – apple strudel from the freezer and custard from the tin—that anyone acknowledges Christmas.

I hadn't planned to tell them about my family Christmas, or indeed my family. However, the relief of being in a Folk-like situation again, combined with the scrumpy, seems to loosen me up, and before I can stop myself I'm telling them about the enormous Red Shoes in the rack, and the rolls of wallpaper that were never hung and are still wrapped in their cellophane.

'Honestly. I wish they'd just split up. They're easier to deal with on their own anyway.'

There is a silence, and I wonder if I've overstepped the mark and said too much. Knowing almost nothing about the circumstances of my hosts, whether they have families or not and the extent to which they get along, my own complaints feel invalid and petty and I worry that I am being just a whinging kid.

'Sorry,' I add, hurriedly. 'The last few months have been a bit weird.'

'Yes,' says Gerry, coming to my rescue. 'It has been a strange time. I can't tell you how sorry I am about the way Folk ended. And I'm sorry, too, about your parents. It sounds miserable.'

He pauses, glances at the others.

'Listen, Mark,' he says, putting down his fork. 'I got you here on false pretences. I mean, we did all want to see you, but there's something else as well. You might have noticed the house is a little emptier than last time you were here.' He smiles, and glances around at the others, who all seem to already know what's coming. 'Long and short of it is this, Mark. There's a room going if you want it.'

I catch Kay's eye.

'What do you say, Sparky. Are you game?'

That name again. Jason is the only person who has ever called me *Sparky*. I have never thought of myself as someone who could take such a name. I've always been plain old Mark. Non-threatening Mark. Mark, your friend but not your lover. Weasel Posh Boy Voice Mark. But, coming from Kay, and with the promise of a new life as one of Gerry's waifs and strays, one of his Children, it becomes almost plausible.

Sparky.

Sparks. Sparkle. Sparkly.

'Now,' Gerry continues, 'about the rent...'

The muscles in my face tighten. The thought of money exchange hadn't crossed my mind. It's not a topic I think very much about. Every month I am informed by my bank that a quantity of money has entered my account, and because of this a hole in the wall spits out cash on request, which I can exchange for things I either need, want or feel obliged to buy.

Okay, that's not quite the whole story. After the UTR party, and moonlighting on the drinks stand, I decided that I would take a job. I wrote a CV on the computer. I printed multiple copies and peddled them around to all the places I could imagine myself working. Outdoor suppliers, bookshops, record stores, a few cafes and bars, a handful of restaurants (though everyone says catering is the pits). At last, becoming desperate, I tried the generic evil capitalist chains, including supermarkets and fast food outlets, who wouldn't accept my CV and insisted I fill out application forms (which took ages). And still nobody wanted to give me a job.

'Er, I could, erm, talk to my parents...' I am mortified by these words I am saying, which sound very Mark Fisher and not at all Sparky, who would walk easily into a job if he needed one, who would be able to hustle and scheme, and somehow – by hook or by crook – pay the rent.

Gerry scrunches his face. 'I've got a better idea.' He pushes his empty plate away and gets up from the table. 'Come on,' he says. 'Let me show you something.'

We trail after Gerry up the stairs, the floorboards creaking under the strain of so many heavy boots. Up, up, up, all the way to the top. Gerry pauses on the landing outside a door I've never noticed before. He fishes in his jeans and pulls out a key.

'Curiouser and curiouser,' says Kay.

He has to give the door a bit of a shove to get it open. He reaches in and switches on a light. It is a small, windowless room – more broom cupboard than a proper room – filled, from floor to ceiling, with files and boxes.

There are papers everywhere. Papers on the floor. Papers piled loosely on shelves. Papers spilling from boxes that have been overfilled and have collapsed under the weight of too much paper.

Gerry picks up a stray sheet and stuffs it into the nearest box.

'This,' he says, 'is the archive!'

'Ooooooh!' we all say.

'What we have here,' he says, tapping the shelf, 'is a record of every major on-the-ground campaign I've been involved in going back a decade, and a good many that came to my attention via our comrades. This is our history. This is our movement. It's all here, you know.'

Badger frowns. 'Bit of a state, isn't it?'

'Ah,' says Gerry. 'Funny you should say that.'

It transpires that Gerry has a proposition for me. The archive has, he admits, been a little neglected of late. What's needed is someone who could take it on as a project, sort out what's there, give it a little attention, a little love.

'A dedicated archivist, if you like. Someone to get it in order.'

He would do it himself, he points out, but he has so much on. He's not sure when he'll get around to it. And besides, he adds, he is too intimately involved.

The position, he continues, while unpaid, would include lodgings and full board. Meals would also be provided. He's been looking for the right candidate for some time, and finding it hard to fill the role.

'I have to be able to trust this person,' he adds. 'Some of the content of the archive is highly sensitive. It must be handled with care.'

Finally, it needs to be someone bright, someone who can grasp general principles even if they are not yet familiar with the detail.

'What do you think?'

'Me? You think I could do this?'

He nods gravely. 'I do, Mark. I really do.'

As it happens, I am not a total novice. At my substandard school we all had to do a work experience placement. I did one at a local architect's because, well, no reason – it just seemed like a good idea at the time. From day one it was clear to me that I was just going to get in the way, but a kindly office manager took pity on me, or she saw my potential, or maybe she was just exploiting me, but she enlisted my help with one of her projects, which were more administrative than architectural. The project was what she called an *unruly* filing cabinet. She said it needed *taming*, like it was a wild animal or, I dunno, Huck Finn.

We worked on this unruly beast every day for two weeks, and I have to say, she taught me loads and by the end of my time there I felt quietly proud of what I had achieved through her patient instruction.

When we returned to school we were required to share our experiences of what we'd learned during our placements and I'd stood up and said that I'd tamed an unruly filing cabinet, hoping to get a laugh, except no one had laughed and afterwards one of the girls in the class loudly suggested that I would make someone a lovely receptionist and someone else said there was no doubt about it now.

We go back out onto the landing and Gerry shows me the room, and I don't mention that I've already had a bit of a nose around, already imagined myself there. And Kay doesn't grass me up either, she just gives me a nod and says, 'Part of the family now, Sparky.'

We all agree that I could make it nice.

Walking home that night, tipsy but not trashed, I experience a rush of excitement and gratitude for this chance to start afresh. I am already feeling more Sparky, less Mark, and eager to immerse myself into my new roles: archivist, private secretary, waif, stray – and, once again, one of Gerry's adopted children.

Chapter Thirteen

I spend the following week clearing my room, soundtracked by a pop radio station. Every song resonates. It is as if the whole universe is telling me to take the plunge, follow my heart and my dreams and release myself from the chains that hitherto had held me back from being the person I can be. I have never felt so understood, by so many people, in so many ways.

When Move Day finally arrives, Dad and I load the car with the possessions I have whittled my life down to. It is perhaps the most father-son thing we've ever done together. There's a lot of jigging and re-jigging and scratching of chins before we get it all in, and I am amused to discover that the obsessive Tetris-playing I did when I got my GameBoy has proven useful for something.

The traffic is unexpectedly heavy, so what should have been a ten-minute journey takes almost half an hour. We listen to the radio and avoid contentious topics, which makes conversation somewhat stilted. When silence threatens to overwhelm, we comment on the traffic and the behaviour of other road users. It helps that I've started my driving lessons. This gives us lots of safe material.

When we get to Mount Pleasant Road there's nowhere to park. We drive up and down the side streets, hunting for a spot, but nothing presents itself. Then he shocks me by stopping in the second row (on the main road!) beside Gerry's car and turning on the hazard lights, which is just the sort of behaviour he deplores.

There is a moment. It occurs just after the engine is switched off. I have not yet reached for the door handle and the only sound is the tick tick tick of the hazard lights, the rattle of cars and lorries going by, and the blood in my brain. It really is just a moment; a deer locking eyes with headlights on a lonely road – and like that deer and that driver along that lonely road, neither party knowing, in that split second, how they or the other will proceed.

'Right,' says Dad at last. 'Best get you unloaded.'

Except we don't. We sit there a little while longer. And I want to say something; something kind or – better – something true (and maybe those two things can be the same): I want to tell him that I don't blame him, that he should not feel bad, that he did his best and that that's enough. Except I'm not sure he did. I mean I'm not *not* sure he did try as hard as he could have done, as he might have done. This, of course, is not something I feel able to say. It is outside of our vocabulary. On matters relating to the management of projects my father is an excellent communicator. He can even communicate in German. If only we had a site to plan, or safety checks to conduct, or a contract to negotiate, we would be fine. Mum and her friends say it's not that he's macho (he isn't), he's just terrified of feelings, his own and other people's. They were just kids when they got together and she hadn't realised that he was so emotionally stunted. Her friends (*their* friends officially) have had similar experiences with their current and former partners. They say she must learn to forgive herself, that it's not her fault that she married a man like that. Zee – obviously I have spoken to Zee about this – says it's 'a generational thing'. She says men of his age had the fear knocked into them as children and it has scarred them for life, emotionally speaking, made them fear their own shadows. I don't know what to think. My only hope is that it's not hereditary.

We unpack the car and Gerry assists, bringing bags and boxes it all into the house, Dad and Gerry making an awkward show at pretending they don't hate one another. It's all 'mate' this and 'Nice One There'. We stick to practical matters, which is fine by me. We load all my stuff into the front room. I can bring it upstairs in my own time, we agree.

Gerry's offer of a cup of tea politely declined, we go back out to the car. It is only the other side of town, we agree, not Timbuktu. I can still nip home to do my laundry or get a decent meal or whatever.

It is nice to say these things, which are the sorts of things people say. Dad glances back at the house. 'You can still change your mind, you know?'

'I know.'

He shakes his head, and I think just maybe I detect a wry smile. He thinks I'm mad for doing this, obviously, but I can tell he's also sort of proud, or at least cognisant, of my stubbornness, which he probably thinks I get from him. After he has driven off, I stand there for a while, alone amid the litter and the dog shit and the traffic of Mount Pleasant Road, and I wonder if I am making a terrible mistake, but it is too late to back out now.

The houses on Mount Pleasant Road were built by Victorians, designed for a single family and staff, which was considered normal then. Today, no one who might contemplate a butler or a maid, or even a cleaner or a nanny, would choose Mount Pleasant Road as a desirable place to raise a family. It is not that kind of place. Meanwhile, as households have divided and depleted, so too have the houses, each one cut up into bedsits or what the Letting Agents call *studios*, which sounds quite arty and bohemian, instead of the truth which is just a bit grim, since most of them have been left to rot by landlords whose only connection to the properties is purely financial.

Gerry explains it better than me. His dwelling, he points out, is an anomaly because he actually lives there, and because he won't have anything to do with these 'sharks' at the Letting Agencies. He says buy-to-let is a *perversion*, an arrangement designed to permanently oppress the non-property-owning classes, whose need for a home is exploited for the benefit of those who already have everything, for whom enough will never be enough.

Behind Mount Pleasant Road there are a few blocks of flats. These came later and you can tell from the concrete, the little balconies and the flat roofs. They are sometimes referred to as 'council flats', which is inaccurate, because while they were indeed built by the local authority, almost all of them are now owned privately after Thatcher decided to sell them off cheap as a sweetener to voters and to reduce what they called the 'burden' on the state.

As well as residential properties, there were also commercial premises, along the cheerily named Mount Pleasant Parade, but where shops had once been most of the windows were now boarded up. All that remained was a grubby video rental library, a bookies and a General Store.

* * *

I am yet to get around to installing window coverings in my room, so at night I gaze out at the backs of the houses, and I am awoken each morning by the sun. When it gets to spring I will need to put in some curtains, but for now I appreciate the connection to nature, however tangential. Even in winter, when the sun does not rise until seven or even eight o'clock, this makes for early starts and I am generally up and about at least two hours before my fellow waifs and strays.

Gerry, of course, is a notorious Early Riser. Several times a week we sit together at the kitchen table and drink tea and eat our corn flakes or, if Gerry is in the mood to make it, porridge. Then we each go off for our respective days. Me to college. Gerry to whatever it is he actually does (it is still not entirely clear to me, although it seems to involve a lot of committee meetings and visits to council offices).

These early morning sessions I regard as precious, stolen hours, and our conversations are wide-ranging and more expansive than is usual, for Gerry has much to say about a great many topics and I have much to learn. I have become increasingly aware that what we pick up at college is merely the tip of the iceberg, constrained as it is by a curriculum designed to meet the dominant ideological forces that control society. Gerry does not accept labels such as 'Marxist' or even 'socialist', nor is he against everything we learn at college, but he does encourage me to supplement my 'conformist' reading with his own more radical reading list. This is all lost on my fellow students. When I start talking, for instance, about E.P Thompson and class consciousness in my A-level history class, people's eyes glaze over, and even my tutor is uneasy about this deviation from the set reading.

Gerry believes that as citizens it is our duty to hold authority to account, including the Authority of Ideas, which he argues is maybe the Most Insidious Instrument of Oppression. I agree. And if it alienates me from the majority of my plodding, intellectually uncurious classmates, then so be it.

* * *

My days usually involve a battle with the shower, a sensitive and erratic beast that has been sent by the gods of bathroom appliances with the sole purpose of testing my will and challenging my resolve. No matter where the dial is set, the blasted thing can't maintain a stable temperature and instead yo-yos between ice cold and scorching hot. I would raise the matter with Gerry were I not living here rent free.

I do not wish to appear ungrateful or precious. The upshot is that after a few weeks I simply resign myself to cold showers, which I have heard are good for the circulation, the cold stimulating the body's own self-regulating heat systems. I am unconvinced about this but we can only live in hope.

More concerning are the dubious stains on the bathmat. Even after I wash it at ninety degrees, they remain. I determine to buy a new one. I will do it as soon as it would be polite, for again I am cautious of coming across as critical or superior.

The tiles on the floor are chipped in several places, which makes them hard to clean. They are extremely cold under my feet. It is always cold in the bathroom. There is an electric heater, which puffs out warmth, but the heat does not spread beyond the immediate vicinity of the heater, and I frequently burn myself by standing too close to the grill through which the hot air comes.

After showering I shave, an act which has no real justification because no matter how much I scrape away, my face remains shamefully smooth, yet I am determined to maintain the ritual, and I place my shaving foam and razor in a prominent position on my shelf, just in case anyone cares to look.

We each have our own shelf. Kay's bursts with potions and vials in exotic and colourful cases, with elaborate labels or no label at all. Badger, meanwhile, keeps only a bottle of shampoo and conditioner, a toothbrush, some toothpaste, mouthwash and some highly pungent cologne, which he wears when he is goes out, an event that recurs at least twice a week, although I am yet to discover where he goes with this marvellous scent of his or the nature of the entertainment. Badger, it should be said, cuts a mysterious figure in the house. He is not unfriendly, yet I can't help but feel he slightly disapproves of me.

My own shelf is a depository of everything anyone has ever left behind, making it a sort of shrine to previous waifs and strays and their personal hygiene habits.

Entering one morning with a black sack and a pair of marigolds, I'm all set to clear away the debris of previous occupants and give myself a Fresh Start. I discover that lots of the bottles and tubes and tubs and pots are down to the dregs, while others are encrusted with stray hairs. Some are so disgusting that even with the gloves I'm reluctant to go near them, but in the bag they go! It feels good to be ruthless.

But one item – a fairly fresh can of Lynx deodorant – jumps out at me. Though I am familiar with the product, I have never actually owned a can of Lynx myself. At school, more than just the male scent of choice, Lynx was regarded as a symbol of virility and, on occasions, it was used as a weapon. A kid in my class used to spray it all the way up his arm, and then set fire to it, making a great display of rolling around on the floor and pretending he had really set fire to himself. I remove my gloves and pick up the can, its smooth metallic coating warm in my hand. I give it a shake. It is much lighter than its appearance would suggest. It is almost full. I give myself a tentative spray. Not bad, actually.

Sparky.

Of course, it is just a can of commercially available deodorant. It could have been purchased (or shoplifted) by anyone. Yet, breathing in the chemically sweetness, I'm pretty sure it belonged to Jason, and I am now wearing his scent.

* * *

During those first few weeks, I make frequent visits to the General Store on the Parade, where I buy industrial strength drain un-blocker and all manner of instruments, foams and fluids promising total annihilation of germs, bacteria and the need for heavy scrubbing. Previously, I never thought of myself as tidy, or what we called a *Clean Freak*, yet Mount Pleasant Road has already changed my perspective on dirt – and value of hygiene.

Yes, cleaning! It is quite the surprise pleasure. While it can be disgusting and physically demanding work, it is spiritually gratifying. After all, it is not often in life that we get to see the product of labour. That gunk that was lurking behind the loo? Gone! The mould around the bath? Zap! Pow! I feel like a fucking superhero. Conan the Destroyer. I'm only half joking. The fridge, meanwhile, no longer gives off the impression that something has died in there. This is my contribution to the common good, my gift to the house, and these tiny victories spur me on and I begin to feel less guilty about living at Mount Pleasant Road.

Food is another voyage of discovery. When Gerry described the setup as 'full board', I wasn't sure whether this meant a Folk-style kitchen (complete with rota) or a looser arrangement of responsibilities and rewards. The reality is that we help ourselves to what we can find, which sounds all well and good, except for one small detail: the supply is, let's say, rather *erratic*. Gerry (being Gerry) doesn't approve of supermarkets, or indeed shops, when it comes to the purchase of food. Instead he *acquires* it, in the same way he acquires all things: via contacts, gifts, favours and happenstance. This means there are days of plenty, where the abundance of options is quite dazzling, and days of hardship, in which nothing comes and hunger must be allayed by whatever is to be found at the back of the fridge and the corners of the cupboards: scary-looking pulses and pickles and pastes and packets, often without labels, or covered in the hieroglyphics of obscure languages. Courage, as well as a measure of creativity, is required. It also helps, in Gerry's house, to possess a strong stomach. At home, sell-by dates were read and respected, and food routinely thrown out if it was 'past its best'. At Gerry's, a sell-by date is a rare sight to behold, let alone one that has not yet passed.

A few weeks in, I get food poisoning, and spend two days in extreme discomfort, moving between my bedroom and the toilet. After this important learning experience, I show more caution on the food front, avoiding precooked rice dishes for instance.

I do not wish to imply that Gerry is ungenerous or neglectful in his duties as a landlord. One evening, for example, early on in my Mount Pleasant life, Gerry arrives home with a giant box of fresh produce – purple sprouting carrots, an enormous head of lettuce, tomatoes of every colour, shape and size, pickled fruit and several varieties of cheese.

The arrival of the box brings untold joy and excitement. We have never seen such riches, we say. Which is not quite the truth in my case, but what is undeniably true is that never have I seen food celebrated or awarded such ceremony as it is at Mount Pleasant Road.

Growing up, my parents did what they called 'Big Shops', involving joyless weekly trips to the supermarket on an out-of-town retail estate, where any connection between the products wrapped in cellophane and the source from which they had purportedly come had long been severed. Gerry regularly describes the food industry as a *perversity* or an *affront to nature*. He once called it the Root of All Evil, which was especially good since the comment was directed at a bag of pre-prepared root vegetables.

The days after the arrival of what soon became known as the Box of Plenty, we feast like kings and queens, safe in the knowledge that nothing passing our lips has been anywhere near a supermarket shelf.

Mostly we sort ourselves out, but Sundays are special, because on Sundays we all cook together. The menu changes week to week, depending on what's in the house, but it is always referred to as *Roast*.

That's the rule: there has to be a roasted element and the roasted element must be the star ingredient.

One week, early on in my induction to the house, the star is cauliflower. My heart sinks on hearing this information, because of all the smells I associate with the community centre canteen, it is the stench of boiled cauliflower that really makes me gag. It's a really fat one as well, this particular specimen that Gerry has procured. Badger wants to roast it whole, like a joint of beef or a whole chicken. We will drizzle butter and juices over the carcass to keep in the moisture and brown it off, he says. He's quite the chef, our Badger.

I have decided in advance that I will not be fussy. I will eat everything served to me, and I will enjoy it. Fussiness had been one of the few real faux pas at Folk. Being picky about what you ate was regarded as pathetic and a bit tragic. Despite his self-sufficient upbringing, Merlin, for example, was shocking about food. He basically wouldn't eat anything.

Still, I do wish it could have been something, anything, other than cauliflower.

I concentrate on trimming the beans and stirring the gravy. But there is no escaping the inevitable, and before I am ready to face my nemesis, the dinner is announced to be served, with much fanfare. Charred at the top and glistening with butter, the steaming cauliflower is removed from the oven. It really is a beast. Gerry carves, chuckling and whooping as the pale flowers fall away from the stalk. 'Get a load of this!' he cries, doling out four giant portions, which are placed before us.

'Mmmm!'

I take a large swig of Badger's scrumpy. Here goes, I tell myself. I try to imagine that it is potato. I am adamant that I will not be beaten.

To my utter and complete astonishment the Beast, as we are calling it, is in fact not too bad. Not necessarily something I would choose, but perfectly edible. Another day, I think, another small victory.

Roast is followed by *Pudding*, which comes in a tin, and has been purchased from the General Store on the Parade. The entire tin, with the contents still inside it, is placed in a pan and boiled for one and a half hours, after which the spongy innards are divided up equally into four servings and served with custard.

In between Main and Pudding, we go through to the lounge, and either watch something on telly or put on a video. Badger has a large horror collection, which we work our way through. There is also the video library on the Parade, where as well as porn you can also rent thrillers and Hollywood stuff and even the odd new release.

If we're still awake after the film, we tend to sit around listening to records and smoking joints, or Gerry will bring out a bottle of something alcoholic and obscure, and we will toast something exaggerated and silly like World Peace or the End of Poverty.

The one snag about *Roast* is that Monday mornings become rather challenging, but I see this as a necessary evil, and while I don't go around telling people at college what I get up to of a Sunday evening, privately I wear my Sunday Service Hangover with pride.

Chapter Fourteen

And so life ticks along. It is 1995 and everything is opening up: lines blurring, borders dissolving, identities loosening, the old rules of what it means to belong being redrafted for a new era– post-Cold War, post-apartheid, post-ideology, post-gender, post-class, post-industrial, post-history, post-everything. And in my own post-Folk life, I see the future unrolling like a marquee across an empty field, ready to be pitched. I see many hands – all the people I've ever known and more I'm yet to meet – each with a designated section, and if we can just work together, pull together as one at the right moment, we can get this thing up. *A tent big enough to hold everyone who wants to come in*, I write in my notebook. With many hands to make light work we can add as many tents as needed. We can move them around, join them up. No borders. No exclusion zones. Like Folk, only everything, and for everyone.

* * *

I run into Zee outside the library. She is waiting for a friend. She is wearing fingerless gloves. Her fingers are long and slender. She sports an enormous scarf that I want to climb inside. She is meeting someone, she says, but he (of course it's a *he*) has not yet arrived. And so she has a few minutes for me. I consider myself lucky. She says she's sorry for not being in touch. I'm sorry, too, I say, wondering if I really am. She has applied for *Erasmus*, she tells me. I don't know what that is but she says it means she can study in Paris, which is what she has dreamed of doing for, like, ever. She thinks I should apply as well. She says it's not too late. She says it would be good for me.

I promise to think about it, which I will, though not as an option for myself.

Yes, it is easy to picture Zee, strolling down those grand boulevards, arm in arm with her beautiful French friends, male and female.

Of course, I don't know if it's like that really, but I feel that Zee's Paris will be. She will make it so. She will go to Matinees. She will have lots of boyfriends... or maybe just the one, who will break her heart, or she will break his, and he will write a book about it. I cannot separate the life I imagine for Zee in Paris from the films we've watched together.

My only personal experience of France is a dull ten days with my parents in the Dordogne, and a prank-filled weekend in Normandy with the school. Other than a nervous teaching assistant, who couldn't control the class, and the exchange students getting in the way of shoppers outside the high street branch of McDonald's, I've never really met any real French people.

Zee's attention is diverted towards a group of students standing at the traffic lights, among them a young man, good looking in a Zee's-latest-boyfriend sort of way. He is wearing the kind of jumper – natural fibres, artisanal – that I know Zee will appreciate.

He's probably a really nice guy, which makes it worse, obviously.

'Anyway,' I say, quickly. 'Better get on. Good luck with Paris!'

'Thanks, babe,' she says, smiling, and I'm not sure if the smile is for my benefit or the benefit of her new fella, who is grinning like the cat who got the cream. 'Come by sometime,' she adds, distractedly. 'Mum was asking for you. They miss you.'

* * *

Another day, another random encounter at college. This time, Seb and Anna. We run into each other on the bridge that connects the original 1930s building to the ugly extension they added in the 1980s. We're between classes so there's not really much time to natter. It's a shame, but without Folk, we just don't see each other any more. I blame myself. I wanted to make a big announcement when I moved into Mount Pleasant Road. There was even talk of throwing a party. But it hasn't quite happened, and as time has passed, it has felt harder and harder to find an appropriate moment to reconnect with the friends from my former Folk life. They are looking well, I comment, and we exchange the sorts of nervous pleasantries that at one time we might have mocked. Yes, we agree, it's been ages. Too long. Seb has a new band. They are called Section 28. I compliment him on the name. Anna has new hair (shorter, bleachier). She looks... different. We move over to the side to allow others to get by. Our position, on the bridge, is not ideal. Like I say, it is not an opportune moment. Yet I am determined. It feels all wrong them not knowing, and I regret not telling them immediately, regret leaving it this long.

'So,' I begin, jauntily. 'I have some news.'

'You're pregnant?' says Anna, drolly.

'Gay?' says Seb.

I laugh. They are a good double act, Anna and Seb. I'm slightly jealous of their friendship to be honest, the way they each seem so comfortable in their own skin, like they don't have a care in the world, which of course I know isn't true.

'Not quite.' I pause, suddenly overwhelmed by shyness. 'I've, er, moved into Gerry's.'

They stare at me, disbelievingly, which makes me even more nervous. I had expected jokes, a gentle ribbing perhaps, but this feels different. Anna's expression is downright hostile.

'Yeah,' I plough on, determined to remain upbeat. 'He had a room going. Can you believe it? I am now officially one of Gerry's waifs and strays!'

'You're one of his *what*?' Anna enquires, icily.

'One of his, er, waifs and strays?'

'Yes, I heard you, Mark.'

'Oh, come on,' I say, panic pulsing through my veins and settling somewhere in my stomach along with residue of the previous evening's *Roast* and home-brew. 'It's not all that bad, you know. A bit... rough around the edges... but my room's quite nice, actually...'

I sense that my words are not helping. Seb looks away. Anna continues to glare at me. 'Well, that's nice for you,' she says at last. 'Glad it's worked out for you.'

I'm trying to think of a response, a way to rescue the encounter, when seemingly out of nowhere, all these people appear, and I'm being pressed into the wall by bodies, perfume and cigarettes and hair and handbags and rucksacks and musical instruments and I don't know what. And, somewhere among them, in this tsunami of students, are my friends, except I'm not even sure they're still my friends. And I don't know what just happened, or what it meant, or what I could have done differently. I wait for the crowd to disperse, hoping, praying that Anna and Seb will wait for me. Because we cannot leave the conversation hanging. Because I don't want them to think badly of me. Because I want a chance to explain and tell them how lost I feel without Folk, how much I miss them. Because I really do miss them, miss us, miss everything. Because I wish we could get back to how we were. But when the crowd finally clears, they are gone too, and I'm not even surprised. And I stand there stranded on the bridge and I have never felt so alone in this world.

I avoid college after that. I still attend classes and do all that is expected of me to ensure that my grades do not suffer. But I no longer hang about. I don't go to the canteen or the common room. If I use the library, I do not linger, and if I must stay I bag myself a quiet corner, somewhere I can hide and not be seen. If the tutors notice a change in me, they have no cause for concern, for I still contribute to class discussions. I am punctual, well prepared and my essays remain predictably 'perceptive' and 'lively'. I am still one of those students that tutors say they don't have to worry about. Everyone assumes, I suppose, that I'm with other friends; that, or I've met someone. I like the idea that folk might think this, that such things could happen for me. Because it is very far away from the truth, but there is no need to dwell on that.

Chapter Fifteen

It takes a while to pluck up the courage to enter the archive. Every time I pass by the secret door, I consider it, weighing up the pros and cons of embarking on the task to which I have been assigned. I always manage to find excellent reasons to delay. At last, the combination of curiosity, guilt and an unexpected free period finally pushes me over the threshold.

I am struck instantly by the room's sound, or rather its soundlessness, which creates the sensation of being in a vault or a bunker, even though it is located at the top of the house and not deep in the ground. The whole room smells of old papers and cardboard and dust. The shelves are in a state of profound disarray. The sheer volume of material is overwhelming and it occurs to me that there is nothing to stop me from just doing nothing. I could pretend to be working and no one, least of all Gerry, would notice or care. Similarly, it is entirely possible that nothing of any historical, artistic or social value is contained in these boxes. That is to say, it may all be junk, just an extension of the clutter that collects in Gerry's car or under the couch. And yet, there is also the possibility that I am standing over a treasure trove of important historical record, a Sutton Hoo for scholars of late twentieth century social unrest and protest movements. Mostly though, I feel I owe it to Gerry to at least give it a go. My only complaint is that I have no partner, no study buddy or team of fellow researchers, the presence of which would lend legitimacy to the endeavour as well as making it a less lonely pursuit. But that's how it is. To keep me company I bring through the cassette player from my room and a tape that Zee made for me back when we used to do things like that for each other. I try to channel Zee's attitude, as well as her brain, for it occurs to me that she would be fantastic at all this. She would know exactly what to do and has both the research skills and the handwriting to turn this mess into something respectable.

I reach up and pull down a random box from a shelf. It is heavier than I anticipated, and I almost drop it, which isn't the best start. I open the lid. The masthead of Juggernaut Press stares back at me. I had rather hoped for more. I flick through the stack of magazines to see if there's anything more inspiring underneath, but it really is just a box of Juggernauts.

The next box is more interesting, in that it contains lots of typed pages. There are loads of them, all loose. Most of the pages contain lists of dates and words that feel strange in my mouth: Black Flag, Contra Flow, Pit Dragon, Red Wedge. They sound like bands.

The entire box is full of this stuff. I spend ages trying to decipher the words. Stripped of context or explanation, the information simply exists.

I look around again. The chaos is not restricted to inside the boxes. The shelves are bursting with documents and folders. I find a letter from the Department of Work and Pensions that is dated March 1986. There is a reminder notice for an unpaid invoice, dated November 1989; an electricity bill from July 1990. There is a birthday card addressed to someone called Sasha.

In a brown A4 envelope I find photographs. I lay them out on the floor. They document, as far as I can make out, what Gerry calls 'Action' – protests, blockades, rallies, marches, sabotage. In one of them, I spot a young Gerry.

He has climbed onto a scaffold and is trying to hang a banner, whose message is obscured in the photo by his own body. He is worryingly high up. It does not look safe what he is doing, but then Gerry has never been a big one for risk assessments or caution.

Another photo shows the lions of Trafalgar Square. I've been there many times, usually for demos, but also with the school. But that is not what I think of. Instead, the memory that pops into my head is the time a cousin I hardly knew came over from America, and Dad had taken us on this mega-touristy Day Out in London. They were staying, her and her father, at a fancy hotel in Mayfair. The hotel, like most things in London, she said, was 'cute' and 'very English', but she wanted to see the famous sights of Big Ben, Buckingham Palace, the Tower and 'London Bridge' (she meant Tower Bridge). In an act of uncharacteristic benevolence, Dad had agreed to take her for the day, even though he usually hated that kind of thing. We started off at an old-fashioned cafe he knew, where we all had what he called a 'Slap-up Breakfast' to 'get us set up for the day', and the staff had made her pancakes, even though they weren't on the menu, and even though when they arrived they turned out to be the English pancakes and not the American ones, she had been sporting about it because her *Mom* (Dad's cousin) sometimes made them like that, and then we had talked about her English mother who we hadn't seen for years because that side of the family never really got on. That day I discovered that doing all this mega-touristy stuff, and hanging around with someone so unashamedly enthusiastic about everything, seemed to bring out something hitherto hidden in Dad, and in me. The day had flown by! And when we dropped her back at the hotel, she said everything had been awesome, the best day ever, and we all agreed it had been heaps of fun.

In the picture, Gerry is in front of the lion, his arm around the shoulder of another man. They are smiling for the camera in that awkward way that men do when someone points a camera at them. I feel I know the guy from somewhere. But the thing with faces and photos, especially old photos, is that we're often so eager for them to reveal truths about ourselves that we find familiarities and connections that never existed. It's all narcissism, obviously. (This is something else that Zee and I have discussed.) Anyway, the guy – the one whose arm is around Gerry – appears in a couple more photos. In another, he is with a female protester. Her angular nose and her cheeks also feel familiar, though again I am conscious that my brain may be filling in the gaps with falsehoods. Nevertheless, I am encouraged by the cheery nostalgia and the camaraderie of the images, and I energetically pull down another box from the shelf. Inside this one I find clippings from newspapers, pamphlets, more photos, which would come under the general heading of 'Action', except these are not the jolly scenes of folk waving placards and shaking tambourines. Instead, this is a world of police cordons, truncheons, violence and fear. A newspaper headline describes 'pitched battles'.

I flick through some of the pamphlets where words like 'traitors' and 'enemies' appear frequently. Folk are being 'stabbed in the back', 'betrayed' and 'hung out to dry'. The photos are even more harrowing, with close-ups of bruised and lacerated skin and limbs hanging limp or pointing in painful directions. In one, a young man stares into the camera, one eye almost twice the size of the other. It is purple-grey with bruising and there are traces of gravel and blood around his nose and mouth. He holds up a broken tooth in his hand for the camera. Doubly disturbing is the slight curl of the lips, hinting at a smile, which reminds me so much of Jason that I have to put the photo away immediately. To distract myself, I pick up a stray photo that has fallen out onto the carpet. A long line of police stand shoulder to shoulder. They are dressed in full riot gear. The shields touch. Their faces are hidden beneath helmets. They stand in a neat row, like authoritarian Morris dancers, their shields glinting against the greys of the sky, the ground, the uniforms.

That night I dream of police lines. I am moving down the line, like the camera at the start of an international football match, picking out the faces of the players during the ritual of the anthems, pausing on each player for the viewers at home to decide if they are really participating or just pretending to sing along. And as I pass down the line the visors on the helmets lift and reveal, not strangers but folk from my life: my old chemistry teacher, one of the blokes who works at the outdoors shop, Anna, Mum, Gerry. I look down. A sea of faces stare up at me. They are bruised and bloodied and bashed. And I hear a voice, a voice I know, a voice saying:

'Happy now, Sparky?'

* * *

One morning I'm sitting at the kitchen table, eating my cornflakes, when a man I have never met pokes his head around the door.

It is early, even for me; the sky that cold dark blue you get just before dawn, familiar to us early risers, but to which most of the population are oblivious.

'Hello,' I say, looking up from my bowl.

'Gosh,' says the man, who is older, older even than Badger and Kay, although it is hard to look at anything other than his eyes, which are almost popping out of his skull. 'Where did *you* come from?'

I inform him that I do, in fact, live at this residence.

'Ah!' he exclaims. 'I've heard all about *you*.' His lip curls into a leery smirk and I wonder what he's been taking. 'I must say though,' he continues, 'from the Badger's description, I was expecting something else.'

I am surprised, and flattered, that Badger has talked about me to his friends. I smile. 'Sorry to disappoint.'

He chuckles. 'I'm on the hunt,' he says, his eyes darting around the room, conspiratorially, 'for tea!'

I point to the tea cupboard and he goes over to it and begins pulling out packets, making a great display of inspecting each one, calling out the descriptions like a bingo caller. Eventually he finds one that meets his satisfaction.

'Do you have such a thing as a teapot?' he calls, opening a random cupboard and peering inside. 'I can't bear the bags, you see.'

We search the kitchen and eventually find a large, bulbous ceramic tea urn at the back of a cupboard. Judging by the dust, which has become encrusted with grease, it has been a long time since this urn was last used. And, force of habit, I feel embarrassed by the dirt.

'Here,' I say, taking it to the sink. 'I'll give it a wash.'

'You are a gentleman!'

'We had a smaller one,' I continue, turning on the tap. 'This one's a bit big.'

He roars with laughter and I can feel myself blushing. I am out of my depth and unsure what is expected of me. I just want to eat my breakfast.

And, suddenly, he is behind me, his breath warm against the nape of my neck, and I can smell him. He smells of cigarettes.

'Got a name, handsome?'

'Erm,' I begin, falteringly, still clutching the tea urn. 'I'm... er... Sparky.'

'I bet you are.'

The tap is still running and water is flowing from the spout, as well as from the large hole at the top.

From behind, he slips his hand under my T-shirt, and I can smell Badger's aftershave now, as well as stale smoke. He presses against me, his fingers moving over my chest and down, sure and probing.

'Badger tells me you're a bad boy,' he whispers, his tongue so close to my ear that I can feel the residue moisture it leaves.

'Please,' I murmur, releasing the teapot. It clatters into the sink.

'Oops,' he says, amused.

Without warning, he violently spins me around, pulling me towards him. And then his tongue is in my mouth, large and muscular. And I am pinned against the sink, his hands all over me. And I try to pull away. And he laughs and reaches for my crotch, a smile playing on his lips. And

I don't know what I should be feeling – I want to be the sort of person who could snog a stranger, male or female, and be cool about it. We have talked (at Folk) about being open to experimentation, about the importance of rejecting received notions about who, and how, one should love. And yet, now it is happening to me, I am repelled, and terrified. And I wonder if this is because I am parochial, and scared, and a closeted homophobe.

Suddenly the door bursts open. Badger is standing in the doorway. 'Are you out of your fucking mind?' he yells. 'I told you, the Kid's embargo.'

Badger is a big guy, a gentle giant sort of a man. This is the first time I've heard him raise his voice. The effect is immediate. The hands are withdrawn.

I am released and the man goes back to making tea, behaving for all the world as if the last few minutes had never occurred. Except I can still taste him: his tongue, his mouth, his tobacco. And where his hands had been I can still feel it. And all I want to do is run.

'Sorry about him,' says Badger. 'Are you all right, Mark?'

I nod.

'I, er, need to get ready for college,' I say.

I do not wish to make a big deal out of what just happened. What didn't happen. Because nothing happened. There is nothing to tell.

Did I lead him on?

Maybe if I wasn't so *Green*, so very green and inexperienced, I would have noticed sooner and he wouldn't have picked up the wrong signals?

On the stairs I overhear them.

'Oh, *please*, Badger. I was merely playing. He's probably done a lot worse. Anyway, I thought you said he was gone? Is the Badger a little jealous? Did the Badger want to keep him for himself?'

'You're thinking of the other one.'

'The other one?'

'I told you.'

'So that's not the *Bad Boy*?'

'No! Jesus. You'll get me kicked out. That's the *Kid*! How much of that shit did you take last night?'

Safely upstairs, I brush my teeth and shower, scrubbing until my skin is raw.

* * *

I do not mention the incident to Gerry, or indeed to anyone, and when Badger brings it up a few days later, apologising once again for his friend, who he says is an idiot and not really a friend, I pretend that I found the whole thing funny.

I will never see the man again.

I cannot help but wonder how it would have ended, and whether Badger's intervention would have been so forthcoming, had I been the *Bad Boy* instead of the *Kid*, or why it is that one seventeen-year-old is 'embargo' and another fair game.

* * *

As the weeks turn to months, my life takes on a new rhythm. Unless I have to be in class, I can be found at Mount Pleasant Road. There is plenty to occupy me. Conscious of living there rent free, and grateful to be allowed to live there at all, I am determined to pull my weight and not be a burden. Twice a week I clean the communal spaces, throwing open the windows to air the rooms, wiping surfaces and scrubbing grime. The vacuum cleaner is useless. I hint that Gerry might invest in a new one – a *Henry* or a *George*, perhaps? Gerry says that's fine. I can get whichever one pleases me, he says. He will reimburse me.

Gerry is far too busy for such things. I've never fully understood what he does in his actual job. It is something for the local authority. Between this, and running Juggernaut Press, and the many other roles he assumes for groups and organisations within the movement, he cannot be expected to maintain an ordered house as well.

Back home, my parents have finally given up the ghost and admitted that the marriage is over. Dad moves into a flat near the station. He takes me for a curry and tells me about a big project he's project managing. It will involve a lot of travel, he warns, which means he won't be around so much, he's afraid. He asks about college. He wonders if I'm managing to knuckle down. I reassure him that I am. He asks if I need anything. He will put some money in my account – to cover any extras. He says he knows it's not been easy for me, with Mum and everything.

Meanwhile, Mum has a mystery boyfriend. It could be Red Shoes, or someone new, or someone old, or someone blue. All she will say is, 'There is someone.'

It is not like her to be coy.

Mostly, though, my world is contained within the walls of Gerry's house on Mount Pleasant Road. Badger is off to New York to make a record with a band that other people have heard of. He's pretending it's no big deal, just a thing he's doing, but Kay says he's really chuffed and he should be because the band are dead good and very cool, which is probably why I've never heard of them. She plays me a record. It's pretty noisy. I don't know what to make of it but Seb would probably like it. I should mention it to him next time I see him. Not that I see much of Seb, or any of that lot, these days.

Kay keeps on boiling up her weird concoctions of flowers and herbs and twigs and oils. She uses a large pot that we all call her cauldron. In less enlightened times, she might have been burned at the stake. These days it seems almost mainstream. She says she's going to start her own herbal infusions range. She wants to take her cauldron to festivals. She will call it the Cauldron, or maybe Witches Brew, she hasn't decided yet.

They insist on celebrating my eighteenth birthday with a special Birthday Tea. There is cake and candles and they sing happy birthday, like I'm six, and it's quite sweet really. I am mortified and touched by Gerry's present – his old SLR camera inside a beautiful leather case. It is far too generous, and I say so, but he insists I keep it. In the evening we drink too much and watch Terminator 2.

* * *

For my next adventure in the archive I go to Harpies the Stationer, a magical emporium for the dedicated stationary-lover. It is hidden from the general public in a backstreet behind the college. You'd have to know it to find it.

There I procure new boxes, folders and box files, coloured dividers, coloured index cards, coloured stickers, and an assortment of highlighters, pens in various thicknesses and ink types and other writing implements. I am awed by the neat rows of slightly different versions of the same thing, how each item in a particular section has been allocated its specific space. The order is impeccable, the staff are knowledgeable. Right down to the nerdy sixteen-year-old girl who works Saturdays, ask any of them for help and they'll tell you what you don't need as well as what you do need. They are serious people. No request is too obscure. No detail too technical. They never play music. The carpet is spotless.

Tooled up with my Harpies bag of goodies, I approach the archive with quiet confidence, again bringing through the cassette player and Zee's tape, which I've now renamed the Archive Selection. It will be the soundtrack to my work until I get completely sick of either the archive or the selection, whichever happens first.

I assign categories based on what I think might be there. Initially, just two – *personal history* and *political activities* – but this system proves tricky because it's not always clear which is which, and a lot of the material seems to be both, neither or too difficult to classify one way or the other.

I make slow but steady progress. By increasing the number of categories, and making them more specific, it is easier to impose order. Folk material goes under *Folk*. Anything connected with Juggernaut is labelled *Juggernaut*.

But whenever I think I might finally have a hold on what the archive contains, something invariably comes along to mess up my system.

The most startling discovery is what at first glance looks to be a box of foliage collected from the woods. But on closer inspection, I discover that the bark scrapings, leaves and mud belong to a single form.

This turns out to be a fairly faithful representation of a bird. Judging by the claws and the large, rather vicious-looking beak, it is not supposed to be a songbird. This bird, I sense, is a hunter. A predator. And I wonder: who could have made this peculiar object? And, further, what does it mean? That is, why did Gerry decide that a sculpture of a bird of prey belongs in this archive?

I try to keep going. I had hoped to get through more material. But the bird is making me feel uneasy. The eyes, which I know are marbles and nothing more sinister, seem to glare at me. I have a strong desire to put the lid back on and tell myself that I never saw it. But I am being foolish. It is not an actual bird, merely a model, someone's craft project. Why does it have to mean anything more than that?

When Gerry comes home that evening the bird is perched on the kitchen table. He seems pretty startled to see it, and I laugh and say, 'Oh, I found him in the archive. Shall we call him Clive? He looks like a Clive to me.'

Gerry doesn't reply.

'Or do you think it's a *she*? Maybe Polly?'

Still no reply.

'Like the pirates?'

I don't even know what I'm talking about.

'Anyway,' I add, 'He-she-it didn't want to go back in the box. Do you, now?'

'That'll do, Mark.'

'Sorry,' I say, feeling the sting of his tone. 'I didn't mean...'

He goes over to the bird. 'Excuse me,' he says, picking it up off the table and pushing past me.

I hear him climbing the stairs. Kay has warned me already about what she calls 'the black dog', how it will visit Gerry and sometimes stay for days, during which time it is sensible to 'keep out of Big G's way'.

So, I grab my coat and go to the chippy.

There is a decent chippy on the corner and, Gerry being Gerry, the Chinese family who run it are friendly with him, adding little extras to our orders if we are with him or if they recognise one of us as *Gerry's kids*. Usually it's just a few extra chips, but sometimes we get a scallop or a pickled onion or a tub of radioactive green mushy peas.

There is a TV on out the back with the sound turned up, the raised voices and music suggesting high drama. I can't understand a word of it because they're speaking Cantonese or Mandarin or something. But the sound of it makes me miss Zee and feeling part of that family. Zee's newish boyfriend – Ben or Matt or something – is a climber, I'm told. Zee likes the outdoors type. I have met him, briefly, and he was friendly in that condescending way that Zee's boyfriends tend to be. I imagine him being really charming with her family. Zee always brings her boyfriends home, even Jason.

It is one of her *things*.

There are a few Formica tables, plus some stools in the window, where one can dine without feeling like one is sitting in a restaurant alone. I flick through the local rag while I'm waiting. The main story is about a murdered pensioner. It happened a while back but the perpetrator has now been convicted and named, and the paper has learned that he was a patient at a secure psychiatric unit which was closed recently as part of the government's Care in the Community programme. Someone in the paper is quoted as saying that it was 'a tragedy waiting to happen'.

My battered sausage and chips arrive, with a bonus pickled egg I didn't order, which wobbles and gleams like something from another planet. I stare at the traffic, the headlamps cut with drizzle. Care – the word so often seems to carry the exact opposite meaning to the one intended, and I think of my parents and how they agonised over sending Granny to a Care Home, which meant (at least for others, based on conversations I had overheard) they were giving up on her, that they had ceased to care about Granny or had perhaps never cared very much about her in the first place. Which isn't true, by the way. Dad was really sad when his Mum died, even if he only cried in private, back at the house, when he thought no one was listening.

Gerry is sitting at the kitchen table when I return.

'Sorry about earlier, Mark. Will you join me? I have beer.'

The way he says this makes it sound as if he's been out hunting and gathering. He gets up and goes over to the fridge.

'You caught me off guard,' he calls. 'The kestrel.'

He hands me a beer.

'Is that what it is?'

He smiles. 'Quite something, huh?'

I nod and take a sip of beer. The label is obscure, the writing contains letters and accents that I wouldn't know how to say. At a guess I would say it is Eastern European or Russian. And I realise that since moving in this is the first time that Gerry and I have sat down, just the two of us, and shared a beer.

'I'd actually forgotten all about it,' he continues. 'So I'm grateful to you, Mark, for reminding me.'

'Where on earth did you find it?' I ask, shaking my head, because even by Gerry's standards the kestrel – if that's what it is – is a curious object to collect.

'I wish I'd never agreed to take it,' he says wistfully.

'It's not yours?'

And so I learn the story of the bird, and its creator – Merlin. Merlin who never made anything, for the whittling was the thing; how he'd spent months and months working on the piece, and how Gerry had been sworn to secrecy until it was finished. Only then would Merlin present it to us at Folk. Except his parents learned of the plan and forbade it, fearing that Merlin would be ridiculed and hurt, although the official reason was that it might get damaged.

'But Merlin was defiant. That's why he insisted I take it. Our plan was to unveil the sculpture, with or without parental consent, the week after the Survival Overnighter.'

I nod. 'Right.'

'I thought we could use it to talk about who owns culture,' he adds, shaking his head. 'It sounds silly, doesn't it? But I had this idea we could do an exhibition.'

'Right.'

Confession: I've not been to many exhibitions. Zee goes to exhibitions. She and Yolanda have a ritual of going to London at least once a year to, as Zee puts it, *Do Culture*. They stay in a hotel and go to exhibitions or screenings that you don't get here, or theatre or ballet or opera. One time she told me about a show they went to that was all about something called 'Outsider Art', which she explained is when artists who aren't recognised by the Art World as artists suddenly get discovered by the Art World (or someone who *is* accepted by that world) and their work is put on show, and the Critics are, like, Wow, we had no idea, this janitor who was ignored his whole life is actually up there with Picasso or whatever.

'An exhibition would have been cool.'

He nods, sadly.

'It was quite a shock,' I add, 'finding it in the archive.'

'Ah, yes. How's that going?'

I tell him about my trip to Harpies and about the categorisation systems I am developing.

'Gosh,' he says, laughing. 'Very impressive.'

I suddenly feel silly.

'Really, Mark. I'm very grateful. I hope it's not taking you away from your A-levels. You know you mustn't let it take over.'

'It's all under control,' I say. 'It makes a nice break.'

'As long as you're sure, Mark. Your Mum would never forgive me if you failed your A-levels.'

'What will happen to the, er, kestrel?'

'Don't worry, Mark. I'll drop it by. I'm up in that part of the world next week. I'm really glad you reminded me.'

He finishes his beer and offers me another, which I'm not going to refuse because I don't know when Gerry will ever have time to sit with me again. Evenings like this were sort of what I'd hoped for when I moved in, not that I'm complaining.

'Any other interesting finds?' he calls, pulling out two more exotic-looking beers from the fridge.

'Some of the images,' I say. 'The brutality, I mean.'

'They say this is a free and democratic country, Mark. We talk about human rights as if we invented them. But the truth is we can be as bad as the worst, it just depends on who you are and what you're up against. Truth is, there are things people don't want to hear. Because they don't fit with certain ideas we have about the world. You understand?'

'I think so.'

He smiles.

'Of course,' he adds, 'when you say stuff like this, people think you're bonkers. But then it's always been that way. Look at Jesus of Nazareth, or, I dunno, Galileo!'

And we both laugh, because obviously Gerry is having a little fun. He doesn't really compare himself to Jesus and Galileo.

Chapter Sixteen

Sometimes Kay and I sit together at the kitchen table, and Kay offers to check my *aura*, which she says is connected to my *chakras*. I always agree to this procedure, because I know it pleases her, and because people are more than they present.

Kay loves hearing me talk about Folk. She says she wishes something like that had been around when she was growing up. Stockport, she says, was a pretty lonely place for a teenager like her. She laughs when she says stuff like this, as if to imply that I shouldn't take it very seriously, and she deliberately exaggerates her accent and says things like, *'Aye, Sparky, it be grim 'p north.'*

But sometimes, when she looks at me, a cloud seems to descend. We'll be talking, and then all of a sudden she'll stop, close her eyes, and they will remain closed for several beats, and it is as if weights are pulling down on her face. And then, just like that, her eyes spring open again and the conversation resumes.

'Are you okay?' I ask, the first few times it happens, and her reply is always the same:

'Okay? Me? I'm grand, Sparky.'

She says it with bravado, like a TV catchphrase, and I can never tell if it's just a joke or not a joke at all, or what she is trying to say or *not* say with it.

In April, Badger goes off to New York. He's not sure when, or if, he'll be back. He says he'll settle down when he's dead. The only permanence in his life, he jokes (in that wry rather intimidating way of his), is a permanent storage box, which he rents on an industrial estate at the edge of town, and where his records, books and musical equipment that he doesn't need this time now go.

The shelves where his records had been are now empty; two gaping holes, like a mouth from which all the teeth have been extracted.

It is with a bittersweet cheeriness that we wave him off. He is excited about New York and working with this band out there. But still, we had been a gang for a little while there, and now it is just me and Kay, so obviously it won't be the same.

My isolation is compounded when Kay, within days of Badger leaving, announces she's going away, too, meaning it's just me and Gerry, except Gerry is hardly ever there so really it's just me, on my tod, which in some ways is pretty sweet. I mean, a whole house to myself and no one to tell me what I can and can't do? What eighteen-year-old wouldn't want that?

And I know that the moment I let on to anyone at college that this is the situation, they'll be trying to get me to throw a party; like, a proper party, which would maybe earn some cool points with the common room crowd. Except I am conscious that it is Gerry's home, and he has been so kind, allowing me to live there rent free. I will not abuse his trust. And so I keep this new state of affairs to myself.

* * *

Kay comes back after a few weeks. She's still Kay, but now she has a bloke, and things suddenly feel very different.

His name is Jonno, and from the moment she returns he is a constant fixture in the house, with his rat's tail, his leather waistcoat and his leathery skin. We pass each other on the stairs, Jonno and I. We never exchange more than a few words. His face is almost expressionless, his eyes sort of dead-looking.

Sitting in the kitchen is now out. Instead, they eat Chinese take-aways in her bedroom, and the empty polystyrene boxes pile up outside her door and stink out the whole house. Those heady days of Sunday Service and Boxes of Plenty are now a distant memory.

For the first time, I sense that Kay is embarrassed by my existence, as if she doesn't like to admit to living with a teenage boy, let alone being friendly with him. And so, not wishing to be anyone's burden, I make myself scarce. Mostly that means keeping to my room, or hiding out in the archive. With regards the latter, I feel I am making some progress.

One day, I go into the bathroom, as you do. There is blood everywhere, all over the sink, up the mirror, the tiles, the walls. Kay is attempting to clean it up with a J-Cloth. It is just a nosebleed, she insists.

Without saying a word, I go to the cupboard downstairs by the back door. This is where I keep the cleaning products. I come back a few moments later with a mop and a bucket, and a pair of heavy-duty gloves.

'You're a love, Sparky,' she says. Her voice has acquired a strange, distant quality, like she's not quite all there. She is slurring her words. She is clearly drunk or stoned or both. 'What would we do without you, Sparky?'

Part of me wishes she'd just stop with the whole Sparky thing. It was okay at first, but now it just feels forced.

I get to work on the blood. I can feel her watching me from the doorway, and I wonder if she is even compos mentis enough to pick up that I am angry with her, that I'm getting a bit sick of clearing up after them all.

'You know you don't have to?' she says, quietly. 'I can sort it.'

'It's fine,' I shoot back – because, really, she can't sort it. She can't sort anything. She was using a fucking J-Cloth to clean up a tsunami of blood.

When I turn around again she is gone. And then I feel guilty.

Because here's the thing: sometimes, when she is alone, I think I can hear her crying, and not just a bit; this is the kind of deep sobbing that overwhelms your entire being, the kind that requires all your strength to keep from spilling over and turning you into a public wreckage.

And then, obviously, I feel terrible for being angry with her, and for humiliating her like that that time in the bathroom, though I know it is not me she is crying for, that it is not about me and it is not my fault she is sad.

This continues for a few weeks more. I hear them: having sex, listening to music, arguing, making up (more sex).

Kay's room is directly below mine and sometimes, I swear it is as if I am in there with them.

* * *

It is late at night and I am alone in my room. I go over to the window. A cat is sitting on the windowsill of the house opposite. I watch for a while as it cleans itself, licking its paws with an air of studied nonchalance, and I think that we clock each other, the cat and I, although I've never been able to read cats well. Gerry used to have a cat called Jerusalem, but having not seen her since I moved in, I assume she is gone, possibly dead, and I wonder if anyone would notice if I just disappeared.

On a whim, I pick up the camera Gerry gave me. I take it out of its leather case. It feels heavy. It is solid kit. I bring the camera over to the window. The cat is still there. 'Say cheese,' I murmur, and I begin clicking, first the window with the cat in it, then the rest of the building, moving left and right and up and down to capture the whole scene. As I do so, lights in windows go out, while others are switched on, and I think of the jittering lights on the stereo downstairs that is no longer used. The cat, meanwhile, gives a flick of its tail, turns and disappears out of sight.

I keep going until I have used up the entire roll of film. I do not use the flash. The light, I feel, must come from outside, and from chance alone.

Tomorrow I will take the film to Harpies to be developed. I'm not a proper photographer and I have no idea if any of the shots will come out, but even if the images are a blur and just blackness, it will, I decide, still be an accurate documentation of the view from this window, which I would love to call *my* window but which will, let's face it, always be *Jason's* window.

The next morning, I'm already standing outside Harpies when it opens, a full hour before most of the shops in town, because Harpies is that kind of place. I hand over last night's roll of film and buy five more rolls. I have an idea, a way to approach the black hole that is the archive.

Armed with my camera, I enter the secret room. My idea is this: as well as categorising the collection, I will create my own record, a sort of archive of the archive. Best of all, my replica archive can exist on a roll of film (or several rolls of film), meaning it can be replicated an infinite number of times and transported easily.

The idea came to me after photographing the backs of the houses, but the spark was something Gerry said. He had wanted to make an exhibition to present Merlin's bird. An exhibition! Exhibitions belong in Zee's world, but never mine, and yet here was Gerry saying that Folk could have them. It had never occurred to me that people like me could have an exhibition.

With a renewed energy, I return to the raw material of the archive. Some of it is beginning to feel familiar, though I know that I have merely scratched the surface of what is there.

Whenever something catches my attention I photograph it. I have a particular fondness, I discover, for lists. Words or names presented without context. I read them aloud. Some of them feel like poems. It doesn't matter that I don't know what they mean. Photos of people and places without names or anything to identify them hold a similar fascination. Or I will find myself admiring the hand-stencilled cover of a pamphlet, poster or flyer. Looked at as a collection of images and words, and free from the burden of having to make sense of them, I begin to enjoy the archive for what it is and I forget to worry about what it is not.

The archive is, for sure, a strange and unpredictable beast; as vast and disparate as any museum collection, and one never quite knows what it will throw up next. For instance, I discover a list of everyone who ever attended Folk – not just names and addresses and emergency contact numbers, but stuff like dietary requirements, health notes and medical histories that – now I've read them – explain quite a lot. There are even details about myself that I had either forgotten or never even knew. It is extraordinary that Gerry managed to gather such comprehensive information. It is still more extraordinary that this resource has outlived Folk and now exists for posterity; a sort of alternative history.

And in this way, the archive becomes a way of reuniting with lost friends and associates. Small details conjure up deep memories, like how Merlin wasn't allowed cow's milk (!) and had never received a meningitis jab (!!!), and now I recall, as if it was yesterday, Merlin being taken away from the Forest of Dean in an ambulance, and how we all thought he had meningitis and was going to die.

* * *

My stomach tightens when I see the ambulance and the police car ahead, their blue lights blinking silently, the evening traffic reduced to a single lane. The moment I turn the corner and see lights, I know, I can feel it in my groin and in my limbs that it is Gerry's house they are stopped outside.

The front door is open. I watch two paramedics come out bearing a stretcher. From the pavement I can't make out much as they load the patient into the ambulance. Everything feels as if it is happening in slow motion. I stand there gawping.

As I approach the steps, Gerry appears in the doorway. He is in conversation with a policeman, nodding in a professional sort of way, and while I can't hear what is being said, they have the air of two people who know one another. Behind me, a door is slammed, followed by another. There is the sound of an engine starting. A single siren wails, like a cry of pain, then is immediately silenced as if it had been switched on by accident.

The policeman takes his leave of Gerry, glancing at me, letting me know that he has clocked me, although he doesn't stop or say anything as he passes me on the steps.

'Gerry?'

He shakes his head and closes his eyes.

'What's happened?

He continues to shake his head. 'I thought she'd stopped,' he says at last, his eyes still shut. 'Silly, silly girl, I thought that was all behind her.' He turns to me, and he seems, I dunno, angry?

'Silly girl,' he says again. 'Did you know? Did you know she was using?'

I shake my head. I am still trying to piece together what is happening. I assume, though I could be wrong, it is Kay he means, and that it is Kay I just saw carried out.

'I just don't understand it,' he says, gazing after the departed ambulance, its blue lights faintly visible in the distance. 'These bright people.'

We go inside. In the hallway there are traces of vomit and what appears to be blood on the carpet. Take-away boxes are strewn about the floor, their gruesome contents spilling out like guts. The place smells musty and unhealthy. Gerry opens a window.

'She was a bit of a mess when I found her,' he says, picking up an empty bottle that had rolled under the window. He shakes his head again. 'It breaks my heart, Mark. It really does. I thought she'd beaten her demons this time, y'know?'

I nod, though I don't know at all, it is all new to me.

'Did you notice anything, Mark? I know I've not been about very much recently. Were there any signs that she was using? Has she been behaving differently?'

He is looking at me, expectantly, and I have no idea where to begin, because it would have been impossible for anyone not to have noticed that something was up with Kay, but at this moment, I want to say, that isn't really the point.

'Is she going to be all right?' I say, because we've just seen Kay, my housemate, a fellow waif and stray and – I thought – my friend, taken away in an ambulance. Asking now whether there were warning signs is, well, a bit late. That horse, as my father would say, has bolted.

In response, Gerry holds up his hands as if we might be better off asking the gods for answers, because he has none. 'It's too early to say for sure,' he says, 'and you know how medics are, never going to diagnose on the spot, but, well, let's just say it's not the first time.'

'You mean it's happened before?'

He nods, sadly. 'Kay puts on a good front, but she's a complicated person. You must have picked that up?'

Again, I don't know how to answer, and I feel guilty for being so self-involved and not paying more attention to what was happening to others around me. Gerry's suggestion that I should have been aware of Kay's problems stings me to the core, and I think of Anna and Seb's reaction to Jason leaving. Maybe that's what they were trying to tell me as well.

'I did have a bad feeling about Jonno,' I say at last, because I have to say something. 'I mean, things seemed a bit, I don't know. Since he came on the scene? You know?'

Gerry frowns. 'Jonno?'

And in that instant I know that he has no idea who Jonno is and I wonder how that can even be possible since Jonno was practically living here.

'The boyfriend,' I say, quietly.

'Anyway,' he continues, picking up a mop, a slight shrug the only indication that he has heard me. 'That's drugs for you. I know we have a bit of spliff here now and again but don't ever get into it. It's a terrible disease. I've watched so many lives ruined.'

'Yeah,' I say. 'Right.'

'But I know you're far too sensible for any of that, Mark. You've got your feet on the ground. I know it is a huge relief to your mum that she doesn't have to worry about things like that.'

I go through to the utility cupboard and fetch us gloves and cleaning products, and together we tackle the mess, filling several black bags and using up nearly a whole bottle of Mr Muscle. It's a relief to be doing something practical. We throw out the mop heads afterwards.

I ask if we should go up to the hospital, but Gerry says there's not much point until tomorrow. He doubts they will keep her in for more than a night anyway. With overdoses it's more of a precaution, he says. And besides, he adds, Kay will be embarrassed when she comes round. It is better for her if we stay home.

That night I hardly sleep. I know I should be worrying about Kay, and I do, but I'm also thinking about myself. What did Gerry mean by *using*? Heroin? I never saw any needles but that doesn't mean she wasn't using them. And I wonder if I have HIV. We have shared joints. We have been sharing a bathroom. I know you can't get it from a toilet seat, but what about the blood I cleared up? Sure, I used gloves, but there might have been a hole in them. I may have had a cut somewhere. Even as I lie awake thinking these thoughts I know I am being hysterical and tabloid. I think of Princess Diana, holding the hands of AIDS victims, and I try to remember what we learned in the Folk session we did when the volunteers from the AIDS clinic came and we talked about society's attitudes and myths around the diseases, and the importance of challenging the lies and propaganda propagated by politicians and the media. Of course, I don't know for certain that Kay is HIV positive. (You usually can't tell by looking at someone, most people don't get symptoms for years.)

In the morning I inspect myself for lesions. I stare at myself in the bathroom mirror and I know I'm being ridiculous, I just can't help it.

After breakfast we get a phone call, which Gerry takes. It is Kay calling from the hospital. They are sending her home. Gerry offers to pick her up. I have an important tutorial at college. I cannot miss it. Gerry thinks it might be better to give Kay a little space anyway.

I consider telling some people at college about Kay, but I'm worried it will turn into gossip, and it is not anybody's business. So I keep it to myself. After my tutorial I rush home.

Her bags are packed. There is a suitcase and a couple of holdalls by the front.

'Hello?' I call.

Kay comes through to the hallway. Her smile, which I know is for my benefit, is full of sadness. Her skin is very pale. She looks smaller somehow.

'You all right, chicken?' She follows my gaze to the bags. 'Just for a bit,' she says. 'I'll probably be back next month. You don't get rid of me that easy.'

I nod. 'Are you okay?'

'Me? You know me, Sparky, I'm grand.'

'But...'

'Bit of a wobble, hun. Sorry to worry you all.'

'Can I give you a hand?'

She looks at me for a moment, and there is something very protective about the way she looks at me, and I think: is this what it is like to have a big sister?

'You're a sweet thing, Mark,' she says, sadly. 'But you're all right, the taxi will be here in a minute.'

'Where will you go?'

'Stockport. For a bit, anyway.'

'I'll miss you.'

'Come here,' she says, and we hug. I can feel her bones, her sharp shoulder blades poking out through the fabric of her shirt. She is thin, very thin. I'd not realised before. She always wore quite loose clothing, and I'd never thought of her as an addict. She was just Kay. *Grand.* And even if I questioned her bravado, her hospitalisation and Gerry's revelations have thrown open everything I thought I knew, and I wonder if she senses this and if maybe this sense of being 'found out' is the real reason for her departure. I cannot believe that Gerry would kick her out.

Outside, a car horn blares, the taxi is here. Kay picks up the suitcase. I insist on helping her with the rest. Kay's cab is waiting in the second row. When the driver sees us, he gets out and opens the boot.

There's not a lot to load in, considering that this is everything she has. It fits in without difficulty. Honestly, I've seen people take more on a two-week holiday.

'Wait a minute,' I say, rushing back into the house, because I've remembered something and, as I suspected, it is still there; her 'witch's cauldron', the one that would go to festivals and fairs; her promise of a new life, or at least a livelihood.

I pick it up. It is heavy. It occurs to me that it will be awkward for her on the journey, and this is probably why she has left it.

I take it out to the waiting taxi anyway. She is already climbing into the back seat.

'Kay!' I call, and I hold up the cauldron, with both hands, like it's a chalice or, I dunno, the FA Cup.

She turns, and smiles.

'Look after it for me, will ya?'

'I'll guard it with my life,' I shout.

And I mean it – that is, I would love to return it to her. And yet, in my guts or my heart or wherever these things are known, I sort of know that it won't happen.

Watching the taxi merge into the traffic, my eyes fill with tears, and I don't even know why I'm crying.

Because no one has died, and Kay and I were never really that close.

Chapter Seventeen

A new tenant moves in. Geoff is a writer, activist and longstanding 'comrade' of Juggernaut. People call him Red Geoff on account of both his complexion and his politics. He calls me *Young Blood*.

In one of our first conversations, before I've really said anything, he tells me that I give him hope, that most of my generation are a write-off, caught up in *consumerist bullshit* and what he calls *the self-improvement industry*. He is going through an acrimonious divorce with his wife, who is a psychotherapist and 'a total bitch'.

'They're confused,' Geoff will rant, over tea and custard creams. 'No solidarity.'

Geoff is a prolific biscuit eater, and a generous one, and in exchange for biscuits I listen to his proclamations about the world, of which there are many.

'Young people?' I prompt, though he needs little encouragement.

'Everyone,' he replies.

'Everyone?'

'Exactly.'

I smile. 'Right.'

But Geoff's all right, at least to me, and with no other waifs and strays left in the house, and Gerry rarely at home, I'm glad for the company. Honestly, if it wasn't for Geoff, I might go for days without speaking to anyone.

* * *

I'm sitting in the back of Mum's 2CV. Next to me is a box of Juggernauts and two bags of moth-eaten clothes for the Salvation Army. Gerry's next to her in the front. We are headed to the Dog's Whistle. I am not sure this is a good idea.

Gerry has been on at me for weeks. He thinks I should get out more. So does Mum. I remind them my A-level exams are coming up. I have a lot of work to do. But the truth is, they're probably right. I have been a little withdrawn of late.

Photographing the archive has proved more tricky than I'd anticipated. The first set of photos didn't work at all. It just looked as if I'd photographed some stuff, which is obviously what I did do; it's just it turns out that doesn't make for interesting photos. When I collected the photos the woman who runs the photography counter at Harpies, seeing my disappointment, said she could see what I was trying to do and that I should try shooting against different backdrops and different lighting setups until I found one that was working.

Mum is looking at me in the rearview mirror. She's up to something, I can tell. She smiles and places a hand on Gerry's thigh. She gives it a squeeze. Gerry lets out a nervous chuckle. She has made him blush. She is delighted with herself for managing to embarrass him. I feel a little queasy, which may be car sickness.

Suddenly it is clear why Gerry has been so distant, and why Mum is so cagey. This 'someone' in her life is Gerry.

'Euew,' I say, because that's what me and my friends say to each other when friendship has spilled over into something more, something ill-advised.

She laughs.

'Sorry for keeping you in the dark,' says Gerry, chuckling. 'We... er...'

'We weren't sure if it was serious,' Mum cuts in, gaily.

'Right,' I say.

At the pub it is clear that everyone knows them as a couple. I am basically the last person to find out. People keep coming over, and every time I have to be introduced, which is excruciating because everyone is being really welcoming and nice. Someone buys me a pint of cider.

Just before the music starts, I spot a couple of girls I know from college, and they invite me to join them. They are impressed to learn that June is my mother. They say it must be amazing to have such a cool mum and I reply that I've never thought of her as cool, that she's just my mum, which makes them laugh.

Sitting with the girls and watching the different performers going up and doing their things, I start to relax. There isn't much time to chat between acts and there's a compere as well, who's actually quite funny, and who keeps it all moving, so little is asked of the audience. It's like Folk but a lot more organised and, I have to admit, it's a higher standard.

Especially when Mum comes on. I'd been dreading this moment because I am convinced she is going to humiliate herself, but she doesn't, not in the slightest. She does a song about a figure called Mack the Knife, who Jason and Zee would probably call a sketchy geezer because he goes around with a blade seducing all the ladies. It's jazz, so it sounds less alarming than it is but when you listen to the words it's pretty shocking stuff. One of the girls, whose name is Laura, says at one point, 'It's like Ella's up there!' and I can't help but feel a little bit proud that my Mum is being compared to Ella Fitzgerald (who even I've heard of).

On the ride home, Mum teases me about Laura, which I don't mind that much.

'So how long has this been going on?' I ask.

'This?' says Mum.

'You two?'

They look at each other and giggle.

Mum grins. 'Oh,' she says. 'A while.'

Then she asks me if I hated the evening as much as I'd expected to, and I say, 'It wasn't too bad,' which makes them laugh again.

They make me promise to come back the following week.

And so, for a while, I become a regular at the Dog's Whistle. A lot of folk know me only as June's son. They all think it's wonderful that I'm living at Gerry's. Someone calls me a *very sussed and mature young man*.

And, despite my misgivings, I do enjoy the sessions. When Mum sings everyone listens. She's good. She has presence. She can occupy the stage in a way that the other performers can't. Her repertoire is wide. She can sing the blues as well as the old ballads. She does what people call 'jazzy numbers' and her own interpretations of songs that people like.

One of her favourite stunts is to pick on musicians she knows in the audience and put them on the spot, demanding they come up on stage and accompany her. Sometimes they've already rehearsed something together and the apparent spontaneity is just show business. But sometimes it really is impromptu, and I can see the fear in their faces, even if they are also flattered to be chosen.

And, all the while, Gerry looks on with adoring eyes.

Mum, everyone tells me, is a real *character*.

* * *

The phone at Mount Pleasant Road rings constantly. Nine times out of ten it's for Gerry. After a few weeks I stop answering it. I'm not his personal secretary. Managing his diary is outside my remit. If it's important, I reassure myself, they can call back.

Every so often, though, I do pick up, not because I must but because I can. And sometimes it's good to hear the sound of someone's voice. The house used to be filled with music and chatter. Now all I hear is Geoff's typewriter. I've got plenty to be getting on with, but it can get a little, y'know, *lonesome*. (I've been listening to too many of Mum's songs, where everyone and even inanimate objects such as roads seem to 'get lonesome'.)

One such evening, the telephone in the hallway rings, and I answer it.

'Gerry about?' says a gruff voice.

The voice recalls for me the first time I heard Jason speak. Back then I doubted its authenticity. I'd only heard voices like it on the telly, never in real life, and certainly not at Folk.

'I'm afraid he's not here right now,' I explain. 'Maybe I could take a message?'

There is a pause, then, 'Just tell him Dee was asking for him.'

'Sure,' I say, and we hang up.

The next time I see Gerry, I mention the call. He nods and says something like, 'Okay,' and that he'll sort it. I think no more of it.

Except a week or so later the same caller calls again. Our conversation runs pretty much the same as last time, the only addition being, the mystery caller asks, sounding a little anxious: 'Is he all right?'

I chuckle, because this person obviously hasn't had a lot of experience with Gerry, who can be rather elusive at the best of times.

'I should think so,' I say. 'To be honest, Dee, I don't see him that much at the moment. But I'll remind him. Maybe try at the weekend? He tends to be around more then.'

He seems reassured by this information, ending the call with an upbeat, 'Yeah, safe. Nice one, mate.'

After that I do make a point of saying to Gerry that he really should get back to this Dee character, that he seems very keen to reach him. When several weeks pass without any more calls I assume contact has been established.

Then, one evening – I'm on my own again – the phone rings and it's him again, except this time he is in a state of some agitation.

'It's Mum,' he says, after we've established that Gerry is once again not home. 'She's had one of her turns. He needs to call the residence. You tell him that, yeah?'

'I'm really sorry to hear that,' I say, thinking of when Gran had to go into a home, how hard that was for everyone, but especially Dad. And I wish that Gerry had confided in me that this was happening, also that he has this brother or half-brother maybe, Dee. I assume, since Gerry has never mentioned him, that they do not get on. 'I'll be sure to tell him as soon as he comes in.'

'Ta. What's your name, anyway, bruvs?'

'I'm, er, Mark.'

'Ah, yeah, he mentioned you a while back. Right, nice one, Mark. You tell him, yeah? He's a hard man to track down at the moment. Has he got himself some sort of girlfriend or something?'

I smile. 'Yeah, he does, actually.'

What I don't mention is that this *girlfriend or something* happens to be my mum. There are some things one doesn't have to broadcast to the world.

'Well,' he says, 'I suppose that's good. You met her? She all right?'

I reply that I have indeed met her and that she is all right, adding, 'They seem to like each other.'

* * *

'Poor Geoff,' remarks Mum, one evening on the way out to the Dog. I've missed the last few sessions, staying in and knuckling down, because while I may not be going to Paris I am determined not to give Mum's friends the satisfaction of seeing me fail. Even from this distance, where I only hear their comments secondhand, played back through the filter of my mother, I sense their desperation to say that they always questioned the wisdom of me moving out of the family home and *not staying with Mum*. (Something I loathe: why do Mum's friends insist on calling Mum *Mum* when they talk to me about her? As in, *Wouldn't it be better to move back in with Mum?*)

Mum says that some of her friends are very disapproving of her, so it is not surprising that they disapprove of me as well, especially since I'm living with Gerry, who is obviously the main subject of their disapproval.

'Poor Geoff,' she says again, smirking, because she finds Geoff an inherently tragic figure. 'Did anyone read that last book of his?'

'Geoff is one of the New Left's foremost thinkers, I'll have you know,' says Gerry, who also seems to consider Geoff fair game for mockery. 'Our readers appreciate Geoff's doggedness, even if you don't, June Fisher.'

They both find this comment hilarious.

'What's happening with the divorce?' she manages to ask between gasps of laughter.

The question draws a grimace from Gerry. 'Ahh,' he says. 'Not good. She's taking him to the cleaners.'

'Poor Geoff.'

There is a moment's pause, then more laughter.

'Sorry,' she says, 'I'm terrible, aren't I?'

'Yes, you are.'

(Etc. Etc.)

I keep quiet. I stare at the traffic. *With friends like these*, I think. I wonder how much Geoff knows. And this: is it better to know what people say about you behind your back, or is it true that ignorance is bliss? It is hard to imagine much bliss in Geoff's life, although if he's already at the end of marriage number three then presumably he's had his moments.

When we get to the pub everyone fusses around Mum and Gerry, who are like celebrities, gracing the evening with their presence. They are charming and self-deprecating, basking in their own brilliance.

As for me, I stand there not knowing what to do with my hands/feet/

face. I can almost hear what people must be thinking when they look at me. Ah, yes, *the son*.

I am the awkward son who doesn't sing, doesn't play an instrument, doesn't do anything really. I missed out on those genes. I have no gift. I am not spontaneous. I am not quick-witted. I am dogged like Geoff; and shy like Dad.

I say hello to Laura and the other girls from college, who politely pause their conversation to exchange pleasantries. The novelty of me has worn off. Once again I'm just Mark from college.

I get a drink and sit in the corner.

A guy goes up and does a song that he's written himself. I don't catch many of the lyrics but it has an emotional chorus which he sings with his eyes closed.

I look around. Is anybody actually into this? It's hard to tell. The song seems to go on forever.

Another guy goes up and does some noodling guitar work. He's probably very good at playing the guitar, but this time it's obvious that nobody cares. He ploughs on, frequently switching guitars. He has a lot of guitars.

More performers go on and do stuff that is slightly less awful, and the mood does pick up a bit. But, really, I'd rather be working on the archive.

It's a relief when it is finally Mum's turn to show them how it's done.

It's a by-numbers performance, a bit half-arsed by her standards, but it's better than everything else we've seen or heard that evening, and I know that I will not be returning. I am already tired of being June's son. The music is boring. Jason and Zee's chemical beats would actually be preferable.

'You're quiet, Mark,' Gerry says on the way home.

'Bit tired.'

'College okay?'

'Yeah, it's fine.'

Mum nods, knowingly. 'You're very dedicated. Not like me, ha! I was a *terrible* student. Far too many parties!'

'It was a different time, though, June,' says Gerry.

And then she starts talking about Glastonbury Fayre and David Bowie and the time she met blah blah blah at the Troubadour, and I zone out and watch the cars with their headlights, like beats in the darkness, rushing by. Gerry nods away, and I wonder whether he finds this stuff interesting or whether he is just humouring her because he fancies her, and because he's flattered that she's taken a liking to him. I get the impression that they both think that, in Mum, he's punching above his weight. Gerry may have a certain charm, but with his paunch and his thinning hair he is no oil painting.

Chapter Eighteen

I try to be modern about Mum and Gerry. It helps, I think, that she never comes round, he always goes to her. That Gerry has been at the house so little of late suggests that the relationship has gone what Anna calls 'Full-blown Obsession' and will soon be over. It is possible that their decision (her decision) to keep their sex sessions in the family home (or do they go elsewhere? In any case, not Mount Pleasant Road) may be to protect my feelings. It is more likely that Mum refuses to come anywhere near Mount Pleasant Road, which is not a part of town she would choose to go and is definitely not up to her standards of comfort or cleanliness. And on this point, I can't help but agree. The house is a health hazard. It could be no one's idea of a love nest.

For instance: one day I'm in the kitchen and the boiler suddenly blows. Well, it makes a popping sound, followed by a loud bang and more popping sounds. And, while I am no expert on boilers, even I know they're not supposed to do that.

There is a bloke – Odd Jobs Dave – whom Gerry uses for this sort of thing. But Gerry isn't home. Because Gerry is never home. Which would be fine, except he hasn't left instructions on how to get hold of Odd Jobs

Dave in such a situation as this.

I hunt in all the obvious places – the hallway, the kitchen drawers, the piles of crap that spring up everywhere like weeds. I have heard stories of explosions, whole streets going up in flames because of a dodgy boiler, and of people (poor folk) dying or developing awful illnesses caused by carbon monoxide poisoning because of faulty boilers. All because landlords fail in their duty to maintain basic safety and hygiene standards in their properties, and while I don't think of Gerry as a slum landlord, obviously, I know (because he's proud of it) how little such things interest him.

I knock on Geoff's door. Perhaps he'll know how to reach Gerry or Odd Jobs Dave or someone responsible. But apparently he's out. So I try calling Mum to see if Gerry's with her. The call goes straight through to answerphone. I mumble a message about the boiler playing up and needing to speak to Gerry urgently. This is how Gerry and I now communicate. Answering machines, relayed messages, notes on the kitchen table. I don't know what I had expected when I moved in. Obviously, I am grateful to him. There is no contractual requirement that he spend time with me. (There is no contract!) He has given me a roof over my head, food in the fridge, heating (when it works) and access to a wider circle of folk than most college students would ever meet. I am grateful. Of course I'm grateful.

I do, however, miss Kay and Badger. I miss *Roast* on Sunday. Hell, I miss Kay's cauldron and chakras. I even miss Badger's smelly aftershave. Most of all I miss the camaraderie, the feeling of being part of something. We were Gerry's waifs and strays, his adopted children. It wasn't quite Folk, but it wasn't far off. We were a ragbag crew, but a crew nonetheless.

I go upstairs. The last remaining rooms I've not yet searched are Gerry's. For obvious reasons I'm reluctant to go in there. I am conscious that Gerry has no locks on his doors, and that this is because he trusts us. Yet at this point I cannot see an alternative. I'm not nosing around, I tell myself, opening the door to his private study. I am merely doing what any responsible tenant would do in the circumstances, taking action to prevent an explosion, carbon monoxide poisoning and death.

The walls are covered in pictures and memorabilia. There's an old black-and-white photograph of a young Gerry standing with a veteran peace campaigner, whose name I forget, who at one time had been something of a mentor to Gerry. When she died, aged ninety-eight, Gerry read a William Blake poem at her memorial.

There are posters: Stop the Bomb. Workers Unite. Free Nelson Mandela.

Above the mantelpiece is a framed picture of us, the Folk kids. The photo was taken one glorious summer's day in the Brecon Beacons by a random hiker who turned out to be a famous photographer. The sun is beginning to dip and the sky is crimson. We had been swimming. Our hair is tousled. Our bare, sun-kissed arms are draped around each other. Look how young and fresh and carefree we are!

There are a few papers on the desk. I check the drawers. A packet of French filterless cigarettes. I always forget that Gerry sometimes smokes. I flick through a couple of notebooks and a diary from 1992, trying not to pry. There are few numbers but no mention of a Dave or an Odd Jobs Dave. The room is surprisingly calm and neat, as if he reserves the chaos for the rest of us, while he himself lives an orderly existence.

I try the bedroom (also pretty shipshape). The bed is made. There are a couple of books lying on the bedside table. I pick one up. Aldo Leopold, *A Sand County Almanac*. I recognise the name from my early morning sessions with Gerry, which have sadly dropped off since he got together with Mum. I open a random page.

All ethics so far evolved rest upon a single premise: that the individual is a member of a community of interdependent parts.

Where the book had been, a handwritten list of names and phone numbers has been cellotaped to the bedside table. Among them, Odd Jobs Dave. I jot the number down on the back of my hand.

But before I go downstairs I steal one last look at the photo above the mantelpiece. Even if it wasn't us, even if it was just a random group of kids, the image would be powerful. The way it captures those feelings – of youth, of trips into nature, of togetherness, of Folk. And when I imagine thinking back on Folk in years to come, it is this image that I think will come to my mind. I go to my room and fetch the camera. I photograph the photograph. I turn to go, conscious that I have already overstepped a line, already overstayed any time I could reasonably justify being in Gerry's private space. And I would have gone, except at that moment I happen to look up and notice the top of the heavy antique wardrobe in the corner, where a cardboard box has been placed and a pair of beady eyes stare at me.

It is nearly two months since Gerry promised to return Merlin's kestrel.

* * *

The sun is shining. Spring is sprung. I have spent the morning scrubbing the kitchen and cleaning the communal areas, including the living room, which although barely used these days, still collects dust and grime.

Back in the halcyon days, i.e. just a few months prior, when there was still talk of throwing a party, establishing a regular film night and generally being a household rather than set of individuals who happen to be in the same house, Badger had rigged up a decent pair of speakers in the kitchen. These he linked to the speakers in the living room, so that with the doors open the music travels through the entire ground floor in full stereo.

Surround Sound, we called it, because everything had to have a name.

I have been listening to the Waterboys really loudly, the windows thrown open, serenading the street, Mike Scott and I, both wishing we were Fishermen.

After attacking a particularly resistant patch of grease above the cooker, I notice I've worked up a bit of a glow.

I'm about to take a tea break when there's a knock at the front door.

The first thing I notice about the young woman standing on the doorstep is that she is wearing Zee's duffle coat, the navy blue one with the tartan lining. Obviously, it's not Zee's actual duffle coat, but I cannot help but stare.

She smiles and holds up her identity card in a practiced sort of way.

'DC Tina Barlow,' she says. 'Jason Templar around?'

'Jason?'

'That's right.'

She has a wide mouth. Good teeth. She doesn't look like a detective, not that I have met many actual real-life detectives.

'Umm,' I stutter. 'He's, er, gone.'

She nods patiently. 'Gone to the shops or gone for good?'

I blush. 'Erm, for good?'

'I see,' she says. 'So he's not in?'

'Is he in trouble?'

'What sort of trouble would that be?'

'Er, I don't know.'

'We just want to find him.'

'Sorry,' I say, scrunching my face.

'How about Roger Clarke?'

'Roger Clarke?'

'The landlord?'

'Oh, er, Gerry?'

She smiles.

'Gerry, erm, Roger's not here.'

'Hmm,' she says, closing her notebook. 'Oh well.'

I feel bad for her that she's having to go away with nothing. I know I'm supposed to hate the police but this one seems all right. I also feel that I need to redeem myself a little with her. I am, for example, capable of speaking more fluently than the monosyllabic ummms and erms and errs.

'Erm,' I begin, 'maybe I can help?'

Her face brightens. Her eyes are hazel and they sparkle when she smiles. I could imagine us being friends. She's no older than Kay and younger than Badger, at a guess, though I'm not good at telling people's ages.

I notice that the tea towel I've been using is still draped over my shoulder and take it away, which makes us both smile.

'Sorry to disturb you,' she says.

I assure her that she isn't disturbing me in the slightest.

I am suddenly aware that the hallway, despite my labours, remains a complete state, littered with unopened mail, laundry bags, a broken toaster and various other bric-a-brac nobody has claimed. Nevertheless, I invite her in, guiding her through the rubble. At least the kitchen is decent. I turn down the music and offer her a cup of tea. She declines, with professional politeness, so I tell her I'm making some anyway and point out the epic array of tea options on the shelf.

She laughs. 'Well, I could go a green, if you have it?'

'Ah,' I say, 'You're in luck there. We've got three different types.'

She asks my name.

'Well, Sparky,' she says, opening her notebook. 'Maybe we can start with when you last saw Jason?'

I hesitate, conscious that the moment I start talking about the Survival Overnighter there will be no way to avoid telling her at least something about what happened.

'It was the last weekend of August,' I begin, once it is clear she is not going to save me from the silence. 'Jason and I, we were part of the same, er, youth organisation.'

This draws a smile. 'Would that be *Folk*?'

'That's right! Do you know it?'

Had she not introduced herself with a police badge, it would have been no surprise to discover that she knows Folk. In fact, I would go so far as to describe her as a Folk person, whether or not she ever actually attended something Folk-like. It's just that I have been brought up to believe that all police are National Front sympathisers and raging Tories.

'Yeah,' she says. 'I do.'

Knowing that she's a Folk person, or at the very least has an acquaintance with Folk, makes it a lot easier. It means I can talk about the Survival Overnighter without having to explain everything.

Obviously I'm aware that she is still police, and there are things I gloss over, parts I skip. But, overall, I think I paint a faithful picture of Jason's connection to the group and the key aspects of the Survival Overnighter.

When I've finished my account, she asks, 'Did Jason seem anxious at all?'

'He was worried about Merlin. Probably more worried than the rest of us, if I'm honest. You see, it was Jason's first trip. He wasn't used to Merlin's... ways.'

'So do you think Jason might have gone looking for him?'

'It's possible.'

'And you didn't see him in the morning?'

'Gerry – er, Roger – said Jason decided to make his own way home.'

'Is that normal? For someone to just decide to make their own way home? Aren't you a group?'

I scrunch my face. 'Well, it's not completely unheard of.'

'Gerry must have got up very early?'

I frown.

'To drive Jason home and then come back again?'

'Erm...'

'Or did he get home some other way?'

'I'm not sure.'

She takes a sip of tea. I chew my lip. I am beginning to doubt the wisdom of being so open with her about the Survival Overnighter. It has opened up more questions than I can answer. I regret, now, not pressing Gerry for more details at the time. Because in the retelling, I have to admit, it does sound a bit odd. How did Jason get home? Did he hitch a ride? But who would have picked him up, in such a remote spot, and at that time of the day?

'May I ask about Merlin?' she says. 'You say his family owns the land?'

I nod.

'And you saw him in the morning?'

'Well, I didn't actually see him.'

'Oh?'

'But Gerry, er, Roger, said he'd been found.'

From the look of quiet scepticism on her face I can tell I've said too much, a suspicion which is confirmed when she asks if I have an address for Merlin. But then, I tell myself, of course she would want to speak with Merlin, and why ever not? It is not as if we have anything to hide.

I consider telling her that I don't know his address, but why not be cooperative? So I run upstairs and fetch the list from the archive.

She writes the address into her notebook. I find myself admiring her grown-up handwriting, and the way she holds the pen in her long slender fingers.

She is grateful. She hands me her card.

'Call me any time, Sparky.'

I show her to the door. On the doorstep I happen to look up at what used to be Badger's window and is now Geoff's. The curtain is drawn but there is a movement behind it.

'How many of you lot does Gerry have here at the moment?'

It occurs to me that Gerry might be breaking the law by letting me stay in the house without a contract or anything.

'Oh,' I say, colouring. 'I don't actually live here.'

'I see,' she says, grinning. 'You just clean for Gerry. Is that it, Sparky?'

It's obvious that she knows I'm lying, but it's equally obvious that she's not going to pursue it. Contrary to what some people say, not all police are like that.

Chapter Nineteen

Seb had been playing in bands forever. The latest outfit, Section 28, were already a band before Seb joined them, and already had a following. Named after a piece of Tory legislation that banned the 'promotion of homosexuality' in schools and elsewhere, as if sexual orientation was a matter of consumer preference that could be corrected in the same way other unhealthy habits such as smoking or eating junk food could be corrected (this at a time when popular newspaper columnists were calling for castration and Electric Shock Therapy as a reasonable step to slow the spread of AIDS among gay men) – the band had been gaining attention. They'd been played on the radio. They'd had a Top 40 single. The singer had been photographed for the cover of a magazine. Major labels were apparently queuing up to sign them. There was talk of a European tour, festivals and *breaking* America. The posters, which were all over town, had stickers on them declaring the event SOLD OUT.

I get to the venue early. The queue snakes round the corner and all the way down to Harpies the Stationer. Seb warned me that it might get busy and that we might have difficulties getting in if we arrive too late. I feel everyone watching me as I walk straight up to the doors and announce to the girl with the clipboard that I am on the guestlist.

Observing those in line, I realise that the jeans I've picked out (blue, straight-leg) are all wrong. As for my fleece, it's terrible. It isn't my favourite fleece, it's not even my back-up fleece, it's the back-up of the back-up, the one I don't mind getting covered in cigarette burns and spilled drink. I can feel people's judgement. And yet, despite my attire, they let me in. They don't even ask to see my ID.

One enters the venue down some steps. The walls and ceiling are plastered with posters of acts who've played the venue over the years. Music drifts up, along with the murmur of voices, all speaking at once. Glasses clink. Feet and furniture scrape the floor.

The bar is still quite empty and I wonder why they don't allow people in a bit faster, even if only for capitalist reasons. I spot Anna talking to some people I don't know. I go over. It takes her a minute to notice me. When, at last, she does, her greeting is cold and distant.

'Oh, hullo, Mark,' she says, not smiling. 'Or is it *Sparky* now?'

The people she has been speaking with drift away. One of the guys raises his eyebrows, possibly in reference to Anna's tone. Thankfully, at that moment Zee arrives, carrying pints of lager in wobbly plastic cups. She gives one of these to Anna and the other one to me, before turning and going back to the bar for more, so she misses me spilling about a third of it down my sleeve.

This draws an icy smile from Anna.

'Never mind, eh, Mark?'

I can't work out if she's angry with me or just messing with my head.

The place starts to fill with noise and smoke and strangers. The floor is already sticky. We find somewhere to perch.

Every few minutes people come by to say hello to Zee and Anna. They seem to know everyone in the place. I sip my beer and search for a friendly face or even just someone to say hi to.

I'm regretting the position I've taken, slightly obscured by a pillar; ideal for parking a jacket, less conducive for conversation. It feels as if everyone is in competition with each other, and with the room, to be heard. The consequence being that the volume continues to rise and rise.

I close my eyes. I'm tired, I'm not really in the right mood. I allow the noise to wash over me.

Eventually, the music and the lights go off, and a hush falls on the crowd. Conversations stop mid-sentence. There's a general movement away from the bar and towards the stage, which is now lit up, and where a young man is down on all fours, his long Jesus-hair falling over his face like a veil.

He is surrounded by a colour spectrum of interconnected boxes, each one linked to the next via an array of cables. A guitar has been laid on the floor, belly up. LEDs blink in the darkness.

I think of my gran, my Dad's mum, who I never really knew, in the hospital. She had been transferred from the Care Home to the Intensive Care Unit, where she had been placed on a drip and connected to a respirator because her lungs had packed up and she couldn't breathe on her own.

I watch the Jesus-guy make his adjustments, moving without urgency from pedal to pedal, going back to the one he's just set, back and forth, again and again, orange, yellow, red, electric blue. It is quite hypnotic to watch his concentration.

After a while he goes over to the guitar and strikes at the strings. Nothing much happens and he returns to his pedals. The process is repeated.

He does not look up. At some point a violin bow comes out, which makes a good spectacle, although it doesn't have any obvious effect on the sound. He plays without pause. There are no endings, no spaces between tracks. It just goes, and then it stops, and then the lights go up, and the people who are still watching clap, and then we all drift back to the bar – where Zee and Anna have taken up new positions and are deep in conversation with more people I don't know.

I join the throng at the bar. Everyone wants to get a drink in before the next act comes on. I glimpse Seb, over by the stage, busy running around, checking equipment, looking very professional, just doing what he does.

He is still there when I return from the free-for-all madness of the bar, drink in hand (more beer down sleeve). I could go over and say hi, but I don't want to be a hanger-on, so I hang back. I make sure, however, that I stay close enough to the stage to keep my spot. I am determined not to be pushed to the back of the room when the crowd pile in from the bar.

I'm on my own, but there's enough going on, I decide. I can stay here and not be too much on the sidelines, at least not noticeably should someone notice me.

Finally the next act comes on – a girl-boy duo with matching keyboards and matching hairdos. She sings and he presses keys and looks fierce. The extent to which what we're hearing qualifies as Live Music in the strictest sense is debatable, but with its pumping beats and shouty choruses, it feels like a breath of fresh air after the heavy meanderings of the Jesus guy, and most of the crowd – me included – start bobbing along and spilling more drinks.

They don't play for very long, but they really throw themselves into it, and by the end I'm not tired any more and when I look up there is sweat dripping from the ceiling. Just from the support band!

I go looking once again for Zee and Anna, but the place is now so packed, and the air so thick with smoke, that the chance of finding anyone is negligible. I give up looking and go to buy another beer. I'm still hoping to run into someone I know.

I get back to my spot just in time before the lights dim. At this point, even if I was to spot someone, I'd never get through all these bodies, which means I can finally relax and stop looking for friends and familiar faces.

Confession: I've not been to all that many gigs before. I am amazed, for instance, by how quickly the crowd forms itself into a single moving mass. I now understand what people mean when they say it's no use fighting it, that you must let it – the music, the moment, the crowd – take you where it's going to take you.

The anticipation is palpable.

All the clichés, it turns out, are true.

My only regret is that I'm not with the girls, not because I need them with me now, but because it means that later we won't be able to look back on this moment together, which feels impossibly sad and for a moment I feel utterly alone in this world, and I picture myself as I imagine I must appear to others, standing there with my pint, dressed like someone's dad.

But when I look around I realise no one is looking my way. That they don't care. That they are not here for me. That it's not about me. And, in this anonymity, this invisibility, I feel free – free in a way that I can't recall ever having felt free before.

Section 28 come on to a roar of cheers and whooping and applause.

Seb looks a lot younger than the rest of them, like someone's kid brother, but as soon as he picks up his bass he's every bit the class act he is: calm, cool and collected. He looks as if he was born to be up there.

The singer, a giant of a man wearing a raunchy black dress, platform heels and a Myra Hindley wig towers over us. He grabs the mic stand and for a terrifying, utterly electrifying moment, it looks as if he's going to launch it into the crowd. We all go wild.

A drum machine starts up, and then the real drummer begins bashing away as well, and they're off.

It's loud. It's fast. It's sweaty. It's glorious.

It is the first time in such a long time I have fully given myself over to anything.

* * *

In the loos at the end, I happen to glance in the mirror. My T-shirt has changed colour and my hair, which I styled with such care before I left the house, has collapsed into a damp, floppy mess. I feel elated. I can hardly recognise myself.

A lot of people have already left by the time I get back out. I spot Seb by the bar and run up behind him and give him a huge sweaty hug.

'That was amazing!'

I know I'm gushing, but I don't care.

He smiles, kindly. 'Thanks, dude.'

I gush some more.

Zee and Anna come over and there are more hugs, more exalted praise.

'Yeah,' he admits, ever the professional. They're pretty happy with how it went. There's a lot happening at the moment. It's a bit confusing. He's trying not to let it go to his head. The music industry is fickle, he says. You'll be flying high and then it will spit you out and you'll never be heard of again. He's seen it happen to too many friends.

Someone buys a round of drinks. A joint is passed around. I'm briefly introduced to the band.

I don't know the circumstances that led up to it, but at some point, several drinks later, I find myself alone with Anna, who is still being weird with me.

'Anna,' I say.

The table at which we are seated is stacked high with glasses and bottles and mountainous ashtrays. I can barely see over it to Anna.

'Anna!'

She can't hear me because the room is too loud and I am too timid.

I get to my feet and lean across the glasses. The room shifts, as if I'm on a boat.

I am really drunk.

I should stop talking now. Except, I have decided. I cannot go back on my decision, I feel. I will not go home while this bad blood between us persists.

It is probably a misunderstanding, I tell myself. Anna can be a little spiky, I tell myself. She might not even be cross with me, I tell myself.

'ANNA!'

This time she hears me, and she turns. 'What?'

The room is moving too much, I should sit down. I squeeze into the seat next to her.

'Anna, I'm sorry if I messed up.'

She stares at me.

'Anna? What is it? What have I done?'

'You really want to do this now?'

'Oh, come on,' I say, and I attempt to flash her a cheeky grin, which probably just looks leery. 'Are you jelly cos I'm living with Gerry?'

I giggle.

'You really don't get it, do you?'

'Woaaaaaah...' I say, holding up my hands as if she's just pulled a gun on me and upsetting a few plastic cups, which topple to the ground.

She moves away from me.

'There's no point,' she says.

I follow her. We are now standing in the middle of the bar. 'Naw, if I've done something wrong, you gotta tell me.'

'Everyone knows it was you, Mark.'

I can feel the blood rushing through my body. My legs feel like mush.

'Did you really think it would work?' she continues.

The lights are too bright. I can feel people looking at me.

'Eh?'

'Did you really think Zee would suddenly want to fuck you? Did you really think that would happen, that all you needed to do was get rid of him?'

My brain is not working properly. The room is spinning. I look into her face.

'Mark, I hate to be the one to break it to you, but Zee wouldn't fuck you if you were the last person on earth.'

'That's enough,' says a voice.

Seb has come over. He touches Anna's shoulder.

She pushes his hand away. 'No, he needs to hear this. He needs to hear that it's not all about Mark Fisher.'

I notice the staff looking nervous. A few people move away. Seb gestures that he has the situation under control. I am conscious of the audience. Seb's whole band. All these music industry types. The only person who's missing is Zee.

'Ah, now I'm the devil,' says Anna, grabbing her coat and heading for the stairs.

Seb hands me my fleece and shepherds me to the door.

'Are you going to be all right?' he says.

I assure him I'm fine. I apologise a lot. I know I must hold it together, at least until I'm outside, preferably until I'm safely down the road.

'I can call you a taxi?' he offers.

No, no, the walk will do me good, I say.

I try to smile. I try to tell him to get back to his people. I try to tell him it's fine.

'You know what she's like,' he says. 'Best not to take it to heart.'

'Yes,' I say. 'I do. Exactly. Thanks. Sorry. Really sorry, man.'

The cold air helps. I find a dark corner and vomit. Emerging from the shadows my head feels clearer already. I'm about to head off when I hear Zee's voice. She's with a group of people I vaguely recognise from college.

My first thought is to flee, but I'm too slow. She's already spotted me, and she's calling my name.

She wants to know which way I'm going. She tells me to wait. She'll walk with me.

'Fuck off,' I hear her say. 'He's my friend.'

And with that she removes herself from the group, and then she's coming towards me, and then she's holding out her arm for me to take, like old times, like everything is normal and fine.

'Come on,' she says. 'Let's go home.'

* * *

We take the back streets, making a detour behind the library and the county court to avoid the yobs on the high street who at this hour will be fighting and tipping over bins and smashing windows and getting out their willies.

Zee, who has been outside for the last hour, missed everything. Someone might have mentioned a drunk girl laying into some kid and getting herself kicked out, but she'd not realised that it was Anna and me.

Our footsteps echo down the empty street and, for a moment, a hush falls on the town, as if the power has been suddenly cut.

'Does everyone think I ruined his life?' I ask.

'Is that what Anna said?'

'Pretty much.'

'I think Jay managed that quite well by himself.'

'Anna doesn't think so'

'Ah, you know Anna, you know how she is.'

'Do I?'

'She has a keen sense of justice.'

'What does that mean?'

'Come on, Mark, everyone knows you tell Gerry everything.'

'What?'

She stops and turns to me. 'Look, Mark, this isn't on you. It's not on any of us. Only a lunatic like Jason Templar would try to turn Gerry's Famous Survival Overnighter into fucking Raindance.'

'Does everyone think it was me who told Gerry?'

'Didn't you?'

I shake my head. 'When would I have?'

'You were gone for ages, Mark.'

'I just went for a walk.'

'You were weird with us all when you got back.'

'I didn't do it, Zee. You've got to believe me.'

'Fine,' she says. 'He must have found out some other way. Fuck it. Let it go.'

Except I can't, and that's the problem. I wish I was more like Zee and could just decide to move on. I don't want to care what happened. I don't want to care about Jason.

We reach the main road, which would normally be thick with traffic and noise, but is now ghostly still, just the occasional taxi and a few delivery vans rumbling by. The traffic lights blink, locked on amber as if in a permanent state of indecision.

Zee says she's hungry. The kebab shop at the end of Paris Street is still open, its lurid lights glowing out of the gloom of all the closed premises.

We enter the brightness. There are a couple of tables in the window. We order and sit down at the table furthest from the door, our reflections in the windows staring back at us against a backdrop of skewered meat behind the glass counter.

I was looking back at you
to see if you were looking back at me
to see me looking back at you.

Zee put that at the beginning of one of the tapes she made for me.

Other than the staff, we're the only ones in the kebab shop, and I realise it's the first time in a long time that Zee and I have dined together. Not so long ago, I ate more meals at Zee's place than I had at home with my parents. It was a running gag that the family had adopted me.

'The police came round looking for him,' I say, biting into my doner. The chilli sauce brings tears to my eyes, but it's good, just what I need.

Zee dips a chip into the sauce. 'Really?'

'I hope he's not done something awful.'

'Fuck,' she says. 'It's my fault.'

'What do you mean?'

'I should have waited to tell him.'

'Tell him what?'

She sighs. 'Mark, I broke up with him.'

'Oh.'

Jason, it seems, had taken it worse than Zee had been expecting. At the time she'd felt that he was being clingy and possessive, but she admits that she was probably just not really feeling it for him, that whatever they had had run its course.

'I know I can be a bit... harsh,' she says, wistfully.

I smile. Classic Zee. Maybe I'm a little bit glad that Jason had to experience it too.

'But I should have waited,' she adds. 'It was bad telling him on the Survival Overnighter.'

I laugh. 'Maybe.'

We move on to to other topics. I tell her about Kay. She doesn't think it sounds like I could have really done anything, that it wasn't my responsibility, that I am not responsible for what happened, which obviously I know, but it doesn't stop me from blaming myself. Then I tell her about Merlin's bird. I remind her about the exhibition she went to that time. The one about Outsider Art. She says she'd forgotten about that. She says I have a good memory. She talks some more about Paris. She'll live in the university accommodation at first, she says. But then she'll get her own place, or maybe a shared apartment with friends.

Future friends.

Anticipated friendships that don't yet exist but will be coming.

Because Zee is someone who has no difficulty making friends.

She has many friends.

She has always had lots of friends.

(Except that time when she didn't, when they moved to the village.)

'You have to promise to visit me,' she says.

Soon – too soon – we reach the corner of Mount Pleasant Road. This is the threshold, the point where she must turn left towards the smart houses at the top of the hill, and I must go in the opposite direction, deeper into bedsit land.

'Well,' she says, and I know this is my chance, perhaps my final chance, and I cannot let this moment pass. And so, before I can stop myself, I blurt out:

'Do you want to see it?'

She frowns.

'The bird,' I add, quickly. 'Merlin's sculpture.'

'Okay,' she says, breaking into a smile.

The lights in the house are off. It takes me a minute to locate my key. In the hallway Zee nearly trips over Geoff's old-man shoes, and we both giggle because it's like the old days, sneaking into someone's parents' house, trying not to get caught.

'Don't wake Geoff!' I whisper.

We go through to the kitchen and Zee takes off her jacket. She is wearing a black sleeveless top that matches and complements the contours of her body.

'Welcome to the palace,' I say.

I watch her reacquainting herself with the house and I wonder how much time, if any, she spent at Mount Pleasant Road, back when Jason was living in my room, before she dumped him.

She grins. 'Got any booze?'

The fridge is a disappointment, but we find one of Gerry's mystery bottles at the back of a cupboard. The liquid is clear, and the writing looks Russian, so we decide it must be vodka. There's a carton of long-life apple juice out the back, and – result! – some ice in the freezer. I have never felt cooler.

Zee fixes the drinks. She already knows where the glasses are kept.

'Mad that you're living here,' she says, pouring two large measures, with that air of confidence that Zee can pull off like no one else.

'It's a step up,' I say, truthfully.

She laughs, because Zee knows better than anyone how desperate I was to get away from the misery that was my parents' marriage.

'I bet,' she says, handing me my glass.

'And Gerry? What's he like as a landlord?'

'I don't see him that much. He's always at Mum's.'

'*Your* mum's?'

I'd forgotten I'd not told her.

'Fuck,' she says, once I've filled her in on the romance of the century. 'How long's that been going on?'

I think about the red shoes. I've spied a similar pair through Gerry's door once, although I can't be certain they are the same ones. And then there's the flirting which, honestly, has been a thing for as long as I can remember. Growing up I'd always dismissed it as my mother and Gerry, doing what they do, being who they are.

'So,' she says, standing up, 'Where's this bird?'

We go upstairs, and I'm relieved to move on, thankful that she doesn't want to talk any further about my mother and Gerry and middle-aged sex. We tiptoe past Geoff's door. She knows which stairs are the creaky ones and avoids them with a ballet dancer's poise.

We reach my room (Jason's room) without incident. I leave her to nose around while I sneak into Gerry's study. Merlin's bird is waiting for me, exactly where I left it.

Standing on a chair, I carefully take down the box from its perch on top of the wardrobe and bring it through to my room, setting it down on the desk. Then I reach inside and, using both hands, release the bird.

'Fuck me, Mark,' she says when she sees it, and I laugh, partly because her reaction mirrors my own feeling, and also because it always amuses me how sweary Zee gets when she's drunk. Even Anna, who's hardly averse to her Anglo-Saxon profanities, calls Drunk Zee a 'potty mouth'.

She bends down and inspects the sculpture, taking it in for several movements. We are standing very close, though not actually touching, and I can feel her proximity, the slight smell of the club on her clothes and in her hair, mingling with her own scent, and I am drunk.

'That beak,' she says at last. 'Those claws.'

I smile. 'Lethal, right?'

'Merlin did this?'

'Who knew, eh?'

She exhales.

Zee's reaction confirms my own feelings. Something else I notice: in presenting it to Zee, Merlin's sculpture has acquired a realness that was previously missing for me. It is now a thing, an actual thing, and no longer simply Gerry and Merlin's sordid secret.

'It's well creepy,' she says. 'But it's good. It's really good.'

She looks radiant. She is everything. I could listen to her talking about art forever.

And it dawns on me that I have been too timid, too nice, and that this is why the Jason Templars of this world get to sleep with the Zee Adams's of this world, and the Mark Fishers don't. Jason never stopped to think, or if he did he never allowed doubt to consume him. He didn't hold back. He didn't wait for permission. No, he got straight in there. And I am convinced, as sure as I am that night follows day, that they fucked right here, right here in this very bed. They fucked long and they fucked loud. Because Jason would, wouldn't he? That's why Zee wanted him. And what woman wouldn't?

You having some of this, Bad Boy?

And I am mortified yet also exhilarated by the shame of this realisation that must have been obvious to everyone except me, of what, all this time, I've been doing wrong.

I pull Zee towards me, more forcefully than I ever imagined myself capable.

She is surprised, shocked even. Of course she is surprised! The Mark Fisher she thinks she knows would never be this bold, would never be this forward.

Fighting away the usual doubts that have plagued me all my life, the voices reminding me that I am not worthy, that I do not deserve happiness and will never be good enough, I push her down into the mattress and press myself against her. Her skin feels incredible, soft and taut, and I kiss her neck, running my hands over her hips, down her thighs. I could devour her.

She is still a little resistant. 'Mark...' she gasps, pushing me away. 'What are you doing?'

I go in for a kiss, tongues and all, but she moves her face away, so I kiss her neck some more.

But something is wrong, or at least not right. This is not how it is supposed to go. By this point she should be giving herself to the moment, overcome by, I dunno, passion or horniness or newfound respect for me; seeing me for the first time in this new light, realising at last what has always been obvious to everyone other than her, that we belong together, me and Zee, Zee and I, that we were made for each other, that this is our destiny...

'Mark,' she says, and it must be said she is recoiling, despite my tender yet assertive kisses. 'I've got a boyfriend.'

'Who cares! I don't care! I want you. Can't you see? I love you, Zee. I've loved you forever. Can't you see? I could love you like no one else. Just give me a chance. I'd do anything for you. I would die for you!'

She pulls away. My resolve is breaking. The doubts are winning. My heart...

'You're scaring me, Mark.'

And suddenly I see myself, as if through the eyes of someone else, someone who doesn't know me, doesn't know us, doesn't know that I'm a nice guy.

The spell is broken. I roll onto my side, my back to her. I cannot look at her.

I hear her getting up from the bed and going over to the door.

'What the fuck, Mark?'

'I... I'm sorry.'

'Is that what you thought was happening? Is that why you got me here?'

She is repulsed by me. I am repulsed by me. Merlin's bird looks on.

'I'm going now,' she says, opening the door.

My eyes fill with tears. 'Zee...'

'I'm going now.'

The door clicks shut behind her. I hear her on the stairs. This time she makes no attempt to avoid the creaky ones. This is no game and we are not kids any more, sneaking around our parents' houses, doing nothing worse than stealing the neighbour's milk from the doorstep. That innocence is gone, departed, dismissed.

I close my eyes but it doesn't help.

PART 3

FLIGHT

Chapter Twenty

The roof of my mouth is stuck to my tongue. My throat feels raw, as if during the night someone has been going at it with sandpaper. When I stand up my brain feels heavy and I know it's going to be a bad one. I stagger to the bathroom and hold my head under the cold tap, gulping at the water, letting it fall down my face. My eyes are puffy and raw from weeping.

In the kitchen I find a stolen pint glass and stand at the sink, downing pints of water as if my life depends on it, like I've been wandering the desert for days.

Gazing out of the window at the day and at the nothing space which could be called a backyard, I watch a crow pecking at the rubbish. A bag has spilled open, its guts spewing out.

Flashbacks of throwing up outside the venue.

If only that was all.

I know I should probably eat something, so I attempt some cornflakes. I'm about to go back to bed when I hear someone on the stairs. I'm guessing it's Geoff and I brace myself to hear about the latest problems with the proletariat, which at least offers a distraction from worrying about real problems, like the fact that I might be a sexual predator, and that I've probably lost my best friend. Correction: after last night's performance I am sure that all my friends hate me, and if they don't then they are fools and too nice and I should stay away from them and stop exploiting their kindness.

But it's not Geoff on the stairs. It's Gerry. He must have slept here. Did he hear me going into his study for Merlin's bird? What else did he hear?

'Heavy night?' he asks.

'Sorry,' I reply, not yet sure what I'm sorry for. 'Was I loud coming in?'

He doesn't answer immediately. Instead he goes over to the window. The crow has now been joined by two more crows and they are feasting on the contents of the split rubbish bag.

'I don't like sneakiness, Mark,' he says at last. 'I don't like dishonesty.'

I look down at my cornflakes, unable to speak.

'I think I've been pretty fair with you, Mark,' he continues. 'Or do you have a different opinion?'

Now I'm panicking. My brain is not working, but it's clear he's furious with me. The last time I've seen him this angry was the Survival Overnighter.

'Were you actually going to tell me?' he asks, the anger rising in his voice.

'Er,' I stammer, burning with shame.

'Your little visitor?'

'Zee? She just... we were a bit... drunk... sorry... I'll replace the vodka. Sorry about that.'

He closes his eyes and silently counts to five.

'You think this is about a bottle of vodka?'

I shake my head. He knows. He heard everything. He is as appalled by me as I am.

'I want to be able to trust you, Mark. But you're making it very difficult.'

'I'm sorry, Gerry, I feel terrible... It got... out of hand...'

'I don't like sneakiness,' he repeats, and suddenly I realise he's not talking about Zee. He's talking about Merlin's sculpture. He must have heard me go into his study. He probably saw it on my desk when he got up.

And for a moment I am relieved, because although going into his private rooms is bad, he also broke his promise to return the sculpture, so in my head we're sort of equal on that front.

'You're right,' I say. 'I betrayed your trust, Gerry. I'm really sorry.'

'I just don't understand what you were thinking,' he says, his face softening, his voice returning to its regular lilt. 'You've seen the archive, Mark. You know better. You have no excuse. Why would you let the police in? Why would you give them that power?'

'Police?'

'Just because they're not wearing the uniform, Mark. Just because they're not coming at you with a truncheon and a canister full of teargas, doesn't mean they won't hurt you.' He shakes his head. 'I don't need to tell you this, Mark.'

'Oh,' I say. My head hurts. There are so many other failings that Gerry could have found in me that I completely forgot about Geoff and the twitching curtains.

I am certain that this is the only way Gerry could have found out about the visit from DC Tina Barlow.

'She was just looking for Jason,' I say, cautiously, because I don't want to rile Gerry again.

'Hmmm.'

'I thought she seemed all right, actually.'

'Did she give a name?'

'DC Tina Barlow.'

He closes his eyes.

'You know her?'

He picks up the kettle and fills it, still shaking his head, and I can tell that he's trying to control his anger. 'So what did you tell her?'

'Not a lot, honestly,' I say, trying to recall what I did actually tell her. 'She just asked me about the last time I saw him.'

'And you told her?'

'Shouldn't I have?'

'You told her about the Survival Overnighter?'

I nod. 'Is that bad?'

'It's fine, Mark,' he says in a tone that indicates that it is not in the least bit fine. 'I mean, they'll have a field day with it, but don't worry.'

'I didn't tell her, er, everything. I mean, I left out the drugs.'

Gerry slams the kettle down on its stand. 'Well, that's good, then.'

I don't know what to say. It is clear that he's cross with me, that he thinks I've done something monumentally stupid and that any respect he had for me has been lost. I'm tired. I'm tired of the fighting and the suspicion. If he had actually met DC Tina Barlow he probably would feel, as I do, that she was just doing her job, that there was no malicious intent behind her enquiry. But he has already decided the story. It was written long ago, long before I ever spoke to any police, before Jason even appeared in our lives it was already written. And, yes, I am tired. I return to my cornflakes.

'I hope Jason's not done anything awful,' I add, because if he's going to be pissed off with me anyway, I think, I might as well try to get some information from him. 'Do you know where he would have gone?'

'He didn't leave a forwarding address, if that's what you're asking.'

'I wondered about the brother?'

Gerry puffs his cheeks. 'He could be anywhere by now.'

'He didn't say anything?'

'Mark, why do I feel like this is an interrogation? Is this the way it is now? Because I've got to be honest with you, Mark, it's getting a bit much. I don't expect you to be grateful but I could live without the constant judgement. We're all doing our best for you and it feels as if it is never quite good enough. Is there something you want to get off your chest?'

'I didn't mean it like that.'

'No,' he sighs. 'I know you didn't, Mark, and I don't want to seem harsh, but I'm a little worried about you.'

'About me?'

'You seem... a little stuck, if you don't mind me saying. I fear that it's partly my fault. It was too much, what I asked of you, what I asked of you all. And yes, I'm talking about Jason now. Maybe I should have been more open with you at the time. I suppose I wanted so much for him to have a second chance – a first chance, really, because life had been hard for Jason – and I thought that could be with us. Maybe I underestimated the task, maybe I didn't want to see the damage. All I can say is that when a line was crossed on the Survival Overnighter I dealt with it in the way that I believed at that time was best for everyone.

'Now—please, Mark, let me finish, this is important – you're asking all these questions about Jason. You say you want to know what happened? But think about it. Would you actually want him back? Because, forgive me for being so bold, but from where I'm standing, you've done quite well out of him leaving. And, yes, I know that Zeenah was here last night, and don't worry I'm not going to embarrass you by asking – but I'm not a complete idiot, Mark. So, I ask you again, do you still want to pursue all this Jason stuff, or do you not think it might be time we all moved on?'

He picks up my empty bowl.

'Finished?'

I nod.

Gerry turns on the tap and starts running a bowl of washing up water. It's the first time I've seen him do any washing up since I moved in, and I instantly feel bad that he's having to wash up after me.

'Here,' I say, getting to my feet. 'Let me do that.'

He waves away my offer. 'Relax, Mark, I've got this one.'

He asks about the gig. Next time, he says, he'll definitely have to come along, and I tell him, almost word for word, what Seb said about the music industry, how it builds people up only to spit them out, and Gerry remarks that Seb is a very wise man.

'And Zeenah's well?'

I blush.

He chuckles. 'Don't you worry. My lips are sealed. I hope the Stolichnaya helped, even if you're suffering for it this morning. Everyone's entitled to let off a little steam from time to time.'

I thank him and say that I'm going back to bed for a bit.

Halfway up the stairs I hear a knock at the door. I'm tempted to ignore it, but Gerry is already cleaning up after me. The least I can do, I think, is get the door.

'I got it,' I call.

I open the door.

'Anna?'

She bites down on her lip and looks me in the eyes. 'Yeah,' she begins. 'That got out of hand. Sorry about that.'

'No,' I say, shaking my head. 'You were being a mate.'

'I was being a dick,' she says with a smile. 'But thanks all the same. Can I buy you breakfast?'

There's a greasy spoon that I went to a couple of times with Kay and Badger, a modest little caff next to the chippy on the corner. The traffic roars by, because it is Saturday morning and shoppers want to get to the shops, and because it's Mount Pleasant Road and there's always traffic. Anna takes my arm in hers and I could cry, but I don't. Instead I warn her to look out for the shit on the pavement, and she says, 'Ain't that the truth, brother.'

There's one table left – and it's a good one, too, by the window. We order two full Englishes and chat about the gig. Anna says that now Seb is going to be famous we each have a moral obligation to make sure he doesn't turn into a rockstar twat, and I laugh and say I don't think that's very likely, to which she points out that that's what they all think before they become one.

'No one sets out to be an arsehole, Mark.'

I consider telling her about Zee, but I realise that I only want to tell her so that she'll reassure me that I wouldn't have gone through with it, that I'm not that kind of guy, except maybe I am that kind of guy, maybe there is no that kind of guy only guys of all kinds and, given the right, or the wrong, set of conditions, we are all capable of doing almost anything. Particularly where sex is involved. And so, I resist the easy confession, and instead I turn to the other thing that had kept me awake for much of the night.

'I need your help, Anna,' I say, lowering my voice. 'I want to find Jason.'

'Do you now?'

'Will you help me?'

'Why do you want to find him?'

'I want to say sorry.'

She puts down the cup and picks up her tobacco. 'So you admit it?' she says, removing a paper from the heavily roached pack of skins. 'It was you who grassed?'

I shake my head. 'No, I don't know how Gerry found out.'

'So what are you sorry for?'

'I don't think we treated him very well.'

The food arrives, mountains of it. We have to move things around to squeeze it all onto the table.

'You know,' she says, picking up a slice of toast, the butter melted in, just the way it should be. 'I reckon that's the first true thing I've heard anyone say in regard to Jason since he left.'

We stay at the cafe for the rest of the morning, nursing our hangovers and drinking cup after cup of tea. It's been a long time coming, this. Talking with Anna. Talking with anyone, for that matter. Rebuilding the closeness that we – I – took so much for granted. When I tell her about my parents, her reaction surprises me, though knowing Anna as I do it shouldn't.

'Go easy on them, Mark,' she warns. 'We'll probably be just as shit at being parents should anyone agree to breed with one of us. Most people are shit at it, just shit in different ways. Mine are fucking hopeless. You should hear the rows with Richie. I'm surprised the Old Bill haven't come knocking.'

'Families,' I say. 'Who'd have 'em?'

'Better than not having them.'

'True.'

'Nah, Markface, the ones you wanna be suspicious of are the ones that look like they've got it made, the ones that look like the fucking Waltons from afar. They're the most fucked up of them all. Always.'

'Are you thinking of anyone in particular?'

She shrugs. 'You went to Folk. Take your pick.'

Chapter Twenty-One

When I get back to the house, there's no one around. I check if Gerry's upstairs, but his doors are closed and there's no answer when I call his name.

I almost jump out of my skin when I go into my bedroom and find Merlin's bird staring at me from the desk. How could I have forgotten those dead eyes and nasty phallic beak after they had tormented me for most of the night?

I must return it, I think. But to whom? Really, we need to return it to Merlin, and I know that I could take that task on myself, spare Gerry the bother. Yet it is Gerry who made the promise, first to Merlin, then to me. Anyone can mess up. We can all let things slide. A missed service on a boiler. A phone call not returned. Words left unsaid. Feelings disregarded. Vows broken. Careless thoughts and selfish actions.

I do not claim to be any better.

But we can try to make things right. And, maybe, the greatest gift that anyone can give anyone is the chance to make things right.

We talk about second chances as if we don't all need them. Like, all the time.

Even Gerry.

With extreme caution – I'd be mortified to damage it now – I lift the bird back into its box and go back out to the landing. It's a bit awkward, the manoeuvre, because I have to put the box down in order to free my hands so that I can open Gerry's door. And it is at this moment, while I'm struggling with the logistics, that I hear someone coming up the stairs.

I freeze, then I remember my vow. I will speak plainly with Gerry. I will give him the opportunity to make it right.

A red-faced Geoff comes puffing up the stairs.

'You okay there, Young Blood? What's that you got?'

The bird's eyes are poking out of the box again. The lid never seems to stay down.

'Oh,' I say. 'Art.'

'Art?'

'That's right.'

He nods, a little puzzled, but apparently satisfied by my response. But when he informs Gerry of this encounter, as inevitably he will, my sneakiness will be confirmed.

Not wanting to take any more risks, the box with the bird goes back to my desk. I close the door behind me. My room smells: of teenage boy, of stale alcohol, of sweat and tears and all my dirty deeds. I open the window. I strip the bed, pulling it away from the wall so that I can remove the mattress protector as well. I will wash it all on 90. I need a fresh start.

I've not inspected behind the bed before. I had assumed that the room was completely clear before I moved in and that any remnant of Jason Templar had been removed, yet now I spot something lodged between the bed and the wall, and when I reach down to retrieve it, I discover it is a cassette tape. There is no label, nothing to identify it, so I stick it in the cassette player and I'm about to press play when I change my mind and I take the whole thing over to the archive. It's time I found a new soundtrack,

I decide, and I'm actually excited by the prospect of hearing something new, something I've never heard before.

Thus far, my relationship with Gerry's archive has been somewhat abstract. There have been curiosities, the odd item that has moved me, shocked me even, or stirred my sense of justice and morality, or reminded me of the person I once was or might have been. But for the most part my interest has been clerical. At times I have felt more like a snoop than a researcher, digging up information that is not my business, and for no purpose other than to possess it and document it and hold it. I have tried, where possible, to impose order where there was disorder. I have endeavoured to create systems where there were none. But what use is an archive without a purpose?

My colour-coded categories and my dogged indexing prove effective and soon I have managed to locate and pull out every item that might assist my trail, including what I now recognise as the ring binder Gerry handed me that first evening Jason came to Folk, which I discover contains all sorts of personal information including medical records that should probably not have been left lying around for us lot to find.

I work fast, conscious that when Gerry learns I've broken his trust with the bird, he may decide that I can no longer be trusted with the archive. I am propelled by the sounds coming out of the little speakers, sounds which are wholly novel to me, the beats almost tripping over themselves; sounds that come from all directions, arriving and departing without asking permission or demanding priority or special treatment. And this is something I notice about Jason's music – for which I have no other name, and which needs no other label: there's no hierarchy. Or maybe there is, but the order is more flexible than what I'm used to, as if any element has the potential to become the dominant force or to drop back or just stay there, doing its thing, being. And I wonder if that's what Jason likes about it, or if there is something he hears that I can't hear, and whether

I could ever learn to hear that. Is that what Zee hears? Maybe she hears something different entirely?

Such are the thoughts I have while I listen to the clattering and the clicks and the whooshes and the waves of the mystery tape, Jason's parting gift to me, though he couldn't have known that I would receive it. To him, he may have just lost a tape, or perhaps he isn't even aware that it is missing.

I think about Gerry, the demands he makes as well as the gifts he brings, his rigid insistence on what he calls trust but which includes loyalty. By speaking to DC Tina Barlow I was being disloyal, which for Gerry is a clear breach of trust. I've seen over the years, longstanding members – other leaders as well as young folk – people who may have regarded Gerry as a friend, breaking rank over a matter of principle or policy, and Gerry simply cutting them off or freezing them out. He could be quite ruthless when he felt he was in the right, which was almost always. 'Popular appeal is the enemy of progress,' he was fond of saying. 'Sometimes you have to accept you're going to rub some people up the wrong way.' It was always someone else who was the enemy of progress. We liked it that we weren't slaves to popular appeal.

Gerry was – is – generous with his trust, until you lose it, and then it's gone and it is not easily won back. That is how it will have been for Jason, I'm quite sure of it. Because that is how it was for Folk. And it is how it will be for me.

Will Gerry drop me, as he dropped Jason, when he realises I can't move on? That I can't just move on? That I won't just move on? That there is no *just* about it. The prospect of Gerry throwing me out raises certain practical issues. Will I crawl back to Mum having been kicked out in disgrace by her lover? Or should I go to Stuttgart and try to find Dad. But I don't even know where Stuttgart is on the map, and I'm not sure I have an address for the site office. Besides, I need to be here for my A-levels.

In the old days, once upon a time, it would have been easy. I would have simply gone to Zee's. It would have been a natural step to go from the 'token white boy' they have taken under their wing, which they – we – liked to joke about, to actual adopted Lost Boy. Yet that door, if it ever was really open, is now firmly closed. Zee would never have me now. How could she? Even if she could, somehow, forgive what I had done, how could we Move On? And, yes, I might try to blame it on the booze, blame it on the boogie, blame it on my cock, blame it on the films I've seen, blame it on the expectations I've absorbed from a society that demeans women and glorifies rape. And maybe there is some truth to all that. But the bigger truth is that I crossed a line.

You're scaring me, Mark.

Meanwhile, in my as-yet-unrealised state of homelessness (can you qualify as homeless if you still receive an allowance from your parents?), I'm running out of options and the clock is ticking, because once Gerry decides you're out, you're out, as Kay and Jason would no doubt testify.

Which leaves only Seb, and after last night's scene in front of all his important music industry types, not to mention the cool-as-fuck band, I wouldn't blame him for barring me from all future gigs. I cannot now ask him for favours.

There is, of course, still Anna, but they are a large family living in a small house. They do not have space to take in some random mate of Anna's who has gone and made himself homeless.

So really there is only one thing for it. I will have to find a job. Someone, somewhere, surely must be able to find a use for me, some purpose. Then I will get a bedsit, or a room in a shared house, and start again. And this time I will do it right. I will not ask for favours or charity. I don't want to be rescued, I just wanna be me.

Ha! Section 28. That's a lyric from one of their songs. It feels so long ago, the gig, feeling on top of the world. My mate on the stage. Jumping around. Everyone happy.

I'm lucky. I have some savings. I could probably already scrape together a deposit. And I can do things. I can be useful.

Independence will involve sacrifices. Where've I heard that before? Gerry. Folk. Everything goes back to Folk. I suspect it will always be so. The frame in which any life I picture always hangs. Then Jason comes along, and whether or not it was his intention, he destroys it. Smashes the frame. Maybe. Maybe not. Maybe he doesn't break anything, so much as he alters the frame, exposes its limitations and opens up the possibility of a new frame or no fixed frame at all?

Incidentally, Jason could do it, what I want to do. And I hope he is, you know, doing something like this for himself, getting it together, finding his way. Doing all right.

I am getting carried away.

I have not fallen out with Gerry. Not yet. And once Gerry learns that I only came across Merlin's sculpture because of the faulty boiler, surely he will appreciate that I was merely acting responsibly and not sneaking around?

Maybe.

(About the boiler: I was right to be concerned. Odd Jobs Dave gave it his best for several hours, going at it with an array of spanners, wrenches and pumps, before finally conceding defeat and calling in a specialist, who took one look and instructed the boiler be replaced, that the existing one was a bit dangerous.)

So, I was right, and in a just world Gerry would be grateful. He isn't, obviously, he thinks I'm being hysterical – about the boiler certainly, and probably also about Jason, Merlin's bird, my upcoming exams, everything really.

Gerry has higher priorities: social justice, solidarity (or lack of it), conflict zones (particularly the ones that go unreported in mainstream media), nuclear energy, western imperialism, the Criminal Justice Bill. How can he be expected to concern himself with the banalities of broken boilers, weird sculptures and missing boys.

Yet I still wish it were possible for him to fight the good fight while also noticing my small efforts and contributions, be it housework or showing concern for former housemates.

One of the things I'm learning at Mount Pleasant Road is how things that start out as small annoyances can escalate and get ugly, whether it's bathroom mould, problem boyfriends or boilers that go bang. Dad was always saying you should nip things in the bud. Not let them get out of hand. Gerry is very different to my father in that regard.

Chapter Twenty-Two

I spend all afternoon in the archive, occasionally nipping to my room to photograph items of special interest. I have finally found a backdrop and a source of light that I like.

I read an essay about a group of homeless people and anarchists called the London Squatters Campaign, who, in 1968, occupied a luxury block of flats in East London to draw attention to the perversity of homelessness when there is so much property lying empty. There's another piece about how squats provided the spatial infrastructure for the feminist movement in the 1970s, and how this led to the opening of women's centres, refuges, nurseries, bookshops, art centres and workshops.

Maybe I could live in a squat?

This line of enquiry leads me to a story about a group of squatters who, in 1992, occupied a palace – a real one – somewhere in Essex, and the violent clashes with police that followed when they were finally evicted.

Under the headline PUNCH UP AT THE PALACE, a newspaper report tells of 'carnage' and 'ritualistic behaviour', alongside a grainy photo of the squatters, dancing and dressed up in eccentric clothing. There are kids in view. A local MP, quoted in the report, describes the squatters as 'irresponsible... an affront to decent British values'.

The Palace is one of those crumbling country piles that are dotted all over rural England. For several years it had stood empty, following the death of Earl Mountbatten of Oxley, who had run the house into a state of disrepair while an ongoing legal battle raged between the would-be heirs, which was when the squatters moved in.

A magazine carries a much longer piece, and a wider range of images depicting life at the palace. The piece shines a light on a world beyond my experience, but is recognisably the world of Folk, just another side of it, a different set of circumstances, a different mix of random and less random factors that determine who gets what, who's in and who's out. I study the faces. They could have attended Folk.

I start thinking of some of the other characters I have met in the archive. In particular, I think of the photo of the guy with the smashed-up face. The one that reminded me of Jason.

Then I notice a smaller picture of a couple of teenage boys. The bigger of the two, who is probably about eighteen or nineteen years old, is standing with his arms protectively around the younger one's shoulders. There is a caption on the opposite page:

Brothers in Arms: Darren and Jason Templar, residents at the Palace.

Even inside the archive, with the door closed, I'm jolted by the thud, the crash, and the sound of voices. I go out to the landing to investigate. Geoff comes puffing up the stairs.

'The filth!' he says between breaths. 'They're here.'

'What?'

'Downstairs, Young Blood. They've got a warrant, so if there's anything they shouldn't find, lose it now.'

I can hear shelves and cupboards being emptied, the static of police radios, boots in the hall, boots on the stairs. I don't know why they've come, but I know I'm to blame. Gerry was right: I should have known that bitch dressed in Zee's jacket was playing me for a fool.

I go into my room and shut the door. It must be a matter of minutes before they come for me. I look around. What to save? I've seen police raids on TV. Once they've decided you're guilty, and given that they have a warrant they must be pretty confident, they don't care what they break. In fact, often they smash things up just for fun, and to intimidate people into confessing to crimes they never committed. That's how they are.

My books. Music, photos – my whole personal archive – these things I should save, for this – Zee and I have discussed it – is what connects who we are to who we were, and to who we might have become, which is sort of like ghosts.

We are haunted by our hopes and dreams, as well as by our failures and regrets. So does that mean I am now a ghost to Zee? Is she a ghost to me?

Caught up in these thoughts, I end up staring at my life and taking nothing, because it's too overwhelming trying to decide what of myself I will keep and what I can lose.

What I do pick up is the box on the desk. A promise is a promise even if I only made it to myself.

Survival instincts finally kicking in, I grab my rucksack, plus a sleeping bag, some college notes, my good all-weather jacket.

Address book. Wallet. Passport.

I can hear them directly below me, and I imagine them going through Kay's old stuff, and I pray that she didn't leave anything precious or incriminating behind. I consider taking her cauldron with me, but I decide it would slow me down too much. Besides, I had no way of ever getting it back to her.

Merlin's bird just squeezes in at the top of my rucksack.

I glance at myself in the mirror. I'm ready. My plan is to simply walk out of the house. I will not stop unless I'm stopped. If you want to get away with something outrageous, behaving as if it is the most normal thing in the world is the most effective move. I learned that from shoplifting with Zee and Anna. We only did it once, and we didn't steal anything worth more than a quid, and only from evil capitalist chain stores. It was (your honour) merely an experiment to see what it would feel like, and to find out if we could. And it turned out that yes, we could, in that none of us got caught, but we all felt guilty afterwards, and for weeks afterwards I would be visited by police in my dreams, and every time I saw a police car I believed it was coming for me.

The door suddenly opens and DS Tina Barlow is standing before me.

'Come on,' she says, taking my arm.

She walks me downstairs. The place is crawling with police. And they're going through everything. Every box, surface, drawer, cupboard. It is a gargantuan task they have taken on. I should know because I have been trying to tame the chaos ever since I moved in.

With the stripped bookcases and tipped over plants, the raid feels more like a heist than due process, or a perhaps game show in which the contestants trash the studio while barking into walkie talkies.

It occurs to me that she hasn't cuffed me, that I could try to make a dash for it. Do a James Bond. But I don't, obviously. Instead I allow myself to be led. Her grip is sure. The fabric of her jumper feels very clean. I think I can smell her subtle perfume.

Outside, on the steps, she turns to me. There's a flicker of a smile on that substantial mouth of hers which – and I know this is wrong – I still sort of want to kiss.

'You don't need to be here, Sparky.'

I stare at her.

'Got somewhere to go?'

I nod.

'Take care, Sparky.'

She hasn't even asked to see inside my rucksack.

'Thank you,' I stammer.

She nods.

'This one's all right,' she shouts across to one of her colleagues. 'You can let him through.'

There are two police cars stopped in front of the house. In the back of one of them I spot Geoff, and I can see him staring at me, letting me know that he has seen this exchange, that he's onto me. He has watched me receiving special treatment at the hands of the law.

I am free, for now, but it will not be long before Gerry hears of this. He will never forgive the betrayal, and neither will anyone else, once this gets around, and I will be a pariah, a turncoat, a snitch, a grass, a traitor. Sneaky. Ungrateful. And after Gerry had been so generous, so good, to me!

The bus stop across from the chippy is deserted. I sit on the plastic perch and stare at the traffic, which roars by, the people going about their lives.

I hail the first bus that comes along, which is only going as far as the bus station, hardly worth the cost of the ticket. The driver eyes me suspiciously and charges me the full fare. I'm the only passenger. I don't know where I'm going. I have no plan.

Chapter Twenty-Three

I am discharged from the bus onto the concourse of the central bus station. Driverless buses stand marooned on the forecourt, as if they've been abandoned in a hurry. There is some fixed plastic seating grouped in sections of six or eight. Most are empty and it is not clear whether the occupants of those that are occupied plan to travel or are just taking shelter.

Some workers are finishing a shift. Their bus company-crested uniforms, complete with blazers and trousers with severe creases down the legs, seem overly formal for the shabby surroundings. The sound of their banter drifts over. I can only make out the odd word, but it's clear they get along. No one is in a hurry, it seems. This is a place where time doesn't so much stand still as pass by without you.

The newsagents on the corner is shut, its windows dark. A sign on the door forbids more than two school-age children from entering at the same time. Another warns that shoplifters will be prosecuted. There is a British Legion sticker, with its Union Jack, and another for a Lifeboats charity. Some kids at my former school claimed they had purchased porn here, though as I peer through the darkened windows nothing on the top shelf looks particularly racy.

A flickering screen lists impending departures to Bournemouth, Manchester, London, Glasgow. I could go, just go, leave this place behind. I start calculating. How much would I need to survive? How long could I go before the money ran out? I have my Youth Hostel Association membership card with me; or I could stay at a YMCA, because that would be fun.

If you're eighteen, and you leave without saying goodbye or telling anyone where you're going, does that still make you a runaway? Maybe I could become a nomad? Or join the circus, except I can't juggle and I don't think I'm brave enough to swallow a sword.

There's a hole-in-the-wall near the toilets. I insert my card and withdraw the daily limit. The machine spits out a fat wad of notes. It feels like drug money. And completely abstract. I stuff it into an inner pocket of my anorak. Then I hoist my rucksack higher onto my shoulders and tighten the straps. I check the screen.

A small line of people waiting at the stand for the Manchester coach. I have no connections to Manchester. I don't think I've ever been there. They have a football team and a good music scene, I think, and it's where the *Guardian* newspaper was started, so it can't be too bad.

I go over to the ticket window.

'Manchester, please.'

This act feels rakish and defiant. I'm just the kind of guy who, y'know, buys a ticket to Manchester. No biggie.

'You're in luck,' says the man behind the plastic glass. 'The last seat.'

I smile (no biggie) and say, 'Meant to be.'

'Single or return.'

Now there's a question. I'm reaching for the zipper of my anorak, anticipating the feel of the notes in my hand, and I'm all set to say 'Single' or even 'Single!' – as in young, free and single – when, without warning, I stop, aware suddenly of what I'm about to do.

'Single or return?' he repeats, tapping his pen on the counter impatiently.

Behind me, I hear what I take to be the coach pulling up to the stand, the doors being released with a sort of sigh, and there is a general sense of movement and eagerness that accompanies an arrival or a departure – any arrival or departure – in a place where waiting is the primary state of being.

Something is said over the Tannoy, but I'm not listening any more because my brain is racing. And I know that I can't do it. I can't just leave. Not like this.

'I'm sorry,' I murmur, turning away from the window.

I flee the concourse, hurrying towards the nearest exit. I come out onto Paris Street. It is not yet dark, not even nearly dark, but the headlights of the cars and the lighted windows of the closed shop fronts seem to insist that it is evening and that the daylight is just an illusion.

I walk fast, crossing the junction at the traffic lights diagonally, while the traffic races by at green, like someone with a death wish.

I picture the people boarding the bus. There is still time. I could run back. Or, if it's too late for Manchester, no matter, I can be Sparky anywhere. Except, I can't, not yet.

For how can I follow the trail, how can I love the sun, when there is still so much to be done?

New North Road. The oncoming cars in my face. The pavement too narrow for the volume and size of the vehicles. I cross the railway tracks. I could jump. Sometimes I have to stop myself from doing things like that, not because I want to die but because I'm curious about the sensation: the falling, the landing, the waiting, the oncoming train, the oblivion. Some poor bugger has to clear up afterwards though. Were I to kill myself, I would come up with a kinder alternative. Maybe try to score myself some of those drugs they gave gran at the end. Then I would take a rowing boat out to sea, sink the needle in and let nature take its course. The seagulls would probably eat some of me and the fish would get the rest.

Not that I'm planning to kill myself, but Zee says it's always good to have an exit strategy. And she would know, having extricated herself from more half-relationships than anyone else I knew. Zee seemed to have no difficulties walking away. Soon she would be leaving us all, not for a boy this time, but for Erasmus. I already loathed Erasmus, just as I loathed Laurent or Tobias or whatever the name was of this latest squeeze of hers.

I pass the prison. It's a mean Victorian relic, with a pompous front for the benefit of the good citizens on the outside, and a decrepit rear where the cells look out onto concrete walls and razor wire. Sometimes you can glimpse the prisoners through the security grills on the windows, smoking or just staring.

You're in luck.

I heard the man. Why couldn't I take the luck and be grateful? Or, forget gratitude, why not just take the luck? Take it as the natural course of the universe, the way things are, the way the cookie crumbles. Why care about finding out what happened to Jason? Why bother? Why care about returning Merlin's sculpture? Would anyone else care? Certainly not Gerry, that much was clear. Okay, Anna, with her keen sense of justice, she cared. She will tell me I'm full of shit, that I always was, and she will no doubt be justified in that verdict. But I will be long gone by that point.

It occurs to me that by boarding the bus I would be resigning myself to the past, a guy that those who remember Folk (also just a memory in this imagined future) once knew, though maybe not as well as they thought they did as it turned out.

At the Clock Tower I have to wait for a gap in the traffic. It's long enough for my mind to wander to the exams, which are coming up and for which I am not especially prepared. But then everyone tells me that these days good A-levels aren't enough. Everyone's got them, these people say, so they don't really mean anything. Yet is having them and it meaning nothing the same as not having them and it meaning nothing? This is a question I would normally put to Zee, who would surely have an opinion, for she has strong opinions about education, and about society. About most things now I think about it. And suddenly it hits me: I have not moved on in the slightest. The epiphany I have waited years to reach still eludes me. I am not healed.

After crossing the big road the streets become leafy and the traffic noises fade, replaced by bird song, drifting on the gentle breeze. I fancy I can hear a nightingale. The ones still singing now, someone once told me, will not find a mate. They are too late. Out of time. What will become of the lonely nightingale singing its doomed song?

Some of these houses I'm passing I once knew, from friends and semi-friends who lived in them, maybe still do. If we ran into each other now, would we say hi? Or would we choose to walk by and pretend we'd not seen each other? It turns out that even in this town things change, and you can't hang on to everyone, you just can't.

The bench at the end of the street has gone. Vandals probably, smashing it up, or else the Residents Committee finally succeeded in getting it removed. The bench had been much maligned for attracting drunks and 'kids', by which they meant other people's children, not the nice ones like me.

Number eight, I note, has a new conservatory. They were always a bit like that. There will have been snarky comments from some of the other residents.

It is odd to think that of all the places in all the world my parents could have chosen for themselves and me, they went for this crappy row of terraced houses in a not very interesting part of provincial England. Maybe they were seduced by the promise of joining the Residents Committee? It is easy to imagine Mum pretending to be aloof – having to, as she would say, 'hold her nose' – and then taking over, wielding that charisma of hers, using her superior language and education to run circles around these provincial bumpkins who thought the pinnacle of culture was a trip to

London to see an Andrew Lloyd Webber musical followed by dinner at Pizza Express. And then there was my father pretending to be grumpy and world-weary, but actually in his element. The shrewd homeowner with his car and his family, well away from the dirt and the riffraff of the big city, his still youthful-looking wife, the life and soul of the neighbourhood. Was that the dream? Would I someday want that too? Of course, the best part of it for him was that he could disapprove of everyone and yet still be invited to dinner parties. They belonged, I could see that. Even if it was all, or mostly, a lie. David and June, such characters!

It was all for my benefit. That was the story they told. They had wanted to start a family and this was the right place for that. The sacrifices they had made, I heard them say time and time again, were worth it. 'So you're an actor, June?' visitors would say in that gushing way people had, which I never entirely bought. '*Was*,' she would correct, gesturing towards the mantelpiece where the posed family photos stood glumly. And Dad, if he was around, would elaborate on her behalf, as if she was too modest to say it herself: 'June went to RADA, you know.' Which always drew admiration. Several acolytes tried on more than one occasion to get her to sign up to the local Am-Dram society.

The curtains are drawn. The light, however, is on in the front room. I press the bell. Greensleeves does its thing, each note underscoring my poor judgement. Evidence of why I shouldn't be allowed to get what I want.

After a few moments the door is unlocked from the other side. There had been a series of break-ins a few years earlier, which had led to the Neighbourhood Watch issuing a request that residents take additional precautions, including more advanced locks and alarms that blinked red in the night. My parents bemoaned these 'draconian measures', dismissing them as reactionary and absurd, then obediently installed new locks and a high-end burglar alarm.

The door swings open and there's Gerry standing before me in a clean sweater and a pair of old man slippers. Less road protestor, more homeowner. He looks almost respectable. He seems as shocked by my presence as I am by his.

'Mark?'

'Hey, Gerry.'

He clocks the rucksack but refrains from commenting. Behind him, the hallway seems tidier and more orderly than I am used to. It is evidently the same house where I grew up yet something feels different. He invites me in, which feels weirder still.

We stand in the entrance hall, neither in nor out, as if waiting for someone to tell us how this thing works. At last I crouch down to untie my laces, which is awkward and takes a while because I'm wearing my high-tops, and you have to loosen the laces to get them off. My eyes fall on Gerry's shoes in the shoe rack. They are so much larger than anyone else's and it is impossible to shake the memory of that day, the day when I had come home too early from college. The farmyard noises. The smell. We had never spoken of the incident. I doubt he knows that I know. I notice my hands are shaking.

While I struggle with the boots, Gerry goes through to the kitchen.

'She'll be sorry,' he calls back.

'What?'

'June.'

Then I remember it is Saturday and Mum will be at the Dog, and I want to kick myself for not realising this prior to knocking on the door, and I wish I could just run away, go back out into the cold and disappear.

'Have you eaten, Mark?'

I watch him from a distance, the way he moves around the kitchen, his familiarity with the space, the dimensions and the appliances my parents had chosen. He knows where everything goes. I had never known Gerry to be house-proud and I realise I am completely wrong-footed by it.

'Come on,' he says, picking his keys up off the counter. 'Let's surprise her.'

'Sorry?'

'I'll drive us to the Dog. That's what you want, right? To see *mum*?'

The word *mum* feels like an accusation.

He smiles, a sickly smile without warmth, but I don't care anymore. I don't care if he knows about the raid or if he blames me for it. I don't care if he thinks I betrayed his trust or believes I am ungrateful. All I want at this moment is to be with the hippies and the hangers-on at the Dog, where I am not a stranger, where I am someone, where I am June's son and she is my mum.

Gerry clicks his cheek impatiently, like you might do to hurry a dog along, and I follow him obediently out to the hall.

'Are you sure?' I say. 'I mean, is that all right?'

'Never been surer, Mark.'

Chapter Twenty-Four

Gerry's car is parked at the end of the row of houses. I came from the other side, which is why I hadn't spotted it before.

The car smells of childhood. PVA glue and old tarpaulins, and the musty, earthy aroma of protest. I keep my rucksack at my feet.

'Should be a good one tonight,' he says, inserting his key into the ignition. The engine growls, and he swings out into the road without indicating.

'Yeah?'

We drive in silence for a while and I look out at the familiar streets passing by and the shadows of the street lamps.

'I believe you took something that doesn't belong to you?'

His voice is calm. We approach the roundabout and I recall the way he drove round and round, teasing us, on the day of the Survival Overnighter. The delight Gerry seemed to take from such games was such a familiar part of Folk and Gerry. Did it even occur to anyone to question all that? Zee never liked all that stuff. She went along with it, because you had to, but I knew it irritated her.

'I get it,' he continues. 'You're angry with me, aren't you, Mark? I said I'd return it, didn't I? And then, three months pass, and the next time you have a little nose around my bedroom it's still there!'

'I'm sorry,' I say. 'I'm sorry I went into your room.'

Gerry offers no response. My words hang in the silence.

We're on the outskirts of town, driving north, into the darkness. When Mum had driven me out to the Dog's Whistle in the past I had paid little attention to the route. The realisation now that I don't know where we're going or how long it will take to get there makes me nervous. I am clutching my rucksack, which is crushed between my seat and the dashboard, and I hope Merlin's sculpture is still in one piece.

Gerry leans across me and pulls open the glovebox causing a few tapes to tumble to the floor.

'Go on, Mister DJ,' he says. 'See if you can find something in all that lot!'

I spy his Guilt Mix. In my haste to find something (anything) that wasn't Gerry's Guilt Mix I grab the first thing to hand, which happens to be the Penguin Cafe Orchestra, an album my parents played often, bridging as it did folk music and easy listening, with vaguely classical pretensions.

The opening jig gets going, but I do not feel like dancing. I search my mind for a talking point that will shift the conversation away from my betrayal, and I remember the mysterious phone calls and another promise I had not kept.

'How's your mum?' I ask as nonchalantly as I can.

'My mum? You want to know about my mum? Why are you asking me, Mark, about my mum?'

'She's in some kind of a home, right?'

'Mark, my mum died in 1987. Why on earth are you asking me about her?'

'Oh, right. My mistake.'

Finally we enter a village, and I recognise it as the village where the

Dog's Whistle is located. Beyond the bus shelter is the pub's big sign, illuminated in white lights, and I never in a million years imagined feeling so pleased to see it.

There are lots of cars parked outside. Gerry was right. It is a busy one tonight.

But as we approach the pub, instead of slowing down, Gerry speeds up.

'Sorry, Mark. Change of plan.'

'What?' I can feel myself starting to panic. 'You can just let me out,' I say. 'I can walk from here.'

He continues driving, staring at the dark road ahead. We have left the village behind again.

'Really,' I say, more forcefully this time, instinctively feeling for the door handle, assessing the practicality of jumping, James Bond-style, from a moving car. 'Let me out, Gerry.'

Back on the open road, it feels darker than before. There are no houses on this section of road and only the occasional vehicle passes us, the head-lights appearing suddenly and then the taillights fading into the darkness.

'You know, Mark, I still owe you a Survival Overnighter.'

I try to remind myself that it's just Gerry and that I have known Gerry forever. He would not hurt me, I know this. He probably doesn't even realise how much he's scaring me. Maybe he actually thinks I care about a bloody Survival Overnighter? Maybe he thinks that this will somehow make everything right between us again? This is, after all, Gerry we're talking about, for whom the usual rules don't apply.

'I think we had one,' I say quietly.

'*That?*' He is incredulous, offended by my comment. 'That wasn't a Survival Overnighter! That was… I don't know what that was, but it definitely wasn't a Survival Overnighter. No, Mark, I mean a real one.'

'I'd rather just go to the Dog's Whistle.'

He says nothing to this. Instead, he reaches over again and turns up the volume. It is so loud that it feels as if the doors and windows rattle as we press on, heading north on the road to Nowhere.

'Gerry,' I try once more. 'Please. I don't want this.'

'When did we get so dull, Mark?' he bellows over the music, like he's on the stage at a rally. 'The old Mark would have jumped at the offer of a wild night under the stars!'

'Gerry...'

'You know what you are, Mark. You're a townie. You weren't always one but it's what you've become. The good news, though, is that you are young. You can fight it. You can push back. Listen, I know you're cross right now, but hear me out. It actually only occurred to me while we were driving. The way you've been cradling that rucksack. I got to thinking, since you've got Merlin's bird in there anyway, why not kill two birds with one stone?'

He chuckles.

I stare ahead into the darkness.

'See! I knew it! So, here's what we're going to do, Mark. Now, listen up. It's a little late to knock on their door this evening, so we'll bed down for the night at a spot I know – you're going to love this place, Mark! – and then, come the break of dawn, we'll hike up to the Cooperage and hand-deliver the creature to its maker. How about that for a plan? Can you live with that?'

'Do I have a choice?'

'We always have a choice, Mark.'

'To be honest, I think I'd rather go another time. I mean... it sounds good... I'm just rather tired.'

'No, no, no, no, no, Mark Fisher. You don't get out of it that easy! You took the bird, now you must follow through! I wouldn't be doing you any favours letting you walk away from this now.'

Since passing the Dog, we have encountered fewer and fewer cars, and no major settlements. Just a handful of isolated houses, dotted here and there, usually set back from the road behind gates or at the ends of gravel tracks.

Gerry's mind is made. That much is clear. We are doing this whether I consent to the plan or not. I realise that I can either continue to protest or try to make the best of it. And it is just one night, I remind myself.

* * *

He thrusts a tarpaulin into my arms and we set off across a field towards a dark mass that must be woods. I don't remember any of this. Our supplies rattle as we walk.

We keep up a brisk pace. Gerry pace, we used to call it.

'We're going to cheat a bit,' he says, a little breathless walking at such a pace in the cool night air. 'There's a log cabin – a shack, really – very basic. It's too late now to build a bivouac or a bender. Next time we'll have to come earlier.'

After a while I begin to recognise certain trees and the curve of the track we are walking along. My arms are beginning to ache from the tarpaulin. Without warning, Gerry starts humming a song we used to sing at Folk. It's a silly nonsense song that the younger ones liked because it's icky and annoying.

Nobody likes us
Everybody hates us
'Cos we live on worms
Big fat juicy ones
Skinny winny winny ones
See them wriggle and squirm!

I try to get into the spirit. This is my history, my world, and I feel I have a right to reclaim it. Gerry's remark about me being a 'townie' had stung, as he knew it would, for there is some truth to the observation. Since the passing of Folk, I have hardly left the town.

We pass the ancient birch trees, which are still majestic but feel even more sinister this time. Should I have put up more struggle? There had been no need to agree to the trip. I could have caught the bus. And even in the car, maybe I should have put up more protest? There had been people standing around outside the pub. Gerry had slowed down. People would have seen us. They would have heard me yelling, had I yelled. The feeling that the position I now found myself in was partly or mostly of my own making overwhelms me. I cannot think. I just want it to end.

Anna and Zee say I am a people pleaser, that I put too much weight on other people's opinions rather than trusting my own judgement. People pleasers, says Zee, may not put authoritarian regimes in place but they sure as hell keep them there. Who do you think shipped their neighbours to the Gestapo? I tell her I agree. But is my agreement yet another example of my need to please? Anna says I should get out more. 'You don't need everyone to like you, Mark. Believe it not,' she says, 'you're actually quite likeable as you are.'

It occurs to me that no one has actually seen or heard from either Merlin or Jason since the Survival Overnighter.

'Are you all right back there, Mark?'

I am lagging behind. If I dropped the tarp and ran, could I get away? The problem is that out here I don't know where I would go. We have passed no houses. It's just us, two lonely figures, the forest and the moor. I don't even have a map this time.

Could I find my way to the Cooperage? If I did, M&S would surely take me in. They may even remember me. And Merlin would be there, wouldn't he?

But I don't know how to get to the Cooperage from here. I wouldn't know which direction to run.

'Not far now!' he calls.

He is waiting for me to catch up.

'Coming!'

We climb a hill, keeping to the track, which is too narrow to walk side by side, and I can hear his breaths, and my own, and I wonder why we are in such a rush.

'I can knock us up some scran when we get there, Mark.'

I think of breakfast with Anna earlier in the day. Why had I not stayed with her instead of returning to Mount Pleasant Road?

My arms are aching and my throat feels scratchy, when suddenly the ground beneath me falls away. I try to grab hold of a bush but I am falling, tumbling, and I can feel the leaves and dirt and branches. Fortunately my rucksack breaks my fall, absorbing the impact as I hit the ground.

Then Gerry is beside me.

'That looked nasty,' he says. 'Are you hurt?'

'No,' I say, embarrassed. 'I'm fine.'

We press on, and I do not complain about the pain in my ankle, which at worst is only a sprain. Still, it is a relief when at last we stop before a wooden hut.

Gerry fishes inside his anorak and produces a large bunch of keys. 'Like I say, it's rather basic. But we can make ourselves cosy.'

He pushes the door open and goes over to the fuse box in the corner, the beam from his torch picking out a gas ring and two bunks along the far wall. After a few moments a light comes on above our heads. The cabin is rustic, about the size of a large garden shed or domestic greenhouse. I recognise the wood, and the construction style, as the same as the bench on which Merlin and I had sat after the camp that time outside the Cooperage.

Gerry gets to work, setting down the box he had brought from the car and rummaging from the contents. He pulls out a packet of Bean Feast.

'Do you fancy setting up that tarp?' He instructs me. 'I thought we could eat under the stars tonight, Mark. I have a few extra blankets should we get cold.'

Outside again I consider making a dash for it. But my foot hurts from where I fell and I wonder if I am being hysterical. It wasn't like he was some stranger.

I wind a rope around two trees and pull the tarpaulin tight, creating a slightly covered area that's protected from the wind. There are a couple of chairs, self-made by someone from the stumps of an oak tree. They look like thrones, like something out of the Middle Ages.

Gerry emerges from the cabin clutching two bowls of mush. 'Here,' he says, handing one to me. 'Get this lot down you.'

We sit on our thrones under our makeshift shelter and eat our Bean Feast, gazing out across the trees.

After a while, Gerry puts down his spoon and turns to me.

'It's all right, this, isn't it?'

'Yeah, thanks, Gerry. It tastes fine.'

'No,' he chuckles. 'I meant this.' He gestures towards the darkness. 'I notice, Mark, that if I spend too long in so-called civilisation it can get a little claustrophobic. Do you know what I mean?'

I tell him that I do.

'Out here,' he continues, 'I dunno, you feel something. Something eternal. Transcendental, you could say. It's important to reconnect with our roots, don't you think?'

I nod.

'You're still cross with me, aren't you, Mark?'

'I'm just a bit tired.'

'You know, I'm sorry about the boiler. Dave told me. He said you were upset by it. Oh, Mark, you know what I'm like. All that 'elf n safety and so forth. It's not really me, but of course you're right, and I apologise if I didn't take it very seriously at the time.'

'It's okay, Gerry.'

'Is it though?'

I say nothing.

'You know I really hoped it would work out for Jason,' he continues. 'When I first met him, he and Darren – that's his brother – were squatting. He was a vulnerable kid. They both were. I couldn't do anything for the older one, but with Jason I felt it wasn't too late, you know, to turn things around.'

It had not occurred to me that the voice on the phone could have been Darren, the famous brother, the *junglist*. I had always heard him asking for 'Gerry' because everyone who called the house always asked for Gerry. But could it have been 'Jay'?

Each time he called I had told him to leave his number, but always he just said: 'Naw, I'll try later.'

And he did try. Again and again and again he tried calling. And every time I faithfully relayed the message to Gerry, who would nod and say: 'Yeah, okay.'

I never checked, never asked Gerry what this meant or why the caller, who identified himself only as Dee, kept calling the house.

Dee. Darren.

Gerry. Jay.

'I don't get it,' I say at last. 'Why did you let me mislead him?'

'Sorry?'

'Those calls. It was Jason's brother, wasn't it? I thought he was asking for you. But all that time he was looking for Jason, and you knew?'

'Does it matter?'

'I made it sound as if Jason was still there. You made me part of the lie.'

'What lie would that be?'

'You let me believe...'

'I let you believe, Mark, what you wanted to believe.'

'But you had no right...'

'Careful, Mark. As I recall, you were all quite happy to see Jason go. Not one of you asked what happened to him. You asked no questions. I told you no lies.'

'But you were supposed to look after Jason.'

'I did.'

'You kicked him out.'

'Who said that?'

'You didn't?'

'Jason decided to leave. I let him go, Mark. Is that wrong?'

He starts clearing away the dishes.

'Fine,' I say, also getting to my feet. 'I'm asking. I'm asking now. What happened out here that night? Why did he not come back with us?'

'Like I told you at the time, Jason decided to make his own way home.'

'And you just let him?'

'What else was I supposed to do?'

'You just left him here?'

Gerry shrugs. 'It was the Survival Overnighter, Mark. Besides, you lot were constantly telling me how grown up you are, how you wanted to be taken seriously. I merely took Jason at his word.'

'Why are the police looking for him then?'

'I don't know, Mark. You tell me.'

It occurs to me that the police may still be looking for Gerry, that we may be fugitives on the run, and also that no one knows I am here.

After we've finished clearing up, I remove my sleeping bag and spread it out across the top bunk. Then I go around the back of the cabin. Gerry joins me, and we pee together, the steady patter of our urine loud against the dry leaves. We watch the bats, their jagged forms silhouetted against the night sky. Nearby, an owl hoots.

Gerry finishes peeing and puts his hand to his mouth, returning the hoot. It's the sort of thing Gerry always did, but this time it feels forced, and I wish he wouldn't. I am struck by how little this feels like Folk.

What's the deal with this Gerry guy?

At the time, I'd been offended by Jason's question.

We brush our teeth. We say goodnight. I get into my sleeping bag, my clothes still on. Gerry turns out the light.

I lie still, listening to him undress. The buckle of his belt thuds against the floor. I hear his footsteps, the squeaky boards on the bunk beneath me, the opening and closing of a zip. The fabric of our sleeping bags rustle noisily in the darkness.

The silence is almost unbearable. I long for the sound of traffic, of drunks shouting in the street or music drifting up from other people's rooms. But all I can hear is the sound of Gerry's breathing and my own short breaths, mixed with the faint murmurings of the woods.

In the silence of the shelter the smallest movements feel loud. After a while I try not to move at all. I try not to breathe. Even my thoughts feel noisy.

I close my eyes but sleep isn't coming. And I wish I was home, home in the house where I grew up. My parents still together, tolerating each other, because they could. In fact, they could be quite good at it, and sometimes it felt as if tolerating each other was actually something they enjoyed doing. And I'm there, too. Not as the main event, just present, just allowed to be. I'm watching the telly, I'm cleaning my boots, I'm eating a slice of toast. It's so... ordinary.

You need the ordinary to have the extraordinary. Zee said that. She also said this: without the ordinary, we are ships without anchors. I wrote that in a notebook. I have notebooks full of things that Zee has said.

Sun. Sky. Skin glistening. We are at the seaside. Red sandstone cliffs jut out, like warts under the microscope, and I can taste the salt. I can smell the suncream. We have been swimming and now we are climbing the cliffs, the sun beating down on our backs. The small sharp stones hurt my feet and my legs are all scratched from the spiky weeds and thorns that grow in stumpy patches out of the stone. We are a long way up, too high, really. It's not safe. Slip now and you could do yourself some real damage, but that's part of the fun. The peril, the danger, the foolishness. Getting to the top has become weirdly important, a primal act, like conquering a mountain or crossing a ravine.

It starts far away, but it moves fast, the rumbling, the shuddering. Birds fly up into the air squawking and screeching. The ground beneath my feet is moving. I reach out to grab at a crag of rock, trying to steady myself, and a chunk of cliff comes away in my hand. I'm just holding this massive piece of the cliff in my hand, and I'm slipping, and everything I reach for is coming away in my hand. And the sun is beating down, scorching, there is no let up, and it makes me feel lightheaded, and somewhere I can hear shouting but I can't understand what is being said, and a dog is barking.

Chapter Twenty-Five

I'm awake. It is still dark, very dark, but the sound of dogs barking persists, and suddenly the door swings open and I am blinded by the light. I shield my eyes with my sleeping bag. I can just make out a figure in the doorway.

He is dressed in work gear. An orange fluorescent jacket, heavy boots, all weather trousers, a beanie on his head.

On the end of a leash, two German Shepherds struggle and strain, saliva dripping from their panting mouths. A flashlight probes the cabin. The beam darts across the walls, picking out items: the saucepan on the hob, the washed-up dishes, Gerry's sleeping bag. Below me, I feel Gerry's weight shift.

'This ain't your land, Gerry.'

Now I recognise him. Where stubble once was, a thick beard now grows, wild and mangy like moorland scrub. The piercing is gone, but the eyes, the eyes are as heavy and as fierce as ever.

The floorboards creak. Gerry groans and sits up in his bunk. He is wearing only underpants and a thin vest, through which scraggly hairs poke out. Even though the dogs growl and he has just been woken up, he seems strangely calm, his demeanour more of irritation at having been awakened than alarm at having been caught. He pulls on some jeans. 'You look well,' he says, mildly. 'We were a bit worried, Jason.'

'You're trespassing.'

Gerry smiles. 'Nice setup you have here.' He picks up a saucepan containing the leftovers of the Bean Feast, and places it down with a noisy clatter on the floor. The dogs lurch forward and begin to eat. 'You made your choice, Jason,' he continues, patting the dogs, who are now wagging their tails ecstatically, their noses pressed to the pot, which rolls and slides noisily around the floor as they tuck into their unexpected late-night treat. 'I simply respected your decision.'

He glances towards me, still cowering inside my sleeping bag. 'Anyway, Mark, you can come out now. There you go! You can say you found him. You can tell them that Jason is doing just fine.'

Jason starts to back away. 'Naw, naw, naw... This ain't real... this ain't happening.'

Gerry, now fully dressed, sits back down on the bunk.

'Now, let me speculate for a moment. This job of yours, Jason, I assume your employers don't really know who you are? I mean, just a guess – or have they forgiven you for what you did to Merlin?'

Jason does not reply.

'Hmm, I thought so.' Gerry taps his nose. 'You know me, Jason, and I hope you know me as a fair man. I believe in second chances, third chances, as many chances as a person requires. Now, you know what, I think I might have spotted a broken fence, ooooooh... way up over by the East Laingleigh Turnstile, was it? Tell you what – why don't you nip over there and take a look?' He taps his nose again. 'It's your choice, Jason. We can make this into a thing or we can make it disappear.'

'No,' says Jason, his voice gruff. He is scared. 'You'll come with me.'

'You can tell yourself it never happened,' Gerry continues. 'We do it all the time. All the time. All those wars going on? All the torture and murderous regimes? How often do you think about them? These things are happening, but if they're not happening to us then they're not happening and never did happen? Isn't that what we do? Isn't that how we live with it? We forget it's happening. We forget it ever happened.'

'You'll come with me.'

'Ooh, I don't think you want that, Jason. Come on, Mark. We're done here.'

I pack my stuff away, pushing my sleeping bag into my rucksack, aware of Merlin's sculpture still in there and hoping it is not damaged. Gerry picks up his holdall, grabs me by the arm and marches us towards the door.

But Jason blocks our way. The dogs, sensing danger, growl.

'As you wish,' says Gerry, cooly.

We are led through the woods. No further words are exchanged, and eventually we reach a fence, and then a gate, and then another fence and another gate, and behind this, lit by the moon and a security light trained on the front door, is the Cooperage.

Their red minivan is parked outside. Merlin used to get dropped off by this red van, not directly outside the community centre but at the end of the lane, where it would also be waiting for him at the end. As if we wouldn't know. I can't remember who it was who started the Postman Pat thing. It may well have been someone who left before Jason's time, but it had stuck. We all used to join in, humming the Postman Pat theme tune, which for some reason we thought was hilarious.

Jason opens the door to a stumpy, windowless outhouse. He wants to wait in here.

'Uh-uh,' admonishes Gerry. Then he turns towards the main house and yells: 'Spencer! Spencer!'

Lights in the house come on.

'Spencer!' Gerry yells again. 'You better come!'

Jason is backing way. He lets the dog lead fall from his hand, then he drops the torch, which bounces and rotates, throwing light around the courtyard like a cinema projection on the brickwork. Then he turns and runs.

* * *

A man dressed in a white dressing gown and slippers is coming towards us. When he gets near I recognise him from drop-offs.

'Roger? What the hell is this?'

'Sorry, Spence, we were in the cabin,' Gerry explains. 'Your new security detail's rather excitable, isn't he?'

'Roger, it's the middle of the night.'

'Yeah, you might want to have a word with him about that.'

'Where is he, anyway?'

Gerry smiles. 'Who?'

'Jimmy. My security bloke.'

'No idea.'

'Jesus, Roger. This has to stop. Turning up like this, at all hours. I thought you had London for that?' He glances at me, as if he has just noticed my presence. 'So, who's this one, anyway?'

'Spencer! This is Mark!'

'Oh, right, I see. Are you staying then? You can have the guest room, I suppose.'

Gerry waves the invitation away with his hand. 'No, you're all right, Spence, we'll get out of your hair.'

'You don't change, do you, Roger?'

Gerry chuckles, and I realise I have seen this man before, and not just glimpses of him at drop-off and pick-up. I know him from the archive. Was it his arm that was around Gerry at Trafalgar Square? Looking at him in his robe, with his security lights, large house, his land and his staff, it is hard to reconcile this version with the veteran protester in the pictures.

But then, as Gerry would say, people are more than they present.

The weirdest thing is that Gerry doesn't seem out of place. He has been caught trespassing and marched here against his will, yet all of it seems to amuse him, as if he is rather proud of his rakishness, his refusal to abide by the rules that apply to everyone else.

There is nothing I can say, I realise, that will change any of this. But there may be something I can do. I put down my rucksack. I reach in. And, as delicately as if it was a real bird I am handling, I remove Merlin's sculpture and place it, like a ceremonial offering, at the feet of the homeowner in his white robe and slippers. out the box. My movement sets off a second security light, so when I lift the lid it is suddenly bathed in white light.

Spencer frowns. He peers inside the box.

'Is this some sort of joke?'

'Please tell Merlin I'm sorry?' I say. 'I wish he had got to show it.'

There is no response from either of the men.

'I know you were worried it might get damaged,' I persist. 'Or maybe... you didn't trust us... not to... laugh? But, honestly, it's great! Really great. Your son...' I trail off. My words do not seem to be getting through. I glance down at the box. The bird is gone. It is just a mess of leaves and mud and sticks.

'Sorry,' says Spencer, reaching inside and taking out a handful of dirt. 'What is this?'

Gerry looks away.

'Roger?'

'Come on, Mark,' he says, wearily. 'I think you've done quite enough.'

'I'm so sorry,' I said. 'It must have been when I fell.'

Spencer inspects the box again and pulls out the remains of one of the wings. It's not much, but it is something, and it's all that's left of the bird.

'Did Merlin make something?'

'Mark. Come on.'

There is a sharpness now to Gerry's voice, and I can tell that underneath his cool demeanour he is seething.

'Where is Merlin?' I ask, suddenly.

Spencer glances up at one of the darkened windows in the house. 'I should imagine he's sleeping. Should I give it to him anyway?'

'Mark, are you coming or not?'

'Will you just give us a minute, please?' I shoot back, not bothering to hide my irritation.

'Look, Roger,' says Spencer, picking up the box. 'I'm off to bed. The offer still stands. Just let yourself in.' And to me he says: 'Thanks, Mark, I'm sure Merlin will be touched that you came all this way.'

He goes back into the house, closing the door gently behind him. The security light stays on. It is just me and Gerry left, standing there in the empty courtyard, in the middle of the night.

'Well, I hope you're satisfied, Mark.'

I stare at him. 'Is that all you can say?'

'What do you mean?'

I pick up my rucksack and pull it onto my shoulders. I fasten the straps. 'You know what, Gerry. I think I might make my own way home.'

'Mark, stop being ridiculous.'

I walk towards the drive, my feet crunching on the gravel.

'It's the middle of the night! You can't possibly get home from here!'

'No? Is that so?'

I keep walking. I do not look back. I feel a drop of rain, then another. I quicken my step. I am running. Down the drive. Crunch. Crunch. Crunch. There's the road. Crunch. Crunch. Am I being followed? Do I even care?

I reach the road. Darkness stretches in both directions. The rain is falling hard now. The upper half of my body is protected by my jacket but my trousers are sodden and the rain is streaming down my face. I can taste it. The sensation returns me to Zee and Anna and Seb and all the others, trudging along after a long day, facing the ongoing traffic, good little hikers that we were. That was the gift of Folk. It wasn't the nature itself but learning to live with it, not just when it was sunny and fine but when it was hard and relentless. Those days when no sensible person would dream of venturing out, we'd be out there. Gerry was the only person mad enough to do that kind of thing and we loved him for it.

I listen for the sound of an engine. Surely Gerry isn't going to just leave me out here like this?

The hedge rises high on both sides. Out of habit I walk on the correct side of the road, facing the non-existent on-coming traffic. I'm cold, I'm wet, I've hardly slept and I don't know where I am or where I'm going. I also know that as long as I keep moving I will, eventually, reach a village or some sort of civilisation. It is not much of a plan, but it's the only one I have.

The rain beats on the road. Droplets ricochet off the surface, lit briefly by the moon's gaze. I tighten the straps around my hood so that only the tops of my cheeks and the area around my eyes are exposed, and I push on, each step a step closer to the next one, and so on and so forth, that's the way we do it: it's not five miles, it's a step, and then another step, and then another, until we get there.

I know this because this is hardly the first time I have had to hike a long trail in uncompromising conditions. But did Jason? I imagine him, after the Survival Overnighter, alone up here, trying to find his way. Trying to find somewhere that could offer him warmth, shelter, security, safety. He didn't even have any gear, thanks to the mix up with Merlin's bag, and nowhere to go. How could Gerry cast him aside like that?

* * *

I must have been walking for an hour when I spot the vehicle, parked at the side of the road up ahead. It is red and a bit dumpy. I recognise it instantly and the Postman Pat theme tune pops into my head. As I approach, the door on the passenger side is flung open and a familiar voice calls out.

'Get in, Mark!'

He has cut his hair short. As I peer into the van, I can't help noticing that now his face is no longer hidden behind the veil of hair and he has the same raised cheek bones and pale eyes as Gerry.

We drive along empty lanes, the headlights bouncing over potholes, rain hammering on the roof, the windscreen wipers beating time.

Merlin had witnessed the whole thing. He saw us arrive, had caught the whole scene in the courtyard, watching from his bedroom window.

'I'm sorry I ruined your bird,' I say. 'It was yours, right?'

'It's okay.'

'Not really, but it is what it is. I hope you don't mind, I showed it to Zee.'

'You did?'

'She thought it was amazing.'

I can't tell if he's pleased or offended, but it feels right that he should know that someone had noticed and found value in his efforts.

'Thank you for this,' I say. 'You really didn't have to come.'

'Couldn't leave you out here on your own.'

'Yes, you could have.'

'No, Mark. We don't do that.'

No, I think. No, we don't.

I learn how Merlin had found Jason a week after the Survival Overnighter. He had been sleeping rough at Ricketts Drop, without a sleeping bag, just his puffa jacket, which was torn and filthy but had kept him alive. He had survived off berries and mushrooms and nettles and whatever else he could scavenge from the woods. Apparently, he even tried eating worms and insects, drying them out on stone, like Gerry had recommended.

Merlin had wanted to take him to a hospital. He had a bad cough and had clearly lost a lot of weight. But Jason had pleaded for him not to, saying he would be sent away, and that he couldn't do that again. And so Merlin had kept him hidden in the cabin, bringing him medicine and food and blankets from the house, and nursing him back to health. Then when the seasonal workers left at the end of September, Merlin somehow contrived to introduce 'Jimmy' to M&S, inventing a story about him being an old Folk acquaintance who had recently moved to the area and was looking for work.

'But why couldn't you just say it was Jason?'

'Come on, Mark. After the Survival Overnighter? After what Gerry told them?'

It occurs to me that, unwittingly, I have just ruined his fresh start. That my attempt to make amends had actually made things worse.

'Merlin, do you think we could find him? Do you know where he might have gone?'

'Maybe,' says Merlin.

At the next opportunity, we turn the car around and start back towards Ricketts Drop. The rain has eased off, and dawn is breaking on the horizon. The sound of birdsong filling the air with chirrups and warbles and clicks and whistles and calls.

'They've switched on the tape,' I say out of habit, and Merlin laughs. Because it wasn't just a Zee thing, it was a Folk thing too.

'Nature's stereo,' says Merlin.

Sitting up the front with Merlin driving the empty country road, I think of the ride home from Under the Radar, and the kindness of my Drinks Stand Guy, whose name I never caught but who made me feel welcome and acceptable and like a someone, not just a nobody.

'Did I ever tell you, Merlin, I went to a rave?'

'You? A rave? That I'd love to see!'

I smile at the gentle joshing, a sensation which maybe comes from a similar place but is so very different to scorn. Then I recount everything I can remember. The ride out with Richie's grumpy friends. Arriving at the quarry and the long, winding path lit by tea lights. The way the sound grew as we got closer. Anna's wings and the bonfire and the glitter and the music with no ends only transitions. When I get to the bit about the DJ only agreeing to the show because he'd heard that there was good hiking in the area, I notice that Merlin is grinning from ear to ear and I am smiling too. Merlin and I have never done this before, never spoken with this openness and lightness. We have known each other for years, yet there was always a cautiousness about the way we interacted, as we were constantly imagining that we were being judged, not by the other person but by unspecific other people. I had feared being put in the same box as Merlin. That this fear was misplaced and kind of crap, I had had to learn the hard way.

'Why did you do it?' I ask, emboldened suddenly. 'Why did you take Jason's drugs?'

'Is that what Gerry told you?'

'Didn't you?'

A sly smile spreads across his face:

'Maybe I wanted to know what all the fuss was about.'

'Hang on, let me get this clear. You found the drugs in Jason's bag, right? And then, what, you just took them?'

'Just one. And then, a bit later, I did another one. But the second one was with Jay.'

'You did drugs with Jason?'

'He came and found me. You lot had all gone to bed by that point. He was, I dunno, really nice. Just wanted to know I was okay. He said it was all right that I stole his drugs, but that I could have saved a few for everyone else. And then, well, we ended up doing another one and staying up all night. It was my idea.'

'And?'

'And what?'

'Was it, you know, worth it?'

His smile fades. 'Worth breaking up Folk? No. Absolutely not. Worth Jason being cast out and almost dying? No way. But if you're asking me if it was fun at the time, sure, we had a laugh. Until Gerry found us. Have you never tried it, Mark?'

All I can do is shake my head. How did I miss all this? How could I have failed to notice so much that was happening in front of my face? Then I think of Gerry and his veiled threat to expose Jason to M&S.

'What do you think your dad will do when he finds out he's been employing Jason Templar all this time?'

'My dad? You think Spencer's my dad?'

'He's not?'

'He brought me up, sure. But he's not my real dad. Not my biological father anyway.'

'No?'

'Oh, come on, Mark. Surely you must know?'

Gerry.

Suddenly it all makes sense. Their styles are so different that it had never occurred to me to notice that Merlin and Gerry look rather alike. But most of it explained why Gerry always treated Merlin differently. I think we all assumed that there must be something seriously wrong with Merlin because Gerry was so weird about him, simultaneously protective and dismissive and constantly embarrassed by him.

'Anyway,' he says, reaching across me and pushing a tape into the stereo. A flurry of beats, all tripping over themselves, rush forth, and I let out a theatrical groan.

'Not you as well,' I say.

With a grin, he turns the volume up, the Postman Pat van rattling and shaking from the onslaught of beats and bass. 'Jay and I have been going to parties all year!' he yells over the music, and I'm no longer even surprised.

By the time we get out onto the moorland road, the rain has stopped completely and colour bursts from every direction. Over a tapestry of rock and gorse and bracken and static white dots that must be sheep, the sky has erupted into deep violet, pink, purple, green, orange, red. I had seen a double rainbow before, but never one quite like this. It is huge. Bigger than any pyrotechnics show. Mixed with the early morning midsummer sun, and my lack of sleep, it is as if my body has been lifted from the seat, my body merged into the light. The road ahead is empty as far as the eye will take you. It's just us, all the way to the horizon. I stick my head out, savouring the cool moorland air that rushes against my face.

Chapter Twenty-Six

In the corner of a motorway service station carpark we gather. We are a ragged band of folk in baggy trousers, neon, novelty sunglasses, shell suits, caps, work wear – and, in my case, a T-shirt and hoodie I borrowed from Jason and some lightweight walking trousers. Lone business travellers get in and out of empty cars, passing through the revolving doors, and disappearing, never to be seen again. But maybe that is not the whole story? Who is to say that on a different day, next week say, or in thirty years, the roles won't be reversed, and today's ravers will be racing off to meetings while those who once wore a suit will be chasing the beat of the drum?

Behind the dinky huts and pebble dash buildings that someone at some point must have thought would look nice, hills stretch like a patchwork quilt, the sun coming up over the crest of fields, the moorland beyond.

A creaky off-white coach appears. It slows to a standstill in front of us, and a cheer goes up. 'Sunny Days' promises the faded logo of a defunct travel operator, emblazoned across the side of the bus. Someone remarks that all the best parties start at dawn.

I have been living at the Cooperage for a little over a month. I am one of six seasonal workers living on-site. Jason, who is still Jimmy to the boss (Gerry did not give him away after all) has the 'drover's hut', which comes with a wood burner and running (cold) water. That's because he's permanent, so he gets special treatment. Which seems fair enough to me. Us seasonal workers stay in a dormitory, adapted from one of the barns. I'll be off to uni in a couple of months, so I'm happy to rough it a little for now. We don't earn much but food is included and unlike at Gerry's there are actual meal times and a menu. It's all very shipshape, which means we can focus on other things, like learning about the land, and tilling and forestry and all manner of topics that previously meant nothing to me but which now are part of daily conversation.

But today is different. Merlin and Jason have been promising to take me to a party, a real one, since I arrived. But they wouldn't do it until my exams were finished. ('You're the brains, Mark. You're not allowed to flunk them now.') And now, finally, the day has arrived.

We file onto the coach, like regular sightseers, moving right down the bus and using all available seats. And then we are on the motorway, going with the flow of commuters and trucks and people with places they need to be; just like us, maybe. And then we're exiting the motorway. Ahead of us is an industrial estate. We rattle along the slip road, a grey crash barrier separating road and scrub, a few more miles and then we reach a high metal fence with anonymous grey sheds behind it, which seems to go on forever. Vehicles with flashing orange lights move to and fro like an elaborate wide game, shepherded by figures in hi-vis vests and hard hats.

At the end of this long road, the warehouses on one side, the motorway on the other, the driver sets us down. We alight, filing off the coach onto the grey concrete, the roar of the road filling our senses.

We set off in convoy. Someone says the party round the back of the warehouse, so as not to be visible from the slip road. Since the new laws, we have to be ultra careful to keep parties like this one off the radar.

The Criminal Justice Act. All the solidarity, the warnings and the protest came to nothing. The government pushed it through with barely a murmur from the opposition, and the tabloids claimed the victory, just as Gerry predicted. But did they really win? And what, exactly, did they win? The irony, of course, is that now even my mother and her friends know about 'repetitive beats', thanks to the rather bizarre wording of the new law. Meanwhile, the music itself is everywhere. What was once the preserve of Anna's brother Richie and his UTR crew, and the pirate radio stations Jason's brother was involved with in London and the other big cities, has become mainstream: it is the sound of a future we all believe is coming and maybe already here. And it's not just Top of the Pops and school discos. Rave is turning up in adverts for banks and political parties. Just walk into any shop on any high street and you'll find something that bears at least a resemblance to the music Jason, Zee and the others were listening to last summer. Although not Harpies, obviously, where they would never stoop to playing music of any kind.

We are directed through an elaborate system of railings and walkways. There are people in hi-vis vests on walkie talkies. Bags are checked. A door opens. A blast of music spills out. A sign says:

No weapons, no glass bottles, no bad attitude.

It is dark inside, much darker than I had expected, and the music is abrasive and pounding. I can just make out a throng of bodies towards the middle and the front. It is not very full. Maybe folk are yet to arrive, or maybe this is all there is. Beyond the barriers there is a hunched figure, who must be the DJ. We find a spot. I let the music, which is unfamiliar and a bit scary, carry me; to trust what is happening. Because it is only by letting yourself go that you can really feel anything.

We dance in one spot for the next two hours, and by the time the

DJ finishes the set, it is as if this is the music I have listened to my whole life. We head outside, where palettes and boxes have been arranged into makeshift seating. The sky is a perfect grey.

Jason and Merlin need to pee. I look for somewhere to sit but there are no free spots, so I squat down on the ground, my back leaning against the fence. Technically, I realise, what we are doing, what all these people are doing, is illegal. I have seen the reports of police coming in and breaking these sort of events up. The thought that at any moment the cavalry might burst in and start waving batons and making arrests makes me anxious. I try to distract myself by thinking about something else. My mind returns to Mount Pleasant Road, my final day and the raid. At the time I believed they were after Gerry. Later it transpired that while they did suspect Gerry of some wrongdoing, it was really a former resident they were hoping to find. They had found nothing incriminating, nor the individual they were looking for, so it all came to nothing, except Gerry now distrusts the law even more, if that's possible.

The sound of my name being called brings me back to the party.

'*Sparky?*' says a voice. 'It is you, isn't it?'

I try to locate where the voice is coming from, but I can't because there are too many people, and I wonder if it is a different Sparky being called. Then I spot the source. At first I don't recognise him, at least I don't know how I recognise him, but when he starts to laugh and says: 'You don't remember, do you?' that's when I realise it's my saviour from Under the Radar.

'No way!' I exclaim.

'This guy,' my Drinks Stand Man explains to one of the people sitting nearby, 'actually saved my life.'

I am introduced. His name is Iggy, which makes me smile, because I know Iggy Pop and the Stooges from Badger, who would regularly play the LPs on the stereo at Mount Pleasant Road.

'Are you here with the drinks stand?'

He guffaws at my question. 'Ha ha, Sparky, are you looking for a job, aye? Naw, had to give that one up. Too much hassle. I'm just a punter now.'

'You know it was actually you who saved my life that night, Iggy.'

'I'm touched,' he says, and he sounds genuinely touched. 'Well, something good must have come of it because you're here now.'

'Yes,' I smile. 'I am here.'

He laughs. 'Can I buy you a beer, pal?'

When Jason and Merlin come back, they find me sitting with Iggy and his crew. Iggy and Jason vaguely remember each other from before.

'Are you still running with Richie's wee sister,' he asks me, which makes me blush

'Sometimes. Not seen her for a little while, to be honest.'

'So you didn't come with her today?'

I shake my head.

'But you know she's here, right?'

* * *

Even in the dark expanse of the warehouse, and in such a colourful crowd, Anna stands out. Her hair, which has turned platinum blonde, has been sculpted with a complicated array of glow sticks, neon hair bands and butterfly clips. With her biker jacket and mutilated beige turtleneck, she looks as though she may have landed here from another planet. She sits perched on the barriers. Next to her is Richie, Anna's big brother, who doesn't seem so big anymore. I might even recognise one of the friends who drove us out to the quarry.

It is in fact Richie who spots me first. I see him point me out to her. And then I see her turn, and I see the grin that spreads over on her face, which is still young, still Anna, and – amazingly – hasn't changed much in the thirty years since.

'Markface!'

People move aside to let us through. And then she is kissing me on the cheek with lip-gloss lips and calling me a dark horse and asking if I have been living a secret double life all this time. 'Who are you here with?' she enquires.

It had not been my intention to keep my living at the Cooperage a secret. On the rare occasions I had gone into college, or even into town, I had half expected to run into Anna or Seb or Zee, or one of the Three Kats, or anyone really. It just never happened. So the news had not reached Anna. Later she would say that the moment she saw me, standing with Iggy and looking like I actually wanted to be there, she knew something big must have happened to me.

Fortunately, I was spared having to explain myself, because at that moment Jason and Merlin appeared, and it was all hugs and wows! and no one was believing any of it, and it being 1995 it was all *completely random*.

We dance some more, all of us together, which means we are now quite the crew, and it feels as if everything is coming together, not how I expected it to, but together nonetheless. At some point Anna and I go outside, just the two of us, and sit down at the seating area where we met Iggy. There is more space now because most people are dancing. We lean against the fence and sip our water.

'Zee told me, by the way.'

Instantly I know what she's referring to. I had been dreading this. Of course I had known it would come out, but I kept pushing it away, wishing it could be erased, knowing that it could not and that this moment would come.

'Bit fucking rapey, eh, Mark?'

'I know.'

'You're an idiot. I mean, what the fuck, Mark?'

'I got... I dunno... I got it wrong.'

'Too fucking right you got it wrong. What? She led you on, did she? By being your mate? By having tits? Mark, you're supposed to be one of the decent ones. You're supposed to be better than that.'

'I know.'

'I know I didn't help matters,' she adds. 'Humiliating you like that. I was drunk and I was angry and I took it out on you, and I'm not proud of myself. But that doesn't change that what you did was way, way, way out of line. You know that, don't you?'

We fall into silence and all I can hear is Zee, warning me, pleading with me:

'Don't put me on a pedestal, Mark.'

Why couldn't I recognise at the time the value of what she had been offering me, which in many ways is rarer and more precious than what she wasn't offering? And why, even when I did realise, did I waste the chance to tell her? Once her A-levels were done, she went away, as I knew she would. First Interrailing, then Paris. There were no more invitations to visit her.

'I'm calling you on it, Markface, because believe it not I actually care about you, and I know you're better, or at least you can be. So, there, I've said it.'

I turn to face her, expecting to find disappointment, maybe contempt. She is looking at me very intently. But it is not hatred I see. It is something else. Something that I now know is bigger and stronger and more complete than any of these other emotions.

* * *

We return inside where the DJ is playing what Merlin and Anna inform me is 'proper old-school jungle', which I reply is proper new to me and sounds like nothing anyone at my old school would have listened to. This earns me a laugh. They know, as I do, that I am playing up to the role. Old before my time. We are all more than we present. Later, I will quip to Anna that I will make a good dad, and to my surprise she will agree, and we will kiss. But for now, it is all about the dancing.

It is a beat that I can get to. Some people are dancing alone, some in pairs, some in smaller or larger groups. Girls dancing with girls and boys dancing with boys. Lads in sportswear with big grins on their faces. Older characters getting down to it in full rave gear. The music builds and builds, weaving in and out, and when it seems as if it can't get any bigger, that there is no more space left where a sound would go, the clatter and boom gives way to a single chord.

The lights go up.

And suddenly, as if the whole thing has been choreographed, everyone begins to cheer and clap and whoop, and the more it goes on, what starts as applause and appreciation for the music, the DJ, the spectacle, the sound, seems to become a salute to something bigger, something for which maybe we don't have language.

I search the faces for Jason. I have not seen him for a while. I had left him dancing with a girl he had just met, which I thought was a little naughty of him since he is also having a thing with one of my fellow seasonal workers. But then, what do I know? As my new friend Iggy once said: isn't he green?

Had they found a quiet corner or gone to the toilets to fuck?

Not these toilets, surely.

I can't imagine this sort of space being conducive to romance, but then nobody at that point had offered me anything of that nature. Maybe there are circumstances when anything might be worth a try?

Safari.

These are my thoughts as I wander around, not finding Jason. I find everyone else. Just not Jason.

At last, someone taps me on the arm. It's the girl Jason had been dancing with.

'Sparky, isn't it?' She fishes inside her pocket and pulls out a napkin.

'Your friend was looking for you. He wanted you to have this.'

I go outside, but instead of staying in the seating area I walk a little further, out onto the asphalt where I can hear the roar of the motorway. It blends with the music, almost as if the DJ intended it so. There are no clouds in the sky. That is, the whole sky is solid grey. Just one tone. On the other side of the fence, the workers, who all look the same in their safety gear, are busy with the day's activities: pointing, directing, loading, unloading, keeping it moving, keeping it tidy; apparently oblivious to the hijinks going on next door. Or maybe they're just used to it. What is remarkable to some can be mundane to others. There are no rules about what we must and must not find remarkable.

When I close my eyes it is starlings I see, weaving in and out, this way and that, diving, soaring, turning, somehow never colliding, never getting into fights or feeling the need to dominate or throw their weight around. They are free, yet bound to each other. One takes the lead and they all create the form. Any one of them might take up a leadership position or drop back behind the others. No one is left behind.

I open the napkin that was handed to me.

The writing is shaky and uneven. I have seen eight year-olds with more confident handwriting.

Sparks. Sory 4 going AWOL. Nufing perssonal. Saw u wiv ANNA (HEART) !!!!!!! U will never beleave it... DARRENS here !!!!!!!! came wi the SE1 crew so Im going back wiv those boys !!!!!! goodbyes ect never my thing as u no but we left a little suprise 4uall so stick around!!!

J (yer bruva)

* * *

Back inside, the music has shifted again. It is slower, more like what I had heard for the first time in the quarry, except bigger chords, chunkier bass, and it feels as if the crowd, which has steadily grown throughout the morning, has settled into a groove that could last all day. I find Merlin, Anna, Iggy and the gang in the centre of a throng of bodies twisting this way and that, which makes me think again of the starlings. I don't tell them about Jason.

A track that everyone knows comes on, even me (thanks to the tape Jason left behind), and all the lights go out. For about a minute, we are plunged into darkness. Then a light comes on. It is way up high, high above our heads. We look up. There's something up there, something large, otherworldly, and it is rotating. We are all mesmerised by this strange twisting object, creature, thing. It slowly descends.

How anyone managed to get up there, into the rafters, and rig up a ten-foot bird to a wire, is a total mystery; but there it is, in all its glory: a monster version of the one I stumbled across in the archive and then never quite managed to return to Merlin.

The bird stops just above our heads. Then it starts to turn. Slowly at first but getting faster, throwing the light through the entire cavernous space, picking out faces and raised arms and then moving on until the whole room had been covered and everyone had had their moment in the spotlight.

Merlin is watching the whole thing with a wry smile on his face.

'Did you know about this?' I ask, but whatever his reply is, I never hear it, because at that moment the whole place erupts into cheers as the music kicks back in, and I realise suddenly that this isn't about Merlin's sculpture, or Jason's exit, or the DJ, or any single link in the great chain of hands that conspired to make this moment happen, and that we, all of us, are no more and no less than a delicate balance of elements, moving through space, dancing our dance, the dance that never ceases to amaze: no ends, only transitions.

Author's Note

A whole band of folk made this book possible.

To Steve, your steadfast belief in the project, your friendship and your counsel kept *Folk* alive at so many points and kept me going. Thank you for everything.

To Beattie, Will, Alina and all my other early readers, thank you for your generosity, enthusiasm, wisdom and patience.

To Joanna, we got there in the end! Thanks for believing in Mark and the gang.

Thank you to Colin and everyone at Velocity Press.

Thank you to my family.

And thank you to my friends at all the different times and in-between points. This book is dedicated to you all.

Thanks to the following people who pre-ordered the book:
Kelly Arnstein, Ruaridh Arrow, John Berridge, Jim Boulton, Gauthier Breuil, Alexis Butterfield, Alison Butterfield, Graham Butterfield, Martin Calladine, Kirk Cheyfitz, Lara Colvill, Alison Eales, Rachel Foster, Celina Fredericks, Liane Fredericks, Stephen Furber, Alan Gardner, Polly Gordon, Kathi Hall, Ryan Hays, Martin Holden, Alina Hoyne, Nick Hughes, Matthew Jackson, Felix Kaufmann, Philippa Kelly, Henriette Lampe, Anna Land, Anna MacKenzie, Emma Mackie-Johnstone, Beattie Maclennan, Hedwig Matt, Stephen McGreal, Andy McKinna, Ciaraleaf Meaney, Jo Millar, Tally Miller, James Morgan, Ravi Motha, Jessica Ormerod, Anne Oxborough, Alexander Raev, Neil Shanlin, Matthew Sillars, Katharine Simpson, Douglas Squires, John Stephenson, Clara Suess, Lisa Thomasius, Scott Walker, Emma Warren, Matt Wilson